Praise for Liz Ireland and her Mrs. Claus mysteries!

Mrs. Claus and the Santaland Slayings

"An exceptional series launch . . . This fun, well-plotted mystery is the perfect holiday entertainment."
—*Publishers Weekly* (starred review)

Mrs. Claus and the Halloween Homicide

"Brings the Christmas cozy to dizzying new heights of cuteness."
—*Kirkus Reviews*

"Entertaining . . . Ireland makes suspending disbelief surprisingly easy. Fans of offbeat, humorous cozies will clamor for more."
—*Publishers Weekly*

"This is a wacky story with a bit of *Elf* meets *Nightmare Before Christmas* meets *Murder She Wrote*. It will definitely entertain readers during the HalloThankMas holiday season."
—*The Parkersburg News & Sentinel*

Books by Liz Ireland

MRS. CLAUS AND THE SANTALAND SLAYINGS

MRS. CLAUS AND THE HALLOWEEN HOMICIDE

MRS. CLAUS AND THE EVIL ELVES

Published by Kensington Publishing Corp.

MRS. Claus
and The Evil
Elves

Liz Ireland

Kensington Publishing Corp.
www.kensingtonbooks.com

KENSINGTON BOOKS are published by

Kensington Publishing Corp.
119 West 40th Street
New York, NY 10018

ISBN: 978-1-4967-3782-3 (ebook)

ISBN: 978-1-4967-3781-6

First Kensington Trade Paperback Printing: October 2022

10 9 8 7 6 5 4 3 2 1

Printed in the United States of America

MRS. Claus and The Evil Elves

Chapter 1

Note to self: Elf clogging should never be the main event.

As the person who'd scheduled the Christmastown Cloggers as part of the entertainment for Santaland's annual ice sculpture contest, I was hardly in a position to complain. Yet it was one thing to have the head of the clogging troupe breathlessly inform me that his group would perform a dramatic "a cappella" dance accompanied only by jingle bells attached to their clogs, quite another to live through ten clomping, jangling minutes of it on a frosty late morning in December.

My friend Juniper Greenleaf craned her neck over her music stand to gaze at the crowd gathered around Peppermint Pond. "I don't see Blinky."

"How would you be able to?"

Half of Santaland had turned out for the ice sculpture competition. Spotting one elf in a crowd of hundreds of elves and people was impossible, unless they happened to be on the dais set up next to the pond for the local dignitaries. Even from a distance I could clearly make out my husband, Nick, aka Santa Claus, on the platform, decked out for the occasion in full Santa regalia. Next to him were Mayor Firlog and his wife, and other town bigwigs. Bella Sparkletoe, whose mercantile was sponsoring this year's sculpture contest, was in her finest purple tunic and elf cap. Most notably, my best friend from Oregon, Claire Emerson, was among the Christmastown elite, standing next to Nick. Claire was visiting me here for the first time, and I could see her pop-eyed expression even from thirty yards away.

Claire, usually a fairly cool person, had been in freak-out mode since Nick and I met her in Fairbanks, Alaska, which was the closest airport to the North Pole. Obviously, it had been a long day of travel for her from Cloudberry Bay, Oregon, and then she'd been greeted with the news that we still had a flying sleigh journey to get to Santaland. Belatedly, I'd realized "flying sleigh journey" was a phrase that probably called for smelling salts.

"Aren't you taking this Mr. and Mrs. Claus schtick too far?" she asked as Nick heaved her suitcase into the back of our elaborately carved sleigh, to which eight reindeer were harnessed.

I'd told her that Nick was Santa Claus, but the reality evidently hadn't penetrated. I could relate. When Nick had first come to stay at the Coast Inn, the small hotel I ran in Cloudberry Bay, I'd had no idea he was Santa Claus. It wasn't until we'd fallen in love that he'd confessed his real identity to me. To say that the news had knocked me for a loop was the understatement of the century. I'd been Mrs. Claus for a year and a half now, but I still experienced moments of amazement.

"How far are we going in this thing?" Claire had asked, hesitating to step in the sleigh. She was looking at us both now as if we were slightly crackbrained.

"Santaland's a two-hour flight away." The reindeer, I could tell, were getting restive. I leaned closer to her and lowered my voice. "We really need to get going. Nick had to call in some favors to get these reindeer to bring us here—most of them are doing it in secret. They didn't tell the rest of their herds what they're up to."

She tilted her head, her wry smile indicating that she was humoring me. "Because . . . ?"

"There's a reindeer strike."

"A Santaland reindeer strike?" She laughed. "You mean these are scabs?"

Nick came around to help her inside. He hadn't dressed in his Santa Suit—outside of Santaland, he only donned the suit on Christmas Eve. I was trying to think of some way to convince my friend that this was serious business. As it turned out, Donner, who was in the point position on the team, accomplished that for me by swinging his head around, ears twitching impatiently. "Are you ready, Santa?"

Claire pivoted toward me, eyes wide. "That reindeer just spoke."

"I think the team wants to leave now," I said.

She gaped at me. "This behemoth can fly?" Her gloved hand lifted toward the reindeer. "*They* can fly?"

"Yes, but it's a long way, and—"

Claire wasn't listening. She was digging around in her fat purse.

"What are you looking for?" I asked.

"If you think I'm getting on a flying sleigh without Dramamine, you've got another think coming."

She downed a Dramamine with a swig of something she'd bought at the duty free. By the time the sleigh reached a deserted side road where the team would have enough room to take off, Claire was out like a dead Christmas bulb and didn't awaken until we'd landed on Sugarplum Mountain. Which was probably fortunate. Even at Castle Kringle, the fantastic ancestral home of the Claus family, surrounded by my Claus in-laws and castle elves, she seemed to find the truth hard to accept. I think part of her still believed my married life was an elaborate Santaland cosplay hoax.

Today was Day Two of her Santaland visit, and she was still looking shell-shocked. I hoped by the end of her two-week visit that she'd get into the swing of things. I'd planned for Claire's visit to be full of music, food, and fun—a dessert potluck, a skate show, the big Kringle Heights Ladies' Guild craft bazaar, elf ballet, and, to top it all off, a fireworks show up at Kringle Lodge.

Elf cloggers aside, this was a day that would make anyone fall in love with Santaland. Christmastown had pulled out all the holiday stops for the ice sculpture event, and nature was doing her best to cooperate. The North Pole in December can dish out weather challenging for even the hardiest elf, but today the sky was clear, the air was still, and the world around us was a Technicolor wonderland. If faeries in sequins had skated across Peppermint Pond, I wouldn't have been a bit surprised. Judging by her already gobsmacked expression, Claire wouldn't have, either.

From my spot standing in the percussion section at the back of the band shell along with the rest of the Santaland Concert Band, I had the best view not only of Peppermint Pond, but of Christmastown, aglow with more than the usual number of lights strung across its streets and in every window. Looking up, I could view where the town gave way to the majestic rise of Sugarplum Mountain and the trees of the Christmas Tree Forest. On the mountain, the cottages and châteaus of Kringle Heights, strung with lights and shiny garlands, twinkled intermittently like distant stars. At a slightly higher elevation stood the elegant spires and towers of Castle Kringle. Against the background of fresh-fallen snow, the whole world shimmered and sparkled.

There was only one fly in the eggnog facing Santaland at

the moment: the aforementioned reindeer strike. My new sleigh, a hybrid model that worked on both electricity and hoof power, had been getting quite a workout ever since Santaland's reindeer had declared a walkout a week ago. I seriously doubted their grievance would last till Christmas Eve, but the strain was beginning to show in Nick's face. Christmas week was a bad time for Santa Claus to be uncertain of his reindeer.

"I wonder what's happened to Blinky," Juniper said, still craning. "He told me he wanted to be here to hear us play."

Blinky was Juniper's latest love interest. Though I hadn't been introduced to him yet, everyone in the Arctic Circle knew about him and his brother, Dabbs. Blinky was a brilliant inventor, and he and Dabbs ran Brightlow Brothers Enterprises, an electronics business that boasted of "Bringing Santaland into the 21st Century."

Smudge, crouched behind the drum kit, couldn't help sniping, "Blinky Brightlow won't show up for an event like this. Everyone knows he's a weirdo."

I took a deep breath. Smudge, Juniper's ex-boyfriend from years ago, always seemed interested in winning her back, but he didn't know the first thing about going about it. For one thing, criticizing Blinky for being eccentric when he himself had cultivated an outsider elf hipster persona was the height of hypocrisy. Of course, he looked anything but cool right now in our band uniform tunic of red and sparkly green, with a billed red hat festooned with a plume of dyed snow goose feathers.

Sure enough, Juniper rounded on him—forgetting we were onstage. "Pot. Kettle. Black." Her vehement tone turned the heads of several band members. Not that anyone in the audience was paying attention to us with twenty elves in spangled harlequin tunics clogging on a makeshift platform downstage. "Blinky isn't weird, he's *brilliant*. Just because he hasn't spent his whole life making candy canes . . ."

Smudge bristled at this slur on his profession. "Candy canes are the lifeblood of Santaland. I've never seen *you* turn one down."

Her cheeks flamed.

Oh God. There was going to be carnage on the bandstand.

Soupy, the tuba player, poked his head around his sousaphone and pinned an annoyed glance on us. "Will you three shush? They're about to announce the ice sculpture competition winner. I've got a box of Twinkle's Fried Pies riding on the Blitzen statue."

That shut us up. Twinkle's Fried Pies were the best. Having a box of their sweet, flaky goodness on the line was no small thing.

The elf cloggers finished to relieved applause and a stir of anticipation. The big moment was here. On the dais, Bella Sparkletoe passed a blue ribbon the size of a door wreath to Nick for him to bestow on the grand-prize winner for best ice sculpture.

In my opinion, Soupy's fried pies were as good as won. The statue of Blitzen the First—a three-times life-size rendering in ice of the legendary reindeer, with very intricate work on the antlers—was a shoo-in to take first place. When Claire, Juniper, and I toured all the sculptures around the pond this morning, we'd marveled at the detail the artist had used to render Blitzen, while at the same time conveying impressive majesty.

"How did they do this?" Claire almost shouted as she'd reached out to touch the ice with her mitten. "It looks like fur!"

The exquisite artistry had amazed Juniper and me, too. Considering how long ice statues lasted here in the frozen north, Blitzen the First would be gazing across Peppermint Pond for decades to come. And from a coldly calculating standpoint, given the situation with the reindeer strike, it was just good politics to award the grand prize to a statue honoring one of the most famous of Santa's original team. It was probably no coincidence that the dais had been set up right next to the Blitzen sculpture.

The entire audience leaned forward eagerly. Luther Partridge, our bandleader, raised his baton, and the band members scooted forward on their chairs and lifted their instruments. After Nick's speech, Smudge was going to do a drum roll. Then, when the ribbon was awarded, we were supposed to break into a rousing rendition of "Deck the Halls," which would turn into a sing-along. No elf gathering was complete without a sing-along.

Nick cleared his throat and thanked everyone again for attending. Public speaking didn't come easily to my husband—he was more at home being a manager than a front man for Santaland—but since taking up the mantle of Santa last year after his older brother died, he was getting better all the time.

I was annoyed, then, at a whining sound in the distance. Nick heard it, too, and kept flicking his gaze up from his prepared remarks like a picnicker being pestered by a mosquito. Each time he looked down again, his words came out a little faster and the whining grew louder.

Just as he walked across the dais with the wreath-sized blue ribbon to where the sculptor-contestants waited, a large mechanical drone buzzed into view overhead, too low for anyone's comfort. The drone resembled a stingray, except it had strange antler-like protuberances coming off both wings. Behind it trailed a long, red-and-white streaming banner, fluttering violently. Elves in the crowd pointed and exclaimed as the drone swooped over the dais. Nick, Claire, Mayor Firlog, and all the other dignitaries hit the deck. Next, the thing banked toward the audience, which emitted a collective shout.

Everyone ducked as the machine passed over their heads, creating a ripple effect. It was like watching a stadium wave, only terrifying.

As soon as the drone had cleared the seats, mayhem erupted. Elves and people darted for safety—but when a drone was still buzzing overhead, where was safety to be found? Audience members pushed over chairs in their hurry to escape from the open. Many stumbled on the overturned chairs, and then one another. Elf pileups created even more mayhem.

We on the covered bandstand watched it all in horror.

"What's going on?" Bobbin, the piccolo player, cried out. "What *is* that contraption?"

"A drone-deer," Smudge said in disgust.

Juniper pivoted toward me, scarlet in her cheeks. The drone-deer was one of Blinky's inventions, and the cause of all the strife between the people and the reindeer—the nonmechanical kind. The reindeer had gotten it into their heads that they might be replaced by these mechanized creatures.

I'd seen smaller models of Blinky's invention. Children had been playing with them for months. Nick's nephew, Christopher, owned one. But I'd never seen a drone-deer so large.

This one certainly wasn't a good advertisement for Blinky's product; it was going berserk. With a tortured whine, it climbed high, and then began to dive in a kind of death spiral—right toward the dais, toward Nick and Claire. Heart in throat, I lurched forward. Shouts of warning went up, and dignitaries dove under chairs. To my relief, the drone seemed to be on track to miss the dais itself. Instead, it crashed right into the magnificent statue of Blitzen the First. A long, sickening crackle like that of an icy branch as it falls sounded, and then the sculpture's elaborate ice antlers shattered into a thousand shards.

After the crash, a hiatus of eerie silence descended across

the pond. The crowd straightened, blinking in disbelief at the damage. Then a collective groan went up. The weight and speed of the drone had sheared off Blitzen the First's majestic head.

Elves and people swarmed toward the crash site. Juniper and I leapt off the bandstand and threaded our way to the front, where Nick and the other local grandees from the dais were inspecting the wreckage. I found Claire and put my arm around her. "I'm so glad you're okay."

"That was surreal!" she exclaimed. "Does stuff like this always happen around here?"

I shook my head. "Objects don't come crashing out of the sky." I thought for a moment, then added, "Except for the occasional drunken reindeer."

The silent shock of the crash passed, followed by a hubbub of outrage on behalf of the beautiful creation of Stew, the ice sculptor who'd created Blitzen the First. Stew pushed forward to view the decapitated head of his ice reindeer. Stew was tall for an elf, and whippet thin. When he fell to his knees beside his fallen creation, it created a sad tableau.

"How could this have happened?" he asked, as much from shock as anger. "Who allows these things to fly around Santaland?"

"Drone-deer aren't usually dangerous," Juniper said, a hint of desperation in her voice as she stood up for Blinky Brightlow's creation. "Something must have gone wrong with this one."

Understatement of the week.

Someone shouted, "It was a targeted attack!"

"Now, we don't know that," Nick said, trying to maintain calm.

"It had to be!" another elf called out. "Those drones go where you program them to."

"If they can't be controlled, they shouldn't be flying

around Christmastown," Bella Sparkletoe declared. "It's bad for commerce."

"What if it had hit a child?" someone else shouted.

"Or me?" said the mayor.

The shouts were drowned out by a siren blare at the back of the crowd. Everyone turned and then parted for Constable Crinkles, who bustled toward the crash site brandishing a bullhorn. Santaland's answer to law enforcement usually resembled a basketball-shaped Keystone Cop, but today instead of his uniform coat he was wearing what looked like a collegiate letterman jacket with *CT* embroidered on one side. He was also coach of the Twinklers, Christmastown's iceball team, whose season started in January. Clearly he'd expected this event to provide a recruiting opportunity.

"Let us pass," he commanded piercingly through the bullhorn. Also unnecessarily, since everyone had already cleared a path for him and his skinny deputy and nephew, Ollie.

The constable stopped next to the wreckage. "What's the problem here?" He was still yelling into the bullhorn.

"You have to arrest whoever killed my statue," Stew announced. "Blitzen the First was going to win first place."

"You don't know that," said Punch, another sculptor. The crusty old elf had been last year's winner. Though his entry this year, a replica of Castle Kringle's old tower, was impressive, he had to be the only one who believed his work stood a snowball's chance in Arizona against the Blitzen statue.

"Santa will tell us," Mayor Firlog declared. "Was Stew about to win first place?"

"Well, yes," Nick admitted, walking over to the headless reindeer. "But now . . ."

Punch whooped joyfully, hopping up and down in his curly-toed boots. "I win!"

"You do not." Stew jumped to his feet and planted mittened fists on his hips. "What's more, if you ruined my statue, you're going to jail."

Punch gaped at him. "What did *I* do?"

"You murdered my statue. Admit it!"

"Wait a second!" Crinkles shouted into the bullhorn, causing us all to wince. "I can't arrest anyone till I have all the facts." The sentence was barely out before the bullhorn let out another eardrum-piercing shriek that sent a wave of groans through the crowd.

"Shut that thing off," Mayor Firlog said, bustling forward. He turned to Nick. "Santa, what should we do?"

"Arrest Punch." Stew gestured his wiry arm out to his sculpting rival. "He obviously wanted this to happen. Look at him gloating!"

"Wanting to win's not a crime," Punch declared. "Besides, if anybody should be arrested, it's Blinky Brightlow. *He's* the one who created this infernal contraption."

"He sold it to someone who programmed it," Juniper pointed out. "That's who did this, not Blinky. Blinky's not even here."

"Then find him and make him tell us who's responsible!" Punch said. "He must know who bought the bloomin' thing."

"But why?" Stew's voice was practically a wail. "Why would anyone but another sculptor want to ruin *Blitzen the First?*"

"If you'd made it better, it wouldn't have been so easy to ruin," Punch sniped.

Just when it looked as if the day's event would devolve into an elf sculptor knock-down, drag-out, Nick stepped forward, holding the banner that had been trailing from the drone. Our gazes met for the briefest of moments. The dread I saw in my husband's eyes sent a spike of foreboding through me. Last year, an incident at the ice sculpture contest had set off a week of murder and mayhem in Santaland. Was history repeating itself?

"This crash was meant to deliver a message," Nick announced. "This banner has words written on it." He'd accordioned the banner so that no one could read all the words, though.

"What does it say?" the mayor asked impatiently.

To Mayor Firlog's annoyance, Nick turned to Constable Crinkles before unfurling the banner. Nick believed in going through the proper channels, and discretion.

The same couldn't be said of Constable Crinkles. He scanned the banner, and as he read he yelled the words into his bullhorn loud enough for all of Santaland to hear. But when I finally glimpsed the message, I could see why. The letters were in all caps, angry red against a white background.

THIS IS JUST THE BEGINNING!!!

Chapter 2

The beginning of what?

A hubbub of speculation followed Crinkles's broadcast of the banner's cryptic message. Were more drone attacks on the way? Glances flicked anxiously skyward as the crowd filtered away from Peppermint Pond. Many of us headed toward the Christmastown Constabulary to discuss the morning's events.

Claire and I walked on each side of Juniper, who was checking her phone for messages. "I don't know where Blinky could be," Juniper said. "He should have been here."

"If his company built that sculpture-beheading drone," Claire said, "maybe it's better that he stayed away."

Juniper opened her mouth to argue, but then stopped herself. Claire was right. Since Blinky's creation was at the center of the trouble, maybe it was just as well that he'd missed the event. That crowd had been itching for a scapegoat.

Claire's eyes widened as we approached the constabulary. "*This* is a police station?"

The constabulary was housed in an old cottage on the edge of Christmastown. It was an elf cottage, of course, and Claire wasn't yet used to the slightly smaller scale. As we entered, the low, coved ceilings made her hunch instinctively, even though she was only a little over five feet tall. It had taken me months to assure my inner spatial barometer that I wasn't going to bang my skull on every doorway.

The interior looked more like something out of an old-fashioned *Good Housekeeping* magazine than a police station. Few signs of law enforcement were on view here in the cottage's old dining room, which was still dominated by a long, lace cloth–covered table and chairs. The sideboard served as a file cabinet, with decorative plates on stands used as paperweights. Cheery mistletoe-patterned paper covered the walls, on which several winter scenes hung in gilt frames. A fireplace almost as long as the table took up one side of the room. A metal grate with reindeer prancing across the top protected the hearth, and from the greenery-and-candle-festooned mantel hung two stockings bearing the names *Crinkles* and *Ollie* in neatly embroidered letters.

At that moment, Deputy Ollie, now sporting a smock apron over his uniform, emerged from the kitchen with a tray of cookies to pass around. The whole point of coming here was to discuss this morning's incident away from the crowd, but a large part of the crowd had followed and were all squeezed inside the constabulary. The sculptors were still arguing, Mayor Firlog was blustering away that something needed to be done, and Juniper broke away from Claire and me to buttonhole Crinkles.

"I've called and texted Blinky," she informed him. "He's not responding."

From Crinkles's flummoxed expression, he didn't see anything odd in the inventor's absence. I wasn't sure I did, either.

Ollie stopped in front of Claire and me. "Cookie?"

"No thanks," I said.

He nudged the platter closer to tempt me. "They're cranberry cashew."

"Oh." There went my willpower. I took one, and Ollie reached into his apron pocket and handed me a dainty paper napkin edged in poinsettias. "They're really good," I told Claire.

She took one, too.

Ollie was gaping at Claire now. "Say," he said, "you're pretty tall! Ever think about joining the iceball team? You should talk to my uncle about—"

"Ollie," I interrupted, "this is my friend Claire, from Oregon. She's not an elf."

He drew back. "Oh! That's too bad. We just lost our forward."

As he continued circulating with the cookies, Claire rounded on me, alarmed. "Do I really look like an elf?"

"You have a hat on." Except for small stature and larger ear profile, elves did resemble humans. Ears were the real giveaway.

We lowered ourselves into velvet side chairs next to where the constabulary's tea trolley was parked. Claire looked quizzically at the china tea service in a traditional elf pattern of cottages against a background of snowy mountains. She arched a brow at me.

"Okay, so it's not *Law and Order*," I said.

She laughed. "It's not even Mayberry."

Juniper came over to us and flopped into a free chair. "Something terrible's happened to him, and nobody seems to care."

Her Cassandra-like tone sent a first stab of real fear for Blinky through me. Juniper had bad luck with boyfriends.

"I'm sure the constable and his deputy will sort it out," Claire said. The words were meant to be soothing, but they had the opposite effect on Juniper, who blurted out a hysterical laugh.

"Crinkles isn't known for his Sherlock Holmes acuity," I whispered to Claire.

Ollie had made his way around the assembled elves and people and come full circle back to us. "You're in luck," he told Juniper. "I still have a few left."

The cookies were the last straw for her. "I don't want a cookie." Her voice cracked. "I just want to know where Blinky is! What's happened to him?"

Shocked stares fell on us. Few had seen shows of temper from Juniper, the mildest-mannered of the Christmastown librarians.

"Blinky's fine," announced a voice unfamiliar to me.

Everyone swiveled toward the elf who had come in. Even though we'd never met, I knew who he was. He'd been featured on the latest edition of *Santaland Today* magazine along with his brother, Blinky. Dabbs Brightlow stood in the arched doorway in a dark green velvet coat and cap with a matching green velvet puffball at the tip. His hands were buried in his pockets. He didn't look pleased about having been dragged from his place of business to account for the damage caused by a Brightlow drone.

Juniper shot to her feet. "Where is he?"

Dabbs shrugged. "Not sure. He wasn't at the office this morning."

"Why not?" she asked.

"Probably because he was crashing that infernal drone into *my* statue," Stew said.

"He wouldn't do that," Juniper insisted.

"Well, Dabbs and Blinky must know who did," the sculptor said.

"It could have been any number of elves—or people," Dabbs said, seeming unconcerned. "We have the occasional friction with customers, just like any other business. We get our share of negative Yelf! reviews."

Yelf! was the review site for Santalanders to vent about service at local businesses. Would an elf announce their evil intentions on a public website, though?

"Who have you sold those drone-deer to?" Stew asked.

"I'll be happy to find that out and provide the constable with a list," Dabbs said. "Brightlow Brothers will cooperate with an investigation in every way possible. As the inventors and distributors of the drone-deer, we deeply regret that this unfortunate event occurred, and we expect an investigation to completely exonerate us of any responsibility. But of course it's not our fault if someone misuses our product."

The words held all the sincerity of a corporate press release. Dabbs was here solely to cover the company's backside.

"If you haven't seen Blinky, how do you know he's okay?" Juniper demanded.

"Because I know my brother. He's a dreamer, and this is how he gets his ideas. He wanders off and thinks."

Juniper shook her head. "But he told me he wanted to be at Peppermint Pond today. Shouldn't we organize a search? What if he's been elfnapped?"

No one hopped up to volunteer for the search party.

"Did Blinky say he wanted to be there, or *would* be there?" Mayor Firlog asked.

Juniper's brow furrowed. "Wanted to," she admitted with a sigh.

"He'll come back," Dabbs assured her.

Strange that Juniper could be sick with worry while his own brother was so blasé.

"How can you be so sure Blinky's okay?" I asked.

Dabbs waved away Ollie's proffered cookie tray and eyed me impatiently. "Blinky's whole life is Brightlow Enterprises. He doesn't have anything else."

"He has me," Juniper lamented.

Dabbs tilted his head, looking at her. "Of course." But the
dismissive tone in those two clipped words spoke volumes.

Juniper reddened, and for a moment it looked as if she
might burst into tears. But she held it together. I had no idea
that she and Blinky had grown so close. For the past few days
I'd been so busy getting ready for Claire's visit, I only listened
with half an ear to Juniper telling me about her exciting new
romance. Now I wondered. Maybe she had misjudged how
well she knew him. After all, if his own family and business
partners felt sure he was okay . . .

"That drone-deer made a direct hit on *my* statue," Stew
said, dragging the conversation back to what concerned him
most. "This was an attack on *me*. Why?"

"And what does this mean for Christmastown, for Santaland?" Mayor Firlog asked. "How can we have our usual holiday celebrations outdoors when elves are worried about
things dropping out of the sky?"

Everyone turned to the constable.

Reindeer-in-the-headlights panic overtook Crinkles. Then
again, it didn't take much to overwhelm Santaland's top law-
man. "What exactly am I supposed to be looking into?" he
asked in a quavering, doubtful tone.

"Blinky's disappearance," Juniper said.

"Public mayhem!" shouted Mayor Firlog. Stew stood.
"What about my statue?"

"It's gone," Punch, the rival sculptor, said. "You'd best
melt it down and start over. What I want to know is, did I win
first place or didn't I?"

"Who cares?" Juniper shot back at him. "An elf's life
could be at stake. Nobody's worried about who got the ribbon for your cockadoodie sculpture."

"Hey now!" Crinkles said. "Simmer down. There's no
call to start throwing that kind of language around."

"What if someone elfnapped Blinky?" Juniper said. "That message on the drone-deer was a warning about something."

At this reminder of the ominous banner, murmurs rumbled around the room. *This is just the beginning.* What was "this"? The targeting of statues? Blinky's disappearance?

One thing about that banner made me doubt that the drone-deer had anything to do with an elfnapping. "The message on the drone didn't ask for anything," I pointed out. The words were menacing, but they didn't indicate anyone was holding Blinky.

Nick nodded at me, understanding. "No ransom demand."

"Not even a statement of what this was the beginning of," I said.

Crinkles scratched one of his chins. "That's true."

Juniper looked at me sharply. "Maybe that just means whoever has Blinky doesn't care about money."

"But an elfnapper would want something," I said.

"No one has been elfnapped," Dabbs said.

"The message said this was just the beginning," Mayor Firlog fretted. "It might be the beginning of a Christmas week crime wave!"

A speculative hum of dread went around the room.

"If the drone-deer was part of a larger warning," Juniper said above the whispers, "maybe the reindeer are the connection between the crash and Blinky's disappearance."

Shocked silence descended. Juniper was implying that the reindeer herds were somehow responsible for an elfnapping, or at the very least the drone-deer crash.

There was no denying that the reindeer were red up to their antlers over the drone-deer. Not only did they find it offensive for their most distinctive feature to be used as a marketing gimmick for the drones, they also worried that drones would prove the final nail in the coffin of reindeer usefulness. The herds had looked on warily as snowmobiles had become popular, worrying that their transport service would become obsolete—which was nonsense. Reindeer sleighs were still the favored method of getting around Santaland, especially by the extended Claus family on Sugarplum Mountain, where the number of reindeer pulling the family sleigh was a measure of status.

"I don't get it," Claire whispered to me. "If reindeer didn't strike over hybrid sleighs and snowmobiles, why should drones trigger a walkout?"

"Because drones do the one thing that only Santaland's reindeer can do," I said. "They fly."

Her mouth formed an O of understanding, and I could see her eyes acknowledge that what I'd told her about the sleigh trip here from Fairbanks was real.

Dabbs finally cast a kindly glance at Juniper. "The librarian actually makes an excellent point. The reindeer *have* been hostile to our product from the beginning."

"Of course the reindeer are at the bottom of this," Stew said, jumping on this new bandwagon of blame. "That crash was all about ruining my Blitzen statue."

He seemed to have forgotten that five minutes ago he was calling for Blinky to be jailed, and his rival sculptor before that. My instinct was to argue against Juniper's reindeer theory, but I bit my tongue. I didn't want to cross my friend here, in front of all these people.

And what if all this *did* have something to do with reindeer? That would be weird, but this was Santaland, after all. A year and a half ago I didn't think reindeer could fly. Once you wrapped your head around that phenomenon, reindeer forming an ice-sculpture vandalizing and elfnapping cabal wasn't too much of a stretch.

Nick stepped up, raising his hands to quiet down the buzz of speculation in the room. "There's an all-herd meeting tonight," he announced. "The reindeer are going to be discussing their grievances. I'll be there, of course, and I'll bring this matter up with them. Maybe the herds know something about the crash." He cast a glance at Juniper. "Or about Blinky's whereabouts."

Crinkles nodded like a bobblehead at Nick's side. "I'll question as many reindeer as I can—and I don't want to hear anything about retaliation against the herds by any elf in Santaland." He sent a warning glare at Stew before turning to Juniper. "And I'll send Ollie out to talk with the snowmen around town. One of them might have seen or heard something about Blinky."

Claire blurted out a laugh. "You'll talk to *snowmen*?"

Everyone turned, and I cringed. I hadn't introduced her to any snowmen yet. "It's actually a good idea," I told her in a low voice. "Snowmen are slow moving, so they sometimes prefer to stay in the same spot for months, or even years."

Her mouth dropped open but no words came out.

"Their charcoal eyes take in a lot," I explained.

"Right . . ." She swallowed and lowered her voice to a mutter. "I probably should have doubled up on my Xanax today."

The gathering finally broke up. Nick had business in town—there was still the controversy around the sculpture contest and the chaos at Peppermint Pond to sort out. Claire, Juniper, and I left him at the constabulary and walked back to Juniper's place, which was an apartment in the second floor of a three-story building not too far from the library. By Christmastown standards it was practically a high-rise.

She'd lived there for several months but had already made it seem like a real home—every place to sit had at least one decorative pillow and a throw blanket or shawl across the back. A corner was set aside for her music stand and euphonium, and one wall was lined with shelves weighed down with an impressive collection of books, fun bookends, framed photographs, and other mementos of her life. Her chunky white rabbit sprawled across the middle of the couch.

Claire squeed at the sight of the rabbit. "What a cute bunny. What's his name?"

"Dave," Juniper said.

Claire looked at me, puzzled. I guess she was expecting the rabbit to be named Fluffy or Snowy, but those were elf names. "You're not in Kansas anymore," I said.

"Like you have to remind me," she muttered.

I sat down next to Dave as Juniper started a fire.

Even Juniper's fireplace showed her love of unique objets d'art—she had a set of snowman andirons and matching fireplace tools decorated with brass snowmen handles. Snowmen and fire seemed like an uneasy combination to me, but they were charming.

Once she'd gotten a few flames to catch in the hearth, Juniper picked up the snowman poker and stabbed fitfully at a log. "I'm a boyfriend jinx," she lamented.

"Stop talking that way," I said. "Nobody knows yet if anything's really happened to Blinky."

"His own brother insists he's fine," Claire pointed out.

Juniper snorted at that. "Dabbs only cares that his company won't take the blame for what happened today."

"You and Blinky just started going out, though," I said. "Maybe his brother's right about his disappearing sometimes."

Juniper had just gotten shed of one disastrous boyfriend in October. When she'd told me about Blinky a few weeks ago, I'd had to bite my tongue to keep from voicing the word *rebound*.

She blew out a breath. "It's true, we only had three dates. And actually he was a no-show for one of them . . ."

"He stood you up?" Claire asked.

Juniper hung the poker back on its holder and crossed to her little kitchen island to pour us all a glass of sweet bearberry wine. "He just forgot. Some people would say he's absent-minded—you know that stereotype. But he's the opposite of absentminded. He's so focused on whatever he's working on that it crowds out everything else."

"Even sex?" Claire asked. Talking about someone's love life—even the love life of an elf—made her seem more like her usual self.

Juniper blushed. "We just—you know—that first time. When he came to the library, it was around closing time, and he wanted to tell me more about a problem he was working on, so I invited him here for a drink."

"What was he working on?" I asked.

"It had something to do with"—her forehead scrunched—"efficiency of movement? I think that's how he put it. I told him that I just needed to do some housework, but he said he enjoyed watching me."

Claire's brows soared. "A housework fetish? That's a new one."

Juniper shook her head. "I think it was more of a scientific study at first. He was really insistent that I do whatever chores I had. He took tons of pictures of me. But then I sat next to him, and . . ."

"One thing led to another," Claire said, taking a sip of the wine. If she was unprepared for the sweetness of it, she didn't show it. Of course, it was probably hard to sweeten something too much for a woman who ran an ice cream parlor. "So, not a strictly-science guy."

"Not at all," Juniper said, before shaking her head. "At

least, that's what I *thought*. The second time he came over he just wanted to watch me making soup."

"Soup," Claire repeated, skepticism oozing into her husky voice.

Juniper plopped down on the other side of Dave. "I was making my grandmother's snailfish chowder, so I invited him over. He was excited about that—said he wanted to come early and watch me cook. And he was very sweet. He even brought me flowers."

Flowers? Blinky wasn't just an inventor, he was a miracle worker. "Where did he find flowers in December?"

She reached for a book on her mantel. It was *A Christmas Carol* in its first Santaland printing—a priceless heirloom, with hand-colored drawings protected by tissue paper. She opened it and a piece of paper slipped out. In its folds were some small, dried flowers. "Arctic buttercups," she said. "They only bloom in a certain place on the tundra here, for a brief time in July. Blinky brought them to me."

"That was sweet of him," Claire said.

Juniper bit her lip. "Well, actually, Blinky said he brought them to me to use as herbs to put in the soup—but they're very bitter and they really don't belong in snailfish chowder. So I set them aside."

Set them aside in her favorite possession.

"That night with the chowder, though, Blinky really was just focused on watching me make chowder. And then he barely stayed to try it. He had to get back to the lab—he said he was working on something life changing."

"Something to do with your soup?" Claire asked.

"I'm not sure. I mean, Granny Greenleaf's snailfish chowder is yummy, but I wouldn't call it life changing." She sighed. "I ended up freezing most of it."

"When was this?" I asked.

"About a week ago."

"And then for the third date he stood you"—Claire caught herself—"forgot?"

Claire and I exchanged a quick glance, and I could tell we were on the same page. This was essentially a one-night stand, and the soup visit had just been an awkward stab at letting Juniper down gently. The third date—the no-show—was Blinky cutting the cord.

"But we'd already talked about today," Juniper said. "I told him I was playing in the band at the ice sculpture contest, and he said he would like to see that."

"From what you've told us, there's no way you should think of yourself as a jinx," Claire said. "You and Blinky were barely—"

Juniper cut her off. "Even if we don't have a romantic relationship—not really—I care about what happens to him. And I have a premonition that something's gone wrong. Maybe something happened to him days ago, and that's why he didn't come over the last time."

I nodded. No sense antagonizing her.

Nevertheless, she focused a hurt look on me. "You barely took my side at all in the meeting at the constabulary."

"I was just trying to figure things out."

"What about the reindeer?" she said, her tone growing more vehement. "You didn't back me up on that line of questioning."

"Because Nick and Crinkles took it up. Besides, I just can't imagine reindeer being able to operate drones."

Juniper crossed her arms. "Maybe the reindeer can't, but what about reindeer advocates?"

It was no mystery whom she was talking about. Nick's sister, Lucia, was the North Pole's biggest reindeer activist and supporter.

"Where *was* Lucia today?" Juniper asked, her eyes steely.

She was right. I hadn't seen her anywhere near Peppermint Pond. Lucia, statuesque and blond, was a hard figure to miss.

"I don't know. She was probably—" *With the reindeer,* I almost said. "But Lucia wouldn't do that."

Juniper laughed. "You think Lucia's not hotheaded enough to pull a stunt like this?"

Was she? My sister-in-law was gruff, but not malicious.

Juniper shook her head. "I just keep worrying that drone-deer banner warning has something to do with Blinky."

But surely she didn't think Lucia would have anything to do with Blinky's disappearance.

"Okay, let's look for him," I offered. "Christmastown's not that big."

"But he could be anywhere—at least according to Dabbs." She sniffed. "No, you shouldn't let my problems ruin your week with Claire."

"It wouldn't ruin anything," I insisted.

"Honestly," Claire said, "if we can be any help finding Blinky, we should start before it gets dark. On TV they always say the first twenty-four hours—"

I cleared my throat. No sense planting a gruesome timeline in Juniper's imagination.

Juniper blew out a breath. "You two should go back to the castle. You have a tea to attend, remember?"

I'd forgotten that my mother-in-law, Pamela, was having a tea this afternoon. "You should come with us. Pamela invited you."

"Yes! Join us," Claire said, smiling encouragingly. "I'm supposed to help her put the finishing touches on the dessert she's serving today, and I think Tiffany will be in the kitchen, too. It'll be like the Great Santaland Bake Off."

Juniper petted Dave. "I should stay here. In case Blinky calls."

The gloom in her expression conveyed that she didn't expect he would call, however.

Outside, as we got into the sleigh, Claire looked at me. "So what do you think? Is this Blinky an absentminded inventor, a heartless lothario, and a reindeer statue destroyer—or an elfnapping victim?"

I wasn't sure. But I couldn't rule out the possibility that he was all of the above.

Chapter 3

Conventional wisdom might say that you can't prove a negative, but that's what I intended to do. The last thing Santaland needed was for everyone to be pointing the finger of blame at the reindeer, especially when the herds already had their antlers in a twist over the Brightlow drones. If I could show that reindeer *couldn't* have crashed the drone this morning, maybe reindeer relations would normalize and elf tempers would simmer down.

Everything I needed for my experiment was waiting for me at home. At Castle Kringle I had access to both a drone-deer and a reindeer. The former, a miniature model, belonged to Christopher, Nick's nephew. Christopher was destined to be the next Santa Claus; Nick was only serving as Santa regent until Christopher reached his twenty-first birthday. In the meantime, he was just another kid, amped up for Christmas and counting down the hours until school lessons were over for the holiday.

When I pulled him out of his mathematics lesson to ask if I could borrow the drone-deer mini he'd received for his recent birthday from his Uncle Amory, his excitement soon turned to disappointment. "You mean I have to study while the adults play with my toys?"

"Not play, exactly. I want to show Claire the drone and conduct a little experiment."

He liked Claire and I could tell he was inclined to be generous for her sake. But he was also a twelve-year-old boy and not above leveraging a little bargaining power during Christmas week. "If I lend it to you, you've got to promise to put in a good word for me with Uncle Nick," he said. "I want a Selfy."

I blinked. Wasn't a selfie just something you took with a camera? I guessed he meant he wanted one of those selfie sticks . . . which seemed like an odd request from a twelve-year-old. But what kids considered cool now was unfathomable to me. In fact, I wasn't even sure the word *cool* was cool. Nothing like being around a preteen to make one feel unhip right down to the hems of your mom jeans.

"It's a deal," I said.

"Yes!" While his tutor waited, Christopher led me to the closet that served as his drone-deer hangar and brought out his toy. Like the larger drone that had crashed into the statue this morning, this device had antlers coming out of its wings and was made of heavy, industrial-grade plastic. The difference was that this model featured a goofy cartoon reindeer face with googly eyes on its triangular body. There was nothing lethal about it.

He also handed me a joystick control panel, like the ones used in remote-control model airplanes. I eyed it dubiously.

"It's really easy," he said. "You just turn it on and use the joystick to control its movements. You know, like with video games? You had those, right?"

I cleared my throat. "I'm thirty-five, not a hundred and five. We had video games."

"Oh yeah, like *Pong*."

"I'm very much post-*Pong*, thank you very much." But my understanding had been that drone-deer were operated by computer. "You can't program the drone-deer on a computer?"

"Well, you *can*. It's not as fun, though." For this, he gave me instructions for an app I had to download on my phone. Even in Santaland, there was an app for everything, and evidently a drone-deer was no exception. He also went over the joystick method, explaining it all with long-suffering patience.

"This is a drone-deer mini," I said when he was finished. "Would a larger model be operated differently?"

His eyes lit up. "Like the big one that caused all the damage today? Did it really score a direct hit?"

I admitted that it had. "Could that one have been controlled by a remote?"

He shrugged. "I guess so."

After giving me a few more instructions, Christopher went back to irrational numbers and I hurried off with my borrowed drone-deer to disprove irrational elf theories.

On the way, I looked down at the joystick Christopher had propped on the drone-deer's nose. If the larger ones could also be maneuvered on the fly and not just preprogrammed via computer, then whoever had crashed the drone-deer could have been anywhere with sight lines of Peppermint Pond. But since it still *could* have been preprogrammed, the culprit might also have been anyone standing in plain sight at Peppermint Pond today. Or someone who hadn't been there at all.

In other words, it could have been anyone.

Anyone except a reindeer. I was sure of that.

I looked up to see my test subject, Quasar, a misfit reindeer Lucia had taken in years ago. He was at the end of a corridor on the ground floor of the castle, his muzzle buried in a greenery display. Belatedly sensing my presence, he snapped his head up and stepped back quickly. He had one bit of antler that had yet to shed—he was always a little later than other males in this regard. That single ragged antler combined with his red nose fizzling nervously and the pine needles stuck to his mouth made him appear as awkward—and guilty—as possible.

"I j-just couldn't help myself," he said in his defense.

He was forbidden from munching on castle decorations, an especially difficult stricture this time of year. Castle Kringle always had tiny Christmas decorative lights strung along the hallways and fresh wreaths put out. But in December we pulled out all the festive stops and every surface was decked with greenery and festooned with ribbons, twinkle lights, and tinsel. It was hard to walk ten feet without bumping against another cheerful tree. From a reindeer's point of view, they were as tempting as the candy dishes displayed everywhere were to me. Every hallway probably seemed like a giant, forbidden smorgasbord.

"I won't tell," I promised. "You're just the reindeer I was looking for. I want to get your help in a little demonstration. Come with me to the salon."

Quasar was usually the most biddable of creatures, but he didn't move a muscle to follow me. "I'd b-better not. Mrs. Claus is having a tea."

He meant Pamela, my mother-in-law.

"That's why I want to do this now. We'll have an audience." An audience of Kringle Heights gossips, no less.

Quasar still hesitated. "She made a special b-bûche de Noël."

"That's okay." My mother-in-law loved making elaborate desserts, but after a previous pastry mishap, Quasar and I were watched with suspicion around her creations. "Just remember it's not a real log," I counseled him. "No lichen on it."

He still hesitated, and I couldn't blame him. Pamela Claus was a matriarch with many excellent qualities, but she'd never been wild about having Quasar wandering around the castle. I suspected that she only allowed his presence inside because she was as intimidated by Lucia as the rest of us were.

"Come on." I beckoned him with my head, since my hands were full. "I'm going to conduct an important demonstration, and you're the essential element."

Quasar might be a misfit, but as his nose clearly showed, he was from the Rudolph herd. If there was anything a reindeer with Rudolph blood loved to hear, it was that he was needed. Suddenly his nose glowed steadily and strong, and his eyes lit up as if he'd just been asked to head up the team of Santa's sleigh on the big night. He clopped resolutely after me to the salon—as resolutely as he could with his slightly lopsided gait.

The large family room on the first floor was where the Claus family spent afternoons when they were in the castle, and today it was the room where my mother-in-law was holding court for a lot of our family, both close and distant. I loved a high tea—and the old-fashioned Christmas music coming from the old cabinet hi-fi in the corner lent the air a cozy holiday buzz. Or maybe it wasn't Perry Como providing the buzz. This tea had been planned as a relaxing event after the do at Peppermint Pond, but everyone was still keyed up from the drone crash.

Pamela was holding court in her favorite armchair. She was dressed in a red-and-green dress in the A-line style favored by Queen Elizabeth, with shoes dyed to match the green. With her gray hair coiled at the crown of her head and a pair of wire bifocals perched on her nose, she was the very picture of a perfect Mrs. Claus.

Claire seemed more relaxed among the human company. She was sitting on the couch next to Elspeth Claus, who draped languorously over one of the sofa's arms. Elspeth lived with Mildred, an older cousin of Nick's. I'd had a run-in with

Elspeth last spring when she'd been accidentally left off my guest list for a Spring Fancy party I'd had here at the castle. I was new in Santaland last year and didn't yet know all the Clauses that well. The party had been a big success—I booked the Swingin' Santas to play, and they're always a hit—and Elspeth had been invited as soon as I discovered the omission. Too late. Elspeth sent her regrets, and ever since then, she'd been sending me resentful vibes.

Nick's cousin Amory's wife, Midge, along with cousin Mildred Claus, and Christopher's mother, Tiffany, were all seated nearby. Tiffany ran a tea shop in town called Tea-piphany and was taking off part of the afternoon to cater Pamela's tea. Partially cater. Pamela's elaborate, fabulous bûche de Noël took pride of place in the middle of the table, an edible masterwork of icing leaves, candy forest animals, spun sugar icicles, and of course a delicious cake log.

I eyed it and then sent a pointed glance back at Quasar. "Not a real log," I murmured as a reminder.

"G-got it."

My appearance brought a crooked smile from Elspeth. "And here's the third Mrs. Claus," she drawled.

She was correct, though it rankled all three of us Mrs. C's for her to say so. Pamela was the dowager Mrs. Claus, Tiffany was the widow of Nick's late brother, the last Santa, and I was the wife of the regent Santa.

"And Quasar," I said, not wanting him to feel snubbed.

"H-hello," he said shyly to the gathered company.

Tiffany laughed at the sight of me standing there with my arms full, and she sprang up to investigate. I always envied her boundless energy. "What did you bring, April? Something for show-and-tell?"

"Christopher loaned me his drone-deer mini. I wanted to conduct a little experiment."

Pamela's lips pursed in disapproval. "We're having tea."

"I'll wait till after tea," I said.

"You'd think we would have had enough of drones for one day," Mildred said fretfully.

"This is a child's toy?" Elspeth loped over and peered down at it. "What does it do?"

"It's a mini drone-deer, and it flies," I said. "Sort of like a remote-control airplane."

"That's not like the one that demolished the Blitzen sculpture, is it?" Mildred migrated over with the others and eyed the hunk of plastic warily, as if it might fly up and demolish her at any moment.

"That one was much bigger," Midge said, puffing up in distaste. "Worthless contraptions, in my opinion. Amory had one at Kringle Lodge. He says those Brightlows are always overhyping themselves."

"You shouldn't fly that thing in the house," Pamela scolded me from across the room.

"I'm not," I assured her. That was the whole point. No reindeer would be able to get the thing off the ground.

"Christopher flies *on* it?" Mildred asked, bug-eyed.

"No—he just operates by remote control, or from an app."

"We should leave flying to reindeer," Pamela insisted. "Real ones."

"I only want to have a demonstration to disprove what people around town were saying about the drone crash," I said. "It couldn't have been the reindeers' doing."

"The reindeer have been behaving abominably," Midge said with an indignant sniff. "Amory and I had to drive down here this afternoon on snowmobiles. So undignified."

"My goal is to de-escalate the crisis," I told her, "so the reindeer will calm down and come back to work."

"It would serve them right if we did replace them all, anyway," Elspeth said, as if Quasar weren't standing right there, able to hear every word. "Seems to me like we coddle reindeer around here too much as it is."

Everyone shifted uncomfortably. Quasar didn't have too many reindeer friends, but what Elspeth said would surely reach Lucia's ears, and Lucia would be furious.

Where is Lucia? Juniper's insinuation about her being the cause of this morning's chaos hovered in the back of my mind.

"So what's this demonstration you want to do?" Claire asked.

"I'm just going to show that there's no way a reindeer could run it. Especially if the drone this morning was run by computer." I looked at Quasar. "Reindeer can't use computers, can you, Quasar?"

He perked up, eager to demonstrate his incompetence. "N–no. Not at all."

"Of course, I've just learned that there's a remote control . . ." I took it off the drone and inspected it, trying to remember what Christopher had told me. It was a puzzling design. There was a red on/off switch, and the joystick with large directional arrows on the four sides of it. I had no idea why the arrows were so large—it was like they were part of a toddler toy. Apart from that, there was just a switch on the back that said EM/RM. I had no idea what either designated.

Right now it was toggled to EM. I frowned. Maybe I should have asked for the instruction book. But how hard could a child's toy be to figure out? Christopher said I just needed to turn it on and manipulate the joystick.

Not that it mattered, I reminded myself.

"The point," I said, "is that a reindeer can't work a joystick." I placed the remote on the floor in front of Quasar. "Can you?"

Quasar put his hoof on the joystick and tried to nudge it, but there was obviously no way for him to achieve purchase.

"You see?" I said. "Without opposable thumbs, it's ridiculous for people to think reindeer could be at the bottom of what happened today at Peppermint Pond. That drone landed a direct hit on Blitzen the First. It would have taken skill to do that."

"So if reindeer can't manipulate drones," Elspeth pointed out, "that just leaves every elf and person in Santaland as a possible suspect."

"Why would elves or people want to ruin a reindeer statue?" Tiffany asked.

"To show that we're not at their mercy." Midge wasn't letting go of her reindeer resentment.

"But we are—we still need them," I pointed out. "Mechanization can't replace everything. We shouldn't want it to."

Pamela crossed the room to ring the bell pull to summon Jingles. "It can't replace food, certainly. I've just rung for the tea tray to be brought in. I received a preview in the kitchen earlier. Between our cooks and Tiffany's shop, we've put together a very impressive tea for you today, if I do say so myself."

We all took our seats expectantly, with Quasar lingering closer to the door, probably in hopes of seeing Lucia.

"Where's Lucia?" I asked.

Pamela let out a little puff of exasperation. "Who knows? Probably running around on some reindeer business. I haven't seen her all day."

Claire looked at me, and I could tell she, too, was thinking about what Juniper had said earlier, intimating that Lucia could have crashed the drone-deer.

The talk turned to the Kringle Heights Ladies' Guild Holiday Crafts Bazaar, a few days away now. Just the thought set off a churning in the pit of my stomach. I wasn't a crafty person, but Pamela had convinced me that anyone could knit tea cozies. She'd even designed an adorable pattern for me to follow—a tea cozy in the shape of a fat Christmas tree, decorated with stars and tiny jingle bells she'd special ordered. She'd also bought all the wool I'd need to make about a hundred of them. Then she'd signed me up for a booth at the bazaar. All I needed to do was knit them. I'd finished exactly zero.

The upshot was, I had a bunch of tea cozies to knit, which I was frantically trying to do in my free time at night. So far each one I'd finished ended up being unraveled the next day when I saw how misshapen it was. I hadn't yet worked up the nerve to tell Pamela, an expert knitter, that I was a knitting washout.

"I have a booth this year," Elspeth bragged as if renting a booth were a great accomplishment. "It's going to be fabulous."

It felt as if the oxygen had been sucked out of the room. Last year for the charity bazaar Elspeth had spent months knitting her own innovation: ear socks. Think little knit shower caps for the ear—that's what they looked like. And she took a lot of care with them, knitting them in all kinds of festive patterns. Even Pamela praised her work. But Elspeth never sold a single pair of ear socks at the bazaar, even though she'd made them for both elf and human ears of all sizes. It turned out, no one in Santaland was clamoring for ear socks. According to Mildred, Elspeth had been distraught for weeks.

"I wonder what's happened to the tea," Pamela said, obviously trying to shift everyone's thoughts away from ear socks.

Claire jumped up. "I'll ring again."

"Thank you," Pamela said.

My friend laughed as she tugged on the pull. "I just love to do that. It's so *Downton Abbey*."

Before Claire could return to her seat, the double doors to the salon opened and a trolley was wheeled in. But the servant pushing it wasn't Jingles, the castle steward, although it bore a certain resemblance to him. The being behind the elaborate tea cart was a mechanical creature with a bulbous body draped in the black-and-white tunic of a castle footman. His head, a perfect oval, had been decorated to resemble a cartoonish facsimile of Jingles's face, including his receding chin and the lock of black hair artfully spanning his forehead to mask a retreating hairline.

Everyone gasped, as much at the mechanical servant as at the impressive tower of sandwiches, cakes, and scones that stood alongside the silver tea service. The trolley was wheeled right up to Pamela's side.

"Oh my," my mother-in-law said, red in her cheeks. "Thank you—" She stopped short, not sure how to address a robot.

"You're welcome," the machine replied, and the gathered company jumped in shock. Tiffany even let out a yelp.

Jingles, the castle steward, looking smug, arrived to check up on his helper's work. "Is everything to your satisfaction, madam?"

"Where did you get this thing?" Midge demanded. Having recovered from being startled by the robot's talking, she circled it in interest.

Jingles preened. He was an elfman—his mother had been a human—and looked like a living image of his mechanical mini-me. "It's been so hard to find a reliable replacement for our last footman, I've been in despair. Then last week I ran across an elf named Velvet who works at Brightlow Enterprises and she convinced me we simply had to try their latest work-saving device at Castle Kringle."

This was cagey marketing on the part of the Brightlows. Planting a prototype of their latest product at the castle in the middle of Christmas season would mean there would be a lot of word of mouth about it.

"It's the perfect employee," Jingles declared. "It doesn't have a thought I don't put into its head. The woman from

Brightlow called it a Selfy—a mash-up of the words *self* and *elf.*" He beamed. "I've named this one Jingleini."

Oh no. *This* was a Selfy? I'd just told Christopher I'd try to convince Nick to get him one. I needed to be more careful throwing promises around. An intelligent robot in the hands of an adolescent had the potential to create all kinds of mayhem.

"Amory and I should get one of these for the lodge," Midge said, jumping on the Selfy bandwagon. "I wouldn't have to worry about all the problems elf servants cause, like wanting days off."

"And you won't have to trouble yourself to be nice to them," a deep voice added from the doorway.

Everyone had been so focused on Jingleini that we hadn't seen Lucia standing there. And she was tough to miss. Tall, with blond hair in a thick braid that reached her mid-back, Lucia dressed for the outdoors even when she was in the warmth of the castle. Now she wore a bright red-and-black checked jacket over her black pants, which were tucked into high boots.

"Lucia," Pamela said, beaming for the company, as if her daughter had arrived decked out in an afternoon formal, "you're just in time for tea."

"Where have you been?" I asked.

"Oh, you know—" Lucia's words cut off at the sight of the drone-deer mini sitting on the floor. "Is Christopher leaving his toys lying around?"

"No, *April's* leaving his toys lying around," Claire said wryly.

I stood. Lucia and I didn't always see eye to eye on things, but on this we would agree, I was sure. "I was just explaining that whoever crashed the drone-deer into the statue this morning couldn't have been a reindeer."

Lucia's mouth twisted into a frown. "What are you talking about?"

"Surely you heard about the crash that brought down the Blitzen ice sculpture?"

She waved a hand. "Everybody knows about that. I mean, why do you think reindeer couldn't handle a drone?"

I turned to wave Quasar over and found him uncomfortably close to the bûche de Noël. He eagerly clopped across the room to again demonstrate his ineptitude.

"I'm assuming reindeer don't have computers," I said to Lucia. "Correct?"

She crossed her arms. "Brilliant observation. Do go on."

I didn't see why she had to be so sarcastic. We were on the same side in this. "So the only other way to operate a drone-deer would be with the remote control. Which Quasar can't do."

Quasar again put his hoof on the joystick.

"Brilliant." Lucia shook her head and sighed. "Look, I think all of this technology is ridiculous—"

"Exactly," Pamela chimed in. "Now come have tea."

"—but even I know that these things are adaptable." Lucia bent down and put the remote on the floor. "See? It's got a switch—EM or RM. Elf Mode or Reindeer Mode." She toggled it over to RM. "There. Try it now, Quasar."

Quasar stepped on the arrow she pointed to. Suddenly the drone lifted into the air with a loud whir and shot off across the room.

Pamela gasped. "Lucia! You stop that this instant."

Lucia was too focused on the drone zigzagging across the room to comply. "Now hit the other arrow, and turn it around," she instructed Quasar in a loud voice.

All the guests tensed as if the drone would come behead them at any moment.

Quasar hit another arrow and sent the drone flying right back across the salon—directly at the tea tower. Eyes flew open in panic, and poor Pamela looked like she was ready to throw herself in front of the tea trolley to save it.

Moving with reflexes that had never exhibited themselves in school sports when I needed them, I dove for the remote and hit the Off switch before the collision could happen. From the floor, I saw the drone stop midair and then fall splat on the other side of the couch.

A groan went through the room.

Dread cannonballed in the pit of my stomach. That *splat* was a bad sign. A very bad sign.

Slowly, I stood, peered over the sofa, and saw that the drone had fallen on the round table before the sofa, right on top of my mother-in-law's bûche de Noël. Quasar was already dipping his head to eat some of the fallen cake.

I didn't need to see Pamela's cold fury. It came at me in waves.

My experiment was a failure, but one thing today was proving certain: Modern technology and Santaland were a dangerous combination. I just had no idea yet how bad.

Chapter 4

The all-herd reindeer meeting that evening provided a welcome opportunity to show off Christmastown by night to Claire. The castle afforded a great view of the city lights from our perch on Sugarplum Mountain, but driving through all the twinkling arches of lights strung across Festival Boulevard and seeing the displays in the shop windows and public parks would be a real treat.

"Aren't you cold?" I asked as I settled a second lap robe over my legs in the sleigh, in addition to the one draped serape-style around my shoulders. "How can it be that I haven't heard a single tooth chatter from you?"

Half the time, mine sounded like those wind-up novelty toys.

"I like the cold," Claire said cheerfully. "My folks used to take me skiing."

"Figures. The one time I went skiing, I sprained my ankle the first day and spent the rest of the weekend by a fire with an Agatha Christie novel and a cup of hot chocolate." I smiled at the memory. "Best vacation ever, actually."

She nodded. "The Agatha Christie part explains why you're so curious about what's going to happen at this meeting tonight."

"That, and I needed to escape the evil eye Pamela was giving me." The flattened bûche de Noël hadn't endeared me to my mother-in-law.

My electric-powered sleigh cut silently down the mountain's winding path. I missed the accompaniment of jangling reindeer harnesses and the soft clop of hooves against packed snow, but there was something to be said for being able to appreciate the stillness of a winter night in silence, with brilliant lights twinkling in the town in the valley, or the occasional illuminated château or tree we passed. The sky overhead provided its own show, too—gauzy veils of pinks and greens layered with the fattest stars I'd ever seen.

"I'm glad you'll have a chance to meet more reindeer tonight," I said, wanting to change the subject. "Usually there are reindeer games going on all this week leading up to the final decision about who'll be on Nick's team on Christmas Eve."

Claire sucked in a deep breath. "Okay, I know you married into this cuckoo world, but you don't believe . . ."

I tilted my head. "That Nick is really Santa Claus? Why else do you think I live in a castle in the North Pole?"

"Lots of people live in fantastic places. There are little enclaves of people who pretend to be living in the nineteenth century. I'll admit, this place *feels* authentic. It's like I'm in a movie! But as for Nick loading up a sleigh with toys on Christmas Eve . . ."

I knew from experience that my life here was a lot to take in, but I couldn't help feeling defensive, and a little exasperated. "Claire, what did you expect when I told you to pack for a visit to Santaland?"

"I thought you were being"—she let out a sigh of frustration—"I don't know, jokey? I just assumed you meant that it was cold here and we'd sit inside bingeing on Christmas movies and gorging on Christmas cookies."

"But I told you Nick was Santa."

"I thought maybe you meant he was a mall Santa or something."

"We don't have malls in Santaland."

"I see that *now*. But how was I supposed to know that when you called me? I didn't know Santaland existed outside of children's Christmas specials. I haven't believed in Santa since I was six."

"Me neither," I said. "And then I started believing again when I was thirty-five. When faced with evidence, you can't not believe. *You've* seen the elves now, and the talking reindeer."

"Yup." She burrowed down in her seat, still looking unsettled. "What am I supposed to swallow next? The Tooth Fairy? Will the Easter Bunny show up at this all-herd meeting tonight?"

I scoffed. "No one in their right mind believes the Easter Bunny is real."

"I don't know what to believe anymore. I'm not even sure if I'm in my right mind."

"Of course you are. You're as sane as I am."

She arched a brow at me, and we burst out laughing.

The all-herd meeting was being held at the Tinkertown Arena to accommodate the expected crowd. To get there, we drove through Christmastown. Seeing the lights strung in twinkling arches over Festival Boulevard was just the treat I hoped it would be. Stores were open late this week, and the streets were bustling. Some elves were doing their Christmas shopping, but occasionally we'd pass a corner where a group was caroling. Peppermint Pond was filled with elves skating or just hanging out and drinking hot cocoa after a long day of work.

Tinkertown was a distant suburb of Christmastown— more of a sister city, really. To get there, we had to cross a section of the Christmas Tree Forest, which formed a border between our country and the wilds of the Farthest Frozen Reaches, and snaked through regions of Santaland like an evergreen garland. Tinkertown was the hub of elf industry, where the big Santa's Workshops were located, along with the Wrapping Works and the Candy Cane Factory. Their surrounding neighborhoods of small cottages caught Claire's attention.

"This would make a whale of a travel article," she said, shaking her head.

"Santaland is secretive. The elves don't want their country commercialized and overrun. They like to stay hidden."

Claire owned an ice cream parlor in the seaside town of Cloudberry Bay, where the Coast Inn was. For years we'd agonized over seasons when tourism flagged. Now here I was living in a place that didn't want tourists at all.

"Like a snowbound Brigadoon." She shook her head. "Not wanting tourists. What a concept."

The Tinkertown Arena stood on the far eastern side of the village—a massive round structure with a thatch-covered roof. In the spring and summer it housed an indoor rink where the elves played iceball, a fast-moving game that seemed like a combination of hockey and lacrosse. There were only two iceball teams in Santaland—the Tinkertown Ice Beavers and the Christmastown Twinklers—although occasionally elves from the wild area up north called the Farthest Frozen Reaches would muster a team, the FFR Destroyers. The Destroyers were so aptly named that they were invited to tournaments as rarely as possible. Luckily, the run-up to Christmas in Santaland allowed no time for iceball, so the arena was free to host the reindeer meeting this evening.

Not many sleds were parked in front of the arena, and only a few pairs of snow skis and snowshoes leaned against the stone wall by the doors. Evidently not many elves or people were attending. All around the arena, though, snow had been churned almost to slush by reindeer hooves. Inside, the arena was well lit, and they'd removed the seating of one section to accommodate as many reindeer as possible.

Claire halted in her tracks at the sight of so many reindeer packed together. Then the smell hit her. Crossing the threshold was like being dropped into a vat of musk oil.

"We're going to smell like Lucia when this is over, aren't we?" she asked.

"It's a distinct possibility."

"Good thing I didn't come on this vacation looking for love."

I smiled. Claire never had trouble attracting male attention. She packed a lot of sex appeal in her small frame, and it had been the rare night out with her that didn't end with some guy hitting on her. Santaland might prove to be her romantic Waterloo, however. There weren't many bachelor Clauses at the moment, and she didn't seem attracted to elves.

My gaze zeroed in on Nick, who was standing in the center area. In his red Santa regalia, he was hard to miss. Amory Claus was next to him, his full salt-and-pepper beard and stocky frame making him appear even more Santa-like than Nick.

A tendril of dread snaked inside of me. I liked Amory, but he had a tendency to shoot off his mouth. And if he saw me he was sure to corner me about the fireworks show at his residence, Kringle Lodge. Ever since meeting up with a pyrotechnician elf named Butterbean, he'd become obsessed with planning this event.

I nudged Claire and nodded to a path through the reindeer crush. The biggest huddle was around a long snack table in the back serving up moss cookies and lichen bars—we veered away from that. I couldn't help feeling slightly uneasy as we moved among the animals. Individual reindeer have names—like Quasar—but elves and people addressed most reindeer by the herds they belonged to, unless they were well acquainted. Lucia knew all their names, of course, while I still struggled even to discern individuals by herd, all of which bore the names of their great ancestors.

So I was pleased when I saw an open space for Claire and me to stand next to a reindeer who was clearly a Cupid, a herd known for its light-colored hides. I also knew at a glance that she was female, since she had all her antlers this late in the year. So did the reindeer speaking at the microphone who was drawling on about the many contributions the Dasher herd had made to Santaland over the centuries.

"Has she been speaking long?" I asked the Cupid.

The reindeer dipped her head to me in greeting, causing both Claire and me to recoil back from those antler tips. "For. Ever," the reindeer responded in a low, slow voice. "And she's a he."

Really? "But his antlers . . ." An impressive rack like that didn't make it till Christmas on males, who were mostly antler bald by December.

The reindeer next to Claire snorted. If I didn't miss my guess, she was a Prancer. "Fake."

The observation caused Claire to swallow her shock at being in the middle of a reindeer conversation. "They look real," she said, impressed.

"From here, maybe," the Prancer drawled. "Up close you can see the glue and wires."

"Notice how still he holds his head," the Cupid pointed out. "One quick move and they'll slip off him like an unbuckled harness."

"Antler toupees!" Claire turned to me, delighted. "Who knew?"

I certainly hadn't.

"That's a Dasher for you," the Prancer declared.

"They think they're God's gift to ruminants," the first reindeer agreed, talking over Claire and me.

"Have we missed much?" I asked them.

The Cupid shook her head. "Every herd selected a representative to speak, but so far, most of them have been doing more bragging and promoting than making a case for the strike."

She wasn't wrong. We listened for a bit and learned that a member of the Dasher herd had been on Santa's Christmas sleigh team 182 times in the past two hundred Christmases, and that they currently held both the fastest recorded time in the ten-mile relay and the cross-country flyover.

Reindeer were very competitive. Usually they put on endless reindeer games and contests, but the strike had stopped those, as well.

The crowd was growing restless. The snorting and pawing in the audience grew more frequent and pronounced, and finally one reindeer heckled, "Get to the point! Do you want to keep us here till *next* Christmas?"

The Dasher speaking drew his head up—carefully, minding his fake antlers—and looked around the audience in consternation.

"Are we going back to work or not?" another reindeer in the audience called out.

"NOT!!!" several yelled.

A Blitzen hurried out to nudge the speaker away from the microphone. "Please, we must be orderly and polite. We have observers here, don't forget."

Several other reindeer rushed to the center area. One, a beautiful dark reindeer that was every inch muscle beneath his full, healthy coat, nudged both Dasher and Blitzen away.

"Here we go," the Prancer next to Claire said with a sigh.

My neighbor drawled to me, "He's the head of the Comets."

"GET AHOLD OF YOURSELVES!" the Comet bellowed into the microphone, a device he clearly didn't need. His voice pierced the air like a trumpet. "This idleness must end."

Many jeering snorts greeted this pronouncement, but the Comet wasn't backing down. "Look at yourselves! Have you ever seen such a miserable, out-of-shape pack of ruminants? No reindeer games in three weeks and you've all gone to flab. Have you forgotten about aerodynamics? If this keeps up, by the end of the week there won't be nine of you capable of getting Santa's sleigh off the ground. You look like a pack of walruses!"

Laughter greeted that last insult. The Dasher pressed closer to the mic. "There's no reason to be rude. Whenever Santa's blown the summoning horn, Dashers have been ready to answer the call."

The Comet exhorted in that shaming tone I remembered from the PE teachers of my youth, "All you're good for now is being summoned to the feed trough. Look at those flabbies back there by the snack table!"

The crowd swiveled to glimpse the reindeer he'd called out, who were caught in bulging-eyed surprise as they munched on birch bark brownies and candy moss.

"We want to uplift reindeer, not make them even more discouraged," the Blitzen admonished.

The Comet was having none of it. "We should respect ourselves enough to not let ourselves get out of shape and then be forced out of our jobs. You don't like drones? Fine! Neither do I. But there's no faster way to make humans and elves want to swap us out for mechanical drone-deer than to refuse to do the work that we can do better than any hare-brained invention!"

Hooves pawed the stadium floor in scattered applause before the Dasher interrupted. "We should not have to work with a threat over our heads. Reindeer made Santaland!"

Mayor Firlog, who I hadn't seen in the crowd, stood up on a chair to make himself visible. "Elves had something to do with that, too!"

Nick lifted his hands, signaling for calm. "You are *all* necessary to Santaland. Nobody wants to replace anyone."

Contentious murmurs spread across the hall, and the Blitzen shot back, "Then what was that drone-deer meant to tell us? It crashed into the statue of Blitzen the First!"

"Purposeful provocation!" a reindeer in the audience called out.

The Comet muscled back to the microphone, every inch the disappointed coach now. "Are you going to let some cowardly, faceless antagonist throw you? That's not the reindeer way! We're not puffin-hearted weaklings."

He'd won over about half the crowd now. Even my neighbors were nodding in agreement.

Just when it seemed that the room was swaying toward ending the strike, Amory Claus ran into the speaker's area. "Comet's right. Dang it, how's this place supposed to function if you all just want to sit on your tails and chew your cud all day? All we have to do is look south to see what happens to unemployed herd animals. Half of you look like you've already been fattened up to become reindeer burgers."

He might as well have tossed an incendiary into the arena. The statement landed to shocked silence at first, then horror, then outrage at the notion of being treated like cattle.

"So if we don't pull your sleighs—what?" the Comet asked. "You'll be *justified* in making us into reindeer burgers?"

"What?" Amory's eyes bulged. "No—I didn't say that. But you need to do something to earn your keep!"

I wanted to slap my hand against my forehead. Why was Amory fighting with the Comet? Didn't the idiot see they agreed?

Nick tugged Amory away from the mic. "Nobody is thinking of eating anyone. Everyone in Santaland values reindeer."

"Comets just want to bully the rest of us," Dasher sniped. The Comet onstage lowered his head. "And Dashers haven't pulled their weight for the past four Christmases."

"There's no point in arguing," Nick called out, but it was too late. Dasher and Comet were facing off, and the audience was pawing and snorting in anticipation of a fight. The Comet rushed, and the Dasher hopped back so fast that his fake antlers slipped off.

The crowd whooped and roared, sending the Dasher fleeing, his newly bald head lowered in embarrassment.

Nick's face turned red. "I know tempers are short now, but please believe me. Your work is valued."

"Then stop the drone-deer!" someone called out.

"They're not going to replace you," he said.

"Then what about the electric sleighs? Your own wife owns one!"

"It's a hybrid," he corrected.

"And she obviously needs it," the Comet interjected, "since you louts are getting too lazy to do what nature intended you for."

Suddenly, a tall figure loomed next to me. Lucia. She tugged my arm and Claire's and then pointed toward the door behind us. We followed her outside. Quasar was already out there.

Snow had started to fall, but the air felt fresh—fresher than inside the arena. I took in a deep gulp.

"What's the matter?" I asked Lucia. "Why did you bring us out here?"

"Couldn't you read the room? Once they brought up that ridiculous vehicle of yours, it wasn't safe in there for you."

"Nick was explaining that," I pointed out. "It's a hybrid. Reindeer usually pull it."

"But they aren't necessary. And that's what has the herds nervous."

I burrowed deeper in my coat, remembering Juniper's earlier questions about Lucia. "So you're *for* continuing the reindeer strike?"

"I just understand why they're alarmed."

"I expected to see you up on the podium during the ice sculpture contest," I said. "Where were you?"

She looked over at Quasar and another group of reindeer who'd left the arena and were pawing the ground for lichen to munch on—probably trying to snack in peace away from the Comet's judgmental eye. "I had somewhere else to be."

"Where?" I asked.

She drew back. "What is this, an interrogation? You could show just a smidgeon of gratitude, you know. I pulled you out of a possible mob situation in there."

I wasn't convinced there was imminent danger, but maybe she had a point. "Thanks. But does my being grateful preclude being curious?"

"No, it precludes your being entitled to poke your nose into my business. I was busy this morning. I've been preoccupied with the strike. Sometimes I'd like to kill those Brightlow idiots for making that stupid drone-deer. It's caused a lot of unnecessary trouble."

That, at least, was something we could all agree on.

The arena doors opened and I looked over, hoping to see Nick. Instead, Amory came out and declared, "Well, this is all a big mess."

"You didn't help matters," Lucia pointed out. *"Reindeer burgers?"*

"I don't see any reason to pussyfoot around the fact that this strike is all a load of nonsense," he said.

Lucia shook her head in disgust. "C'mon, Quasar. Let's go back inside. It's gotten crowded out here."

As soon as the two left, Amory leaned closer to me. "I need to talk to you about the entertainment you chose for the fireworks event at the lodge."

I bit back a huff of exasperation. Originally I'd booked the Reindeer Bell Choir, but the reindeer had pulled out as part of their protest. After some scrambling, I'd found a great replacement. "The Wonderland Winds are one of the most in-demand groups in Santaland."

"Sure, sure, they're great. But they're a dance band. For the fireworks show, we need to go big." After the words "go big," he made an expansive gesture, like he was Florenz Ziegfeld. "Like the Christmastown Orchestra along with the Civic Choir doing the 'Hallelujah Chorus.'"

Was he kidding? "I can't just order up a 'Hallelujah Chorus' on a few days' notice."

"Why not? They sing it every year, and the darned thing hasn't changed in four centuries."

I sighed. "I'll talk to their conductor about it, but it's a busy week, Amory. You might have brought this up earlier."

"I know, but I was just going through the final plans for the fireworks display with Butterbean." His eyes lit with an almost fanatical glow for Santaland's maestro of pyrotechnics. "You wouldn't believe what that genius elf has come up with—it's going to be the most magnificent display the North Pole's ever seen. The fireworks will be visible all the way down the mountain—maybe even all the way to Tinkertown."

Something about Amory's big fireworks show at Kringle Lodge—located just below the summit of Sugarplum Mountain—had been bugging me. I leaned in, lowering my voice. "Aren't you worried about setting off an avalanche?"

This was a touchy subject, I knew. Amory's parents had been buried in an avalanche when he was a boy. Frankly, it surprised me that he was willing to take this risk.

He waved away my fear as so much ignorance. "Butter-bean's looked into all that. He's an engineer, you know."

No, I didn't. "Really?" There was no Santaland equiva-lent to MIT that I was aware of. "Where did he study?"

"Well, he's self-taught," Amory admitted. "Butterbean says all the great men of engineering and science were autodi-dacts. Edison, Bell, Einstein—"

Claire laughed. "I'm pretty sure Einstein went to college."

Amory's brow scrunched. "Really?" He shrugged. "Well anyway, Butterbean says an avalanche being caused by loud noise is pure Hollywood. It would have to be a truly earth-shaking percussive sound to set off an avalanche, and he as-sures me that fireworks are nothing close to that."

Butterbean had designed a little fireworks display at Pep-permint Pond for the summer solstice celebration last June. Nick and I had been in Oregon running the Coast Inn, my bed-and-breakfast in Cloudberry Bay, so I hadn't been able to witness it, but by all accounts it had been nice. Butterbean's ambitions had evidently advanced beyond simple Roman can-dles and ground spinners, though.

"Okay, I'll see if the Christmastown Orchestra is avail-able."

"And the choir?" he asked hopefully.

That would be a lot of people to transport up to Kringle Lodge. "The entertainers will outnumber the guests," I said.

"It's going to be spectacular," he promised again.

"Okay, I'll ask."

"Let me know as soon as possible. I don't want Butterbean getting stressed out over lack of preparation. He's an artist, you know. Very sensitive." He headed off toward his snow-mobile.

Claire shook her head in amazement as she watched him drive off. "Butterbean must be some kind of arctic Svengali."

"I haven't met him yet," I said. "But you're right. He's got Amory completely under his spell."

Nick finally emerged from the arena. He looked at Claire and me in surprise. "I didn't know you two were here."

"We were standing in the back," Claire told him.

Nick put his arm around me and drew me to him. The warmth of his body was welcome.

"What's happening inside?" I asked.

"They voted to extend the strike, but Comet convinced them to recommence the games."

I wondered if all the anxiety I'd witnessed among the reindeer in the hall really could have caused a reindeer to crash that drone. *THIS IS JUST THE BEGINNING!* I shuddered at the thought of worse to come than a damaged ice statue.

And what about Lucia? Was her evasiveness just masking one of her silly projects, like last year when she'd sneaked a cat that was half lynx into the castle? Or was she hiding something more sinister?

The words she'd spoken about the Brightlows echoed in my head. *"Sometimes I'd like to kill those Brightlow idiots for making that stupid drone-deer."*

Maybe Juniper was right to worry about Blinky Brightlow.

Chapter 5

"Have you taken leave of your senses?" was the response of Nippy Goldmitt, conductor of the Christmastown Symphony Orchestra, to the idea of the CSO providing a "Hallelujah Chorus" to Amory and Butterbean's fireworks spectacular. "We don't have time for a fireworks show. *The Nutcracker's* this week."

"Oh right. I forgot."

Nippy's face collapsed into a mask of astounded horror. "You forgot *The Nutcracker?*"

The others around the table at the Christmastown Board of Activities meeting regarded me with similarly dumbfounded looks. Heat crept into my face. The annual performance of *The Nutcracker* was a major deal. "I didn't actually *forget*," I said quickly. "It just slipped my mind for a moment."

When I looked over at Luther Partridge, the leader of the Santaland Concert Band, his face was set in disappointment. "I can't believe you didn't ask the Santaland Concert Band to the fireworks show first."

Hope flickered inside me. "Do you think we can do it?" We'd never played that piece of music, and while our band was good, we weren't sight-read-Handel-at-a-performance good.

"No," he admitted, "but you could have asked. Where is your band loyalty?"

I hated to disappoint Amory. "There must be *something* we could play. It doesn't have to be the 'Hallelujah Chorus.'"

Luther's face pillowed in thought. Then he brightened. "What about the *1812 Overture?*"

"During Christmas week?" asked Mrs. Firlog, the committee's chair.

"It *does* go with fireworks," Luther said.

More important, the concert band could play it. An overture in the hand was worth two hallelujah choruses in the bush. "It could work," I said.

"All right. We'll do it." Luther drummed his fingers. "But it's last-minute, so our numbers might be reduced. Everyone's scheduled up to their eyeballs this week. And I'm not going to make everyone stand around in their uniforms in the freezing cold at the top of Sugarplum Mountain."

I nodded, grateful for that last bit especially. "It will be perfect—thank you." Even if we could only muster a triangle and piccolo player, at least I wouldn't be returning to Amory empty-handed.

The meeting moved on. During a discussion of sleigh parking for *The Nutcracker,* my phone vibrated in my jacket pocket. As surreptitiously as possible, I peeked at the screen.

It was Claire, whom I'd left having coffee with Juniper at the We Three Beans coffeehouse. Juniper had the morning off from the library, and she and Claire seemed to enjoy each other's company. But apparently Juniper had other things on her mind this morning besides eggnog lattes. **Juniper going to Brightlow Enterprises to search for Blinky,** Claire warned. **Can't dissuade her, so I'm going 2.**

Trying to locate Blinky was one thing, but running off half-cocked to Brightlow Enterprises struck me as a dubious strategy. Did Juniper think Blinky was hiding from her in his office?

How does J seem? I texted.

The bars on my screen blinked before the answer appeared. **Anxious, agitated.**

Not good, in other words. **I'll meet you there.**

When I looked up, the others around the table were staring at me with various degrees of disapproval.

I stood. "I'm so sorry. Something's come up that requires my immediate attention."

I rushed off to pick up Juniper and Claire.

Brightlow Enterprises' headquarters was in the large brick structure originally built to be the Christmastown pottery works, before the pottery moved to a larger building in Tinkertown. It was the last of the old factory buildings standing in Christmastown, although technically it was just at the edge of the city limits. A Brightlow Enterprises logo had been painted over the old pottery works sign, next to the now-unused domelike kiln chimney.

As we entered the lobby, an elderly guard perched on a stool stopped us. He had on a green jumpsuit tucked into black work booties, and a nametag that read *Cookie*. "I need to know your business here," he said.

"We're here to see Blinky Brightlow."

He scratched at the gray stubble on his chin. "Mr. Blinky Brightlow didn't come in today."

The quiet in the building made me wonder if anyone had come in.

"What about Dabbs Brightlow?" Juniper asked.

He crossed his arms. "Yep. He's here."

I had a feeling we were going to get an automatic rebuff, so I pulled rank. "Please tell Mr. Brightlow that Mrs. Claus is here to see him."

"Mrs. Claus?" He blinked at me. "My goodness. I'm sorry, ma'am, I didn't recognize you. I'll go see if Mr. Brightlow is available."

After he'd shuffled off, Claire turned to me in amazement. "Holy cow, you really are somebody in this town."

"Of course she is—she's Mrs. Claus." Juniper touched my arm. "Thank you for goosing him. They don't seem to want visitors here."

Why would that be?

A svelte, blond-haired elf wearing a scarlet-felted wool tunic and artfully tied silk scarf met us and introduced herself as Velvet Sprucebud, public relations representative for Brightlow Enterprises. "We're so honored to have you visit us today, Mrs. Claus. What can I do for you?"

"I need to see Dabbs," Juniper piped up. "About Blinky."

Velvet eyed her with the same look she might have bestowed on a fly that had landed on her jacket. Then, catching herself, she pulled her lips back in a smile. "Do you have an appointment?"

"Well, no," Juniper admitted.

Velvet's smile remained fixed. "He's very busy."

"We just want a word," I said.

She hesitated, but relented at last. "I'll show you up to the executive offices."

Those turned out to be on the third floor, which was reached via an old-fashioned birdcage elevator. When she shut us in, I marveled at its antique mechanism. "It's funny, having this here," I said. "Brightlow Enterprises specializes in modern electronic gadgets, yet you have an antique elevator."

"We look to the future, but we value tradition," Velvet said, as if she spent half her life speaking in slogans.

As the elevator rose, I could look out and glimpse a large workroom floor—the kilns had been removed. I didn't have an unbroken view, but it seemed a little barren, frankly. The offices on the two floors above encircled the work floor on three sides.

When the car stopped, Velvet opened the gate for us. She got out last and beckoned us to follow her. "Right this way, ladies."

Once upon a time, the hallways on all three levels had opened up on the work floor below, but at some point the Brightlows had screened off the hallways that overlooked the main floor.

We were shown into an office with Dabbs Brightlow's name on it. A decorated Christmas tree stood in the corner, and the arched window afforded a spectacular view of the slope leading up to central Christmastown. A desk the size of an iceball rink took up a large chunk of floor space. Dabbs Brightlow sat in a leather armchair so large it appeared to be attempting to swallow him whole. He looked every inch the prosperous business elf in a navy blue velvet suit. Prominently displayed on the polished wood surface in front of him was a Golden Icicle good citizenship award, which the Christmastown Chamber of Commerce gave out to a select business every year.

"Good day, ladies. Have a seat."

"Would you like some refreshments?" Velvet asked us as we settled into plush guest chairs. "Eggnog?"

"We just came from We Three Beans," Claire said.

Velvet smiled wider. "I'll bring some munchies for you. We received a delivery from Merry Muffins this morning."

I love Merry Muffins. Then again, I love almost anything made of dough.

After she left, Dabbs clasped his hands together. "What can we do for you today?"

"I'm concerned about Blinky," Juniper said, scooting to the edge of her seat. "I still haven't heard from him, and everyone acts as if it's no big deal."

His smile faded into a frown of sympathy. "That isn't true. In fact, we're hoping his disappearance is a very big deal. Unlike me, Blinky gets some of his best invention ideas when he takes off by himself."

"You invent things, too?" I asked.

Dabbs drew back, smiling modestly. "I do. Ever heard of the Twist-Eez jar opener?"

"Um . . ." I didn't want to insult the guy.

Juniper sucked in a breath of recognition. "My grandmother has one—I gave it to her years ago."

Dabbs looked pleased. "That's gratifying to hear."

Interesting. "I got the impression that you were the business brain of this enterprise, and that Blinky—"

He cut me off. "That Blinky is the genius inventor?" He smiled again, more stiffly this time. "Well, he is. Still, I keep my hand in, ideas-wise. I consider myself something of a Renaissance elf."

Juniper shifted, impatient that the conversation had turned away from Blinky.

Dabbs saw her concern and held up his hands. "Sorry, I didn't mean to get sidetracked. I know you're concerned about my brother, but I'm certain Blinky will be back. In fact, as soon as I hear from my brother, I'll ask him to contact you. Perhaps you'll even hear something from him today."

A quick rap sounded on the door, and an elf in a gray-beige tunic sped in with a folder of papers. He skidded to a stop when he saw us sitting there. His hair and eyes were also beige-ish; he was an elf who gave the impression of fading away. "I'm sorry, sir, I didn't know you had—" His gaze fell on Juniper and his mouth dropped open. "Oh! Hello!"

She smiled at him. "Hi, Virgil. I didn't know you worked here."

"Virgil is our accountant." Dabbs leaned forward, looking between them with interest. "You two know each other?"

Virgil blushed.

"We played Bob and Mrs. Cratchit in the school play once," Juniper said.

"That's wonderful." Dabbs really did seem delighted by this news—or perhaps just by the change of subject from his brother's whereabouts. "And did this theatrical coupling lead to romance?"

"No," Juniper said, a little more vehemently than necessary.

Virgil shifted from one bootie to the other during the uncomfortable silence that followed, looking as if he'd be happy for the carpet to swallow him up. "Well. It's good to see you here with . . ."

Juniper introduced Claire and me. "We came here to ask after Blinky. You haven't heard from him, have you?"

His face turned crimson. "No." He swallowed and faced Dabbs. "I, uh, just had these reports, sir."

"Thank you very much, Virgil."

Virgil all but bowed and started to back out of the room. "It was nice to see you again," he said to Juniper. "I suppose I'll see you at the library sometime."

"Yes," she said.

After he was gone, Dabbs rubbed his hands together. "There seems to be a little history between you two. Perhaps today could be the rekindling of an old flame."

"I doubt that," Juniper said.

He seemed awfully eager to concoct a romantic alternative for Juniper. Why? From the set of Juniper's jaw, it clearly wasn't working.

She turned to Claire and me. "We should go. I don't think we're going to learn any more here today."

Baffled by her abruptness, Claire and I got to our feet. A little regretfully, too, because it was just at that moment that

Velvet brought in the tray of muffins. They looked and smelled delicious. She must have warmed them up for us.

"You're leaving?" she asked, surprised.

I hesitated. *I* hadn't gone to We Three Beans that morning, and I was feeling peckish. "Well . . ."

Juniper looped her hand around my arm. "We have somewhere we need to be."

I didn't know what she meant, but I reluctantly played along. "Right. Thank you, though."

I hoped Velvet would offer a muffin to go, but no such luck. A few minutes later, we were back in my sleigh, and I was grumbling about the muffins. "Come by my place," Juniper said. "I've got a coffee cake I stress-baked last night."

She didn't have to ask me twice.

When we got back in Juniper's apartment, however, Juniper opened a storage tin and let out a groan. She held up the empty tin. "I forgot that after I stress-baked, I stress ate."

I wasn't very successful at concealing my disappointment.

Juniper brightened. "I still have some snailfish chowder. It won't take a second to warm it up."

"That's okay," I said. "I'm really not hungry." Not hungry enough to eat snailfish.

Juniper nodded and joined us in her living area. "Did you all notice how nervous Virgil was? I think he knows something about Blinky."

Claire picked up Dave the rabbit and cuddled him in her lap. "Who is this Virgil guy? Did you have a thing with him?"

Juniper rolled her eyes. "No—we were sort of friends in school. He was awkward even then. I think he had a little crush on me, though."

"Little?" Claire said. "He's still blushing fifteen years later."

"I heard he hasn't had much luck in the romance department," she said, then sighed. "We have that in common."

Just then, a short jingle sounded on Juniper's phone on the kitchen counter. She rushed over to check it. "It's from Blinky!"

"A text?" I asked.

It had to be a long one, for the time her gaze remained fastened on the screen. Her smile of anticipation melted away.

"Not a love note, I take it," Claire said.

"Read for yourself." Juniper handed the phone to her.

I hurried around the sofa and read over Claire's shoulder.

Am having a few days' retreat to do some work important to myself and to Brightlow Enterprises. I am sorry I did not warn you of this, and that I missed the sculpture event. Although, given what happened, perhaps it would have been best if the whole town had given it a miss. Thank you again for allowing me to observe you making chowder. It helped immeasurably. Sincerely, B

Juniper sank down into her armchair. Her brows pinched together. "Do you think he signed his name 'B' like a familiarity thing or a rushed thing?"

"A guy who types out *immeasurably* in a text is not in a rush," Claire said.

"It was thoughtful of him to text me, though." Juniper drummed her fingers in thought. "But his brother guessed that he would."

Quite a coincidence, that. Dabbs had predicted Juniper would hear from him, and then just a half hour later here was a text from Blinky.

"Could Dabbs have gotten hold of Blinky's phone?" I wondered aloud.

Juniper closed the phone's cover. "Why?"

"To make us think that Blinky is still . . ." My mouth snapped closed.

Juniper looked unhappy. "Here I was all glad that he'd written, and now you're implying that he didn't. And when I was first worried something had happened to him, you thought I was being alarmist. Now you're suggesting . . . what?"

"That someone wrote it for him," Claire said.

"Because he's been elfnapped?" She turned to me. "Yesterday you didn't seem to think that was a possibility."

Yesterday I hadn't talked at any length to Dabbs Brightlow. The fellow was too smooth for my liking. And the way he was trying to facilitate some kind of romance between Juniper and Virgil seemed odd, not to mention completely inappropriate.

Juniper plucked the phone up and gave the text another look. "He mentions the chowder. That's a personal touch, isn't it? Dabbs couldn't know about that."

She was right. I was letting my imagination go wild.

"I guess Dabbs was right about Blinky," I said. "He's just off being inventive."

Juniper sighed. "I'd better get ready for work. I'm working the afternoon shift."

Outside, back in the snow, Claire shook her head as she pulled on her gloves. "Poor Juniper. That was a brush-off note if ever I saw one."

My stomach rumbled, and I thought longingly of Velvet's muffin tray. Then a happy thought occurred to me—Merry Muffins was just a few blocks from Juniper's apartment. "I'm starving. Let's go to the muffin shop."

"I'm not going to fit into my clothes by the end of my vacation, am I?"

"We'll walk there," I said. "Walking in these temperatures boosts your metabolism."

She sent me a skeptical look.

"It's Santaland science," I said.

Walking did have the proven benefit of relieving me from parallel parking the sleigh on the busy street where Merry Muffins was located. I was never the best at parking, and a sleigh was far more cumbersome than a car. Also, my time here being driven around by reindeer had spoiled me. Reindeer were like a combination motor and chauffeur.

I took Claire's arm and steered her toward one of my favorite scenic byways. "There's a quaint backstreet over here I want you to see."

Wishful Lane was a narrow old street, with lights strung in swags overhead from old lampposts. For a moment Claire and I were the only ones there—and it felt magical. At least it did until a swishing, whirring sound came up behind us. We turned just in time to glimpse a startling sight—a snowman on some kind of motorized board, barreling toward us at high speed.

The snowman's low voice called out a panicked warning. "Waaaaaatch ouuuu—"

Claire dove out of the way, but shock made me sluggish. I'd never seen a fast-moving snowman . . . especially not one hurtling straight at me. I stepped aside, but not fast enough. The snowman's stick arm clipped my shoulder, which sent me sprawling to the snowy ground and knocked the snowman off-balance. He wobbled, and the board he was on, which had some kind of wagon attached to it, careened out of control until it hit a lamppost. The snowman crashed and then fell, his three-sectioned body coming apart in a sickening explosion of powdery snow.

Chapter 6

A moment of shock passed before Claire and I picked ourselves up from the snowy ground and processed what had just happened.

"I've never seen a snowman move so fast," I said.

Claire eyed me incredulously. "I've never seen one move at all!"

Snowmen were a friendly presence all over Santaland, but getting from one place to another was a challenge for them—until now. I could have sworn that the snowman who'd just run into me was Fezziwig, who'd occupied the same spot in the park across from Christmastown's city hall since I'd lived here.

What the heck had happened?

A muffled groan came from the pile of snow by the lamppost. I gasped. Was he still alive?

Claire and I skidded over and looked down at the blobs of snow strewn across the street. One pile had a vertical stick and a lone piece of charcoal still attached, staring up at the sky. Other charcoal bits, a carrot, and longer sticks littered the snow nearby, as well as a black bowler hat. "I think I need some help," the blob said. The stick mouth was apparently still working. "If it wouldn't be an inconvenience?"

I positioned myself directly over a chunk of coal, although it was hard to know where to look when I spoke to him. "You're Fezziwig, aren't you?"

"Oh, Mrs. Claus! What a pleasure."

I knelt in the snow—hoping I wasn't crushing some part of him. "Are you in pain?"

"No pain, no. But I feel rather . . . scattered. Someone might have to patch me up a little."

Claire and I exchanged looks. It was a good thing the snowman couldn't see himself strewn all over Wishful Lane, or he might be more panicked at how much damage his crash had caused. Another bonus was that he had no idea that I hadn't built—or rebuilt—a snowman in thirty years. I doubt Claire had, either. The Oregon coast wasn't known for its snow.

"Let's start with your base and move up." Claire leaned over the snowman's former head and said soothingly, "You just relax right there and we'll have you back good as new in no time."

"I'm very much obliged."

We got busy repacking his base, which was mostly intact and still on the infernal contraption he'd been riding. As we worked, I studied the thing. It looked like a very wide snowboard, although it appeared to have runners below it, as well as some kind of power source. A wagon hitched behind it contained packages, which had survived the crash intact. The snowboard's being slightly raised off the ground made me suspect that there was a slight undercarriage, maybe with a battery. I remembered hearing a humming whir after it had turned onto the street. A snowman riding an electrified sled seemed a recipe for disaster—and Fezziwig was proof.

After fixing his lower segment, the rest of him was trickier. His center section had to be completely rerolled. While we worked, I asked him, "What were you doing driving this thing?"

"Oh, I got bored, I guess, and this opportunity came up."

"Opportunity?" Opportunity to kill himself, maybe.

"I was delivering packages."

I put my hands on my hips. "Who on earth—"

Claire laid a mittened hand on my arm. "Let Fezziwig rest, and help me with this." We had to heave the center snowball onto the base, which was no easy feat. After much grunting and lifting, we'd put the trunk and torso together, although they appeared a little mismatched. The snow on the street that we'd rolled him in was whiter than the original snowman body, which had endured years of weather. He was now a patchwork of old and new. Did that matter? I wasn't up on my snowman anatomy.

His head was the biggest challenge. We packed the snow to the biggest remnant and hoped that we weren't scrambling him up hopelessly. But he seemed okay, talking to us throughout the entire operation. Maybe snow was a natural anesthetic.

"My nose usually has a slightly upward tilt," he said.

I smiled. "I've noticed that about you. Your hat is always at a rakish angle, too."

"I like to look nice. Especially when I'm in front of City Hall. It's a rather public role."

"You should go back to your spot instead of zooming around town carrying packages."

"No doubt you are correct," he said soberly. "Yet it's a thrill. We snowmen don't get many of those."

Over his head, Claire caught my gaze. She was holding up one of his charcoal eyes, which was pulverized. The biggest chunk was now the size of a pebble.

"I'm sorry, Fezziwig," I said. "One of your eyes is just a coal chip. It might not work very well."

He sighed. "The hazards of locomotion."

"I bet you can get a replacement at Sparkletoe's Mercantile." They had everything there. Bella Sparkletoe was gruff but kindhearted—she'd probably replace it for free.

"Maybe I'll get an eye patch," he said. "That would be jaunty, wouldn't it?"

Claire found his muffler on the street, shook it out, and wound it around his neck. With his bowler once again perched on his head, he looked like a slightly dilapidated version of his old self.

I returned my attention to the snowboard he was perched on. The back had a retractable ramp that made it possible for the snowman to get on it. "How does this thing move?"

"It's pressure sensitive," he explained. "I move my weight forward, it goes forward. It's the opposite for reverse, and so on. Ingenious, no? It's ideal for snowmen."

Ideal, except that snowmen's reflexes weren't made for speed.

I toed the wagon attached to the back. Fezziwig couldn't have attached that and gotten on the thing. Someone had to have helped him. A close inspection of the packages revealed that they were all from Walnut's Bootie World.

"Walnut hired you?" I should have known. Walnut was Santaland's big box entrepreneur.

"He offered me the opportunity," Fezziwig corrected. "He said if I delivered enough packages, I could keep the board."

Right. He could keep it until the Christmastown municipal workers were called out to scoop up his remains with snow shovels after the next crash. Then the board would be offered to another snowman as an "opportunity."

I rubbed my freezing hands. "Let's go talk to Walnut."

"I can't," Fezziwig said. "I have to make my deliveries."

Was he serious? "After this experience, you still want to ride around on this thing?"

"I'll be more careful. I think I'm finally getting the hang of it."

I couldn't stop him, of course. Snowmen had free will, and there was no law against them careening around on motor-powered vehicles.

We watched anxiously as Fezziwig backed away from the lamppost. He was only slightly more adept at maneuvering that thing than I was at managing a sleigh. Just getting himself straightened out to drive off down the street made him emit several exclamations of "Whoopsie!" and "I got it!" before he set off again, shakily. Neither Claire nor I breathed until he had turned the corner and sped out of sight.

"Those things will be snowman death mobiles," I said.

Claire shook her head, dazed. "You know, I thought I was getting used to this crazy place. The elves are sort of like more compact, weird humans, and talking reindeer are freaky but I can sort of accept that because, well, parrots talk. Why not a reindeer? But I've just performed emergency surgery on a snowboarding sentient snowman. Forget muffins, I need a drink. Is there a bar around here?"

I felt rattled, too. "The Mistletoe Tavern is close. They've got mulled hard cider."

But after one drink, I realized there was a certain elf bootie impresario I needed to have a word with.

Walnut's Bootie World was in full holiday swing when we arrived. Outside, a banner across the front of the building shouted *Slipper Extravaganza!!!* in tall red letters. The sign reminded me of the smaller one attached to the drone-deer's tail yesterday. Same colors, same overuse of exclamation points.

A giant inflatable Santa stood sentry by the entrance.

Claire stopped by its oversize boots and stared up at it. "Nick's better looking than that."

I laughed. I was so glad she was here, and that she could appreciate Nick's good qualities now. Last summer, when she was first getting acquainted with him and before she knew who he really was, she'd taken him for a bearded beach bum. Part of that was my fault. I'd commanded Nick to relax and let me tend to the work around the inn, and I hadn't confided the truth to Claire. "By the way, I married Santa" wasn't the kind of thing that fit easily into conversations. But not telling her the truth about my life had become a strain on our friendship, so I'd invited her to come stay for the holiday.

Yes, her visit had gotten off to a bumpy start. Maybe my expectations had been too high, and I hadn't explained things well enough before she arrived. But for someone who'd gone from complete skeptic to snowman paramedic in two days, she really was handling being dropped into Santaland as well as could be expected.

The elf booties delighted her. Walnut's inventory ran the gamut from simple elf work boots to handcrafted, elaborately curly-toed fashions that even the most style-conscious elf would covet. The showroom was huge and staffed by elves in colorful tunics who rushed down aisles laden with towers of shoeboxes to show customers.

Walnut's office was in the back, one floor up, where a plate glass window overlooked the showroom.

Claire and I headed back, delayed a few times by attentive employees and Claire's need to inspect a few of the fancier booties more closely.

"I need to take a pair back to Cloudberry Bay as a souvenir." She inspected a particularly flamboyant pair of purple dyed musk-ox leather with a French heel and toes that curled into a spiral. "I wonder if they have my size."

I wondered that, too. For a human, Claire's feet were tiny. By elf standards, they were canoes.

"Maybe I should buy a pair of slippers instead," she said.

"You have plenty of time yet to mull it over. I'm going to talk to Walnut."

She put the shoe down. "I'm going with you."

Walnut was a wealthy elf, and he dressed the part. His tunic was deep green velvet with purple piping and he paired it with a multicolored striped tie. Purple-and-white stockings stuck out of a pair of dark green stamped alligator–patterned patent leather booties with squared, upturned toes.

When we entered his office, Claire gaped at him, and he returned the favor, barely able to take his eyes off her even as he spoke to me. "Mrs. Claus! What a delight to see you. And who did you bring to my little emporium?"

"This is my friend from Oregon, Claire Emerson." I smiled at Claire and gestured to him. "This is Walnut Lovejoy."

He took her hand. Several chunky rings winked from his fingers. "Enchanted. Maybe Mrs. C didn't mention this, but I'm a bachelor."

Claire didn't look interested, and I was too impatient for this nonsense right now. "Walnut, what is this insanity of using a snowman as a package deliverer?"

His smile fell away. "Did one of my men misplace something you ordered?"

He had more than one snowman working for him? "Fezziwig just collided with a lamppost."

"Oh fudge, when was this? I'll send someone to retrieve the merchandise right away." He reached for his phone.

For heaven's sake. "The merchandise is fine, but Fezziwig had to be rerolled."

"He made it?" His expression was equal parts astonished and pleased. "Well, that's wonderful. What's the problem?"

"The problem is that this new contraption of yours is hazardous to the health of snowmen, and probably a hazard to the rest of us, as well. It's only a matter of time before another accident happens. It's a horrible idea."

"The snowmen don't think so. Everyone I approached was very gung ho. Imagine being plopped out in the cold for decades and then suddenly being offered the opportunity to be mobile, and useful."

"Useful to you. It's exploitation. You're not even paying them."

"They get to keep their Snomaneuvers, and believe you me, those things aren't cheap."

"Sno-ma-what?" I asked.

"Snomaneuvers. That's what she calls them. Very clever. I ordered a whole fleet."

"Who is this 'she' you're talking about?" I asked.

"Holly Silverpick. The Snomaneuver is her invention. She's a very clever elf—used to work for Brightlow Enterprises, but she quit in a huff when they rejected her plans for the Snomaneuver."

"Because they realized it was a snowman killer?"

His lips twisted. "I believe it had more to do with the fact that she wanted the company to spend money developing a product for snowmen, who have no disposable income. No income at all, actually."

"You can't blame the Brightlows for not wanting to run with the idea," Claire said.

"No, rejecting it was probably a sound business decision from their perspective, but Holly foresaw that it might have other uses, by business elves like yours truly, for instance."

"Business elves with no scruples," I said in disgust.

"Well, what are we supposed to do when the reindeer don't show up for work?" he said peevishly. "It's the busiest time of the year."

"So you just stick a bunch of snowmen with defective reflexes on fast-moving snowboards. What could go wrong?"

"Yours is the first complaint I've had."

"When did you start using them?" I asked.

"This morning."

I tilted my head. "So . . . one crash in three hours?"

He shrugged off the odds. "We're revolutionizing snowman lives and ushering in a whole new era of snowman usefulness."

"They're useful now," I said. "They're citizens, and they're the eyes and ears of Santaland."

He sighed. "Would *you* trade places with a snowman?"

"Well, no . . ."

Claire laughed. "April hates the cold."

"Is that so?" He turned to me with real interest. "I have some fantastic bootie warmers in the showroom. They might be perfect for you."

Honestly. Every conversation was a sales opportunity with this guy.

On the other hand, bootie warmers did sound good.

"We were going to browse a little on the way out," I said. "I'll look for some."

"Be sure to take advantage of our visitor discount," he told Claire. "Twenty percent off."

It was late afternoon and full dark when Claire bought her slippers—and the purple booties, which she couldn't resist and were in stock in elf size XXXXXL. We needed to get back to the castle before they sent out a search party for us. Tomorrow, though, I would be returning to town to speak to Holly Silverpick—and not just about the Snomaneuvers.

From what Walnut had told me, I had a sneaking suspicion I'd discovered who was responsible for that drone-deer crash. Holly was a disgruntled ex-employee of Brightlow Enterprises, bringing out a project they'd rejected, so she had every reason to make a Brightlow product look bad by having it nose-dive into the ice sculpture contest's most spectacular statue. She'd probably had plenty of experience working on drone-deer at Brightlow Enterprises and knew just how to program one for a precision hit.

What worried me now was that banner. If the drone-deer strike had been just the beginning, what did Holly Silverpick have up her sleeve for a follow-up?

Chapter 7

The next morning I cranked one eyelid open to see Nick perched on the side of the bed, dressed and pulling on black boots shined to a mirror gloss. The lights strung overhead were dimmed to low. I pushed myself up and plumped my pillows against the headboard of our sleigh bed.

"I'm going to Tinkertown to check on things today," he said.

All the workshops and factories had very competent managers from among the elf ranks or, in a few cases, from the Claus family, but Nick liked to double-check that there wouldn't be any critical production shortages. Of course, there might be a critical Santa shortage if the reindeer didn't field a sleigh team in time for Christmas Eve.

I reached out and ran my hand along one velvet-covered shoulder. "Do you want to borrow my sleigh?" His two were both reindeer-powered.

"Jingles offered me the use of his snowmobile."

"There's something undignified about Santa Claus reduced to puttering around on a snowmobile," I said.

"Don't let Jingles hear you say that."

Jingles was inordinately proud of his Snow Devil 1100, a top-of-the-line model. It was snazzy—for a snowmobile. But even the snazziest, most souped-up snowmobile lacked the grandeur of Santa's grand sleigh, an intricately carved and brightly painted wooden conveyance. Or even his less ornate working sleigh, which was pulled by a team of four.

He kissed me. "I want you and Claire to have your sleigh today."

Immediately, thoughts of all I had to do today popped into my mind. "This morning we're going to talk to Holly Silverpick."

He arched a brow as he finished pulling on his boots. I'd told him my new theory about the drone-deer crash last night, and about Holly Silverpick's terrible invention. "I promised you I'd bring up the problem of snowman boards at the next Christmastown Council meeting," he reminded me.

"That won't be till *after* Christmas. By then the remains of former snowmen will be piled up all over town."

"I'll stop by Mayor Firlog's this morning," he said. "Maybe he can influence Walnut."

"I still want to talk to this Holly person to see if my hunch about her involvement in the drone-deer crash is correct."

After Nick left, I showered and got changed. This afternoon was Mildred's dessert potluck, which called for stretchy fabric. I was finishing dressing as I heard a gentle tap at the door. I perked up at the prospect of Jingles bringing my morning shot of caffeine. Coffee in my bedroom before I had to face the day was my favorite perk of being Mrs. Claus.

"Come in."

The door opened, but instead of Jingles, Jingleini whirred in, a tray balanced on his rigid, outstretched arms. If those plastic protuberances of his could be called arms.

"Good morning, Mrs. Claus," he said in a voice that was somewhere between Jingles and Hal the Computer from *2001*.

Was I supposed to answer? "Where is Jingles?"

"I am Jingleini."

"I know that."

There followed what could be described as an electronic hesitation before Jingleini cycled back to the beginning of his script. "Good morning, Mrs. Claus."

He'd obviously been programmed with limited responses— and I wasn't giving him the expected cues. I tried again, taking care to enunciate carefully. "Good morning, Jingleini."

He rolled closer. "Please remove the tray at your convenience."

Well, this was spooky. I took the tray.

"You are welcome!" he said.

"Thanks," I muttered.

"Here is a joke to start your day: Where do elves vote?"

Did Jingles expect me to play straight man to an automaton?

A confused moment passed before he repeated, "Here is a joke to start your day: Where do elves vote?"

I bit my lip. "I don't know, Jingleini. Where do elves vote?"

"The north poll. Ha-ha. Will there be anything else, Mrs. Claus?"

I crossed my arms. "Please somersault your way out the door."

At my unexpected command, he hummed without moving. "I am Jingleini."

"That's all," I said. "Thank you."

"Good day, Mrs. Claus." He backed up, rotated, then headed to the door. Unfortunately, the carpet edge sent him off course and he ended up heading toward the couch of our entertainment center in the corner of the room. Soon he was pressing into it, whirring helplessly like a trapped Roomba and repeating, "I am Jingleini."

I got up and yanked the bell pull. Suspiciously fast, Jingles appeared. His smile faded when he took in Jingleini's predicament.

"We're still working out a few kinks," he said. "He'll do better tomorrow."

"Wouldn't it be easier just to hire an elf?"

"You haven't seen the job candidates I've interviewed. Incompetents and half-wits."

"Do they face-plant into couches?"

Jingles put a protective hand over his protégé's head. "It's just first-day jitters."

"He's a robot. Robots don't get jitters."

"Tomorrow will be better. You'll see."

I was all for second chances, although I didn't know if that should extend to Selfies.

"Is anyone else up downstairs?" I asked.

"Christopher's having his last day of studies, Tiffany left for her tea shop an hour ago, and the dowager Mrs. Claus is in the kitchen putting the final touches on her peppermint pavlova for the dessert potluck."

"Have you seen Claire?"

"She's also in the kitchen, making ice cream for the potluck." He noted my thoughtful frown. "You did remember the potluck, didn't you?"

I nodded. An afternoon of desserts wasn't likely to slip my mind. I felt a little bad that Claire was spending her holiday making ice cream, though. "I'll go down to the kitchen and see if Claire's ready to leave."

Jingles blocked my path. "I'm sorry. I have instructions to keep you out of the kitchen."

"Why?"

He shot me a loaded glance. "Do I really need to say it?"

Just because of the incident with the bûche de Noël, I was being banned from the kitchen?

"I am *not* dessert-cursed," I said, with perhaps a tad more defensiveness than was warranted.

"It's not me you need to convince," he said.

After Jingles and his mini-me left the room, I applied the finishing touches to my outfit and face. My clothes were designed by Madame Neige at the Order of Elven Seamstresses, the finest in Santaland couture. Today I was wearing a stretchy green sheath dress with a white long-sleeved bolero jacket, which was light-years from the practical, housework-ready outfits I wore in Cloudberry Bay. The knee-high black boots I pulled on wouldn't have served me well as the proprietor of the Coast Inn, either. Being an innkeeper was a combination of Martha Stewart and maid-of-all-work. In Santaland, most of my work was ceremonial. Showing up really was 99 percent of the Mrs. Claus job, and no one wanted me showing up in jeans and sweatshirts.

I hurried downstairs to rescue Claire. A swing through the breakfast room told me that everyone had already eaten and scattered. I was just as happy to grab something in town while we were there.

I headed down the servants' corridor that connected the breakfast room with the kitchen. The latter was a kingdom to itself, a gleaming world of white and stainless steel. Overseen by the dictatorial hand of Felice, even the butcher-block tables were polished until they shone. Elves in starched white uniforms crowded around several workstations. Claire and Pamela had commandeered one long butcher-block table for themselves, the top of which was sprinkled with powdered sugar. As I walked in, the two of them were laughing uproariously at something. How often had I seen my mother-in-law laugh like that—a full-throttle belly laugh? Not many. Claire had a knack for making everyone like her.

As if sensing my surprise, the two looked over at me.

"You look fantastic," Claire said.

Pamela's greeting was less complimentary. "You shouldn't be here."

I lifted my hands in surrender. "I just came to fetch Claire."

"Mildred's potluck isn't until this afternoon," Pamela said.

"Claire and I are going into town this morning."

Claire's face fell. "Oh—I forgot. I still haven't finished here." She gestured to the baking mess around them. "Plus I'm going to make rum raisin ice cream for the party. You don't mind, do you?"

The hostess in me trumped my disappointment. As I knew from my experience as an innkeeper, the guest is (almost) always right. "Of course not. We've been running around nonstop since you got here. And your ice cream will be a hit at the potluck."

Claire's ice cream shop made Cloudberry Bay a memorable stop for tourists driving down the scenic Oregon Coast. Ice cream wasn't a treat often served in Santaland—cold foods weren't a big craving here—but Santalanders hadn't tasted Claire's ice cream yet.

"I'll see you before the party, won't I?" Claire asked.

"Of course. I'll be back to pick everyone up and drive to Mildred's."

I headed into town on my own. I had a little extra time to kill, so I took the opportunity to see Juniper. I texted her to meet me at Tiffany's Tea-piphany, my sister-in-law's tea shop. Tiffany was behind the counter as I entered. She looked uncharacteristically unhappy.

"Nothing's wrong with the ice show, is there?"

Her Little Gliders ice show, a showcase for her figure-skating students, was tomorrow morning.

"I'm just worried that I don't have a really good gift for Christopher this year," she said.

"I'm supposed to tell you he wants a Selfy."

"As if Jingleini isn't bad enough." She sighed. "It was so much easier when he just wanted a dog. All this electronic stuff—who knows where it could lead? What if he expects it to do his homework for him?"

"If my interactions with Jingleini are any indication, you don't have to worry about that. It would be like asking a hair dryer to do your homework."

Juniper came in already dressed for work. Her distracted air made me suspect she didn't have much time.

"I ordered for us," I assured her. "A pot of Good Morning, Sugarplum, and a Tower of Scones."

Even the prospect of the best scones in Christmastown didn't smooth the lines from her brow.

"Is something wrong?" I asked.

"This morning I went back to talk to Virgil."

"Already?"

"I got an uneasy feeling from him yesterday. You saw how he acted."

"Like a shy person running into his old flame."

"He and I were never really an item—not in the way you mean." She shook her head. "That anxiety from him was about Blinky. I'm sure of it."

That wasn't how it seemed to me, but maybe I just didn't have all the facts yet. "What did Virgil say to you?"

"He said he couldn't talk to me, especially about Blinky. That it wouldn't be prudent."

"Well, from his perspective, maybe that's true. Especially if he has lingering feelings for you. You're involved with his boss."

"But I don't think he *has* lingering feelings. It's not like we haven't bumped into each other since school. He comes into the library when I'm there sometimes. He's a big reader."

"And does he always turn the color of a beet when he sees you?"

She cast back, then shrugged. "Yes, but he's usually not so jumpy."

"Because before you weren't declaring that you and his boss were an item."

Juniper drummed her fingers lightly on her teacup. "His *missing* boss."

"You got that text yesterday," I reminded her.

"But what if you were right and it wasn't really him? Or if he was forced to write it?"

We seemed to be back to square one.

"I'm sure Virgil must know *something*," Juniper said. "Maybe if you talked to him, he'd give straighter answers." She fished in her handbag and brought out a business card. "Here's his work number."

"Why would he talk to me?"

"Because you're Mrs. Claus."

"I'm not sure that's the magic phrase you assume it is." Nevertheless, I tucked the card into my pocketbook. "I might not have time to meet with him today. This afternoon's Mildred's potluck, and I'm speaking to Holly Silverpick this morning." I filled her in on Fezziwig's crash yesterday and my subsequent conversation with Walnut.

Juniper listened, then glanced up at the teapot clock on the wall. She put her cup down. "I need to get to the library. Let me know how things go after you call Virgil. You won't forget, will you?"

"Of course not."

After she left, I finished my tea and gave Virgil's number a ring. A receptionist picked up and I asked for Virgil.

"He isn't available right now," she said.

"Could you please leave a message for him to call me at his earliest convenience? I'm Mrs. Claus."

"I'll leave it on his desk. He'll see it when he comes back in."

I frowned. "Wait—isn't he in the office today?"

"He fell ill soon after he got here this morning and went home."

He fell ill? Right after he saw Juniper, maybe?

"Thank you." I ended the call.

Juniper hadn't mentioned that Virgil looked sick. Maybe he was malingering. In spite of Juniper's protestations, my diagnosis was lovesickness.

I paid my bill, waved good-bye to Tiffany, and headed out. Holly Silverpick's business, Silverpick Industries, was located on Sparkletoe Lane. The street brought back a host of memories, not all of them good, but walking past Sparkletoe's Mercantile was always a treat. This month they had an old-fashioned animatronic display behind their plate glass window. The mechanical wooden elves looked astonishingly lifelike.

As I watched, an actual elf swung out of the mercantile door, clasping multiple bags close to his chest. He was a ragged creature, with rusty long hair and beard, and was all dressed in leathers and mangy-looking furs. He sidestepped me, grumbling to himself as he shoved a handful of licorice into his mouth.

I stared after him as he scuttled away on bandy legs like a little goblin. Other elves on the sidewalk gave him a wide berth. He was obviously one of their brethren from the Farthest Frozen Reaches, known on this side of the border as a wild elf. They weren't often seen in town. This one had obviously been on a shopping spree, which was odd. Wild elves usually survived off the land and by barter.

I continued farther up the street to the two-story building that housed Silverpick Industries. The office was on the second floor. Holly Silverpick was not what I expected. Even for an elf, she was small, and also very fit. She was dressed in a sensible jumpsuit, low booties, and had her dark brown hair cut short. The minute I opened the door, she was on me like sprinkles on a sugarplum.

"What can I do for you today, ma—" Her eyes bugged. "Mrs. Claus. What an honor! Can I get you some eggnog?"

My stomach full of scones clenched at the suggestion. Unlike everyone else in Santaland, I'd never taken to eggnog. "No thank you."

"Tea?"

"No thank you."

"I've got gingerbread spice, bearberry citrus—"

"That's okay, I just came from the tea shop."

"Tea-piphany? That's where I buy *my* tea. What's your favorite? Peppermint?" She held up a little sachet.

I wavered. "I do like peppermint . . ."

She raised a hand, bidding me to stay put. "I've got the kettle boiling, so I'll pop this in and have it for you in a jiffy."

I watched her bustle around a tiny kitchenette area.

"I really just came to talk to you about the Snomaneuvers," I said, which wasn't the whole truth. I also hoped to finesse my way to getting her to open up about her relationship with the Brightlows, and to confess to crashing the dronedeer.

"Sit down, I'd love to tell you how a whole fleet of Snomaneuvers could be of service to Castle Kringle."

I remained standing. If I sat down, I'd probably get talked into buying Snomaneuvers in bulk. Holly Silverpick seemed like a very persuasive elf. Although her powers of persuasion had failed to work on the Brightlows.

As she finished prepping my cup of tea, I examined the spacious room. Plaster walls had built-in shelves stuffed with boxes and jars of materials. A few worktables with various half-built contraptions on them were pushed close to the walls, but the long room with its wide wood-plank floors felt as un-cluttered as a roller rink. One Snomaneuver stood alone in the middle of the floor. I didn't see signs of other employees.

"Do you run this business by yourself?" I asked as she handed me the tea.

"That's right! I'm a one-elf operation. Are you interested in the Snomaneuver?" She led me over to the floor model. I took a closer look. The top was just like a massive skateboard, with a lip lowering at one end, presumably for the snowman to get on. This model was painted in four colors, giving it a Piet Mondrian art appearance.

"Isn't it a beauty?" she asked.

Its mod design did appeal to me. "The one I saw yesterday had a little wagon attached."

"The wagons are sold separately. Would you like to see the optional extras?"

"That's not necessary." I was getting sidetracked. "I heard you used to work at Brightlow Enterprises?"

Traces of doubt etched in her forehead as suspicion dawned that her efforts here wouldn't result in a sale. "Yes. I worked there for a few years after I was apprenticed in Santa's Workshops. Toy Division D."

"And you developed the Snomaneuver at Brightlow Enterprises?"

"No." Her voice was emphatic. "I developed it *while* I was there—but on my own time. When I pitched it to them, they turned me down cold. The Brightlows didn't share my vision."

"They didn't think there was profit in marketing products to snowmen, you mean."

Her features tensed. "They're very short-sighted. It's the Brightlow way or the highway—not that I was fired. Lots of elves have been fired there lately, but I chose my own path."

Her story might have been inspiring, if the product she

was pushing weren't so dangerous. "They obviously had a valid point about the snowman boards. I witnessed a snowman crash yesterday."

Her eyes widened. "Which one?"

"Has more than one crashed?"

She waved her hands in front of her. "There are a few kinks that need to be ironed out."

"Fezziwig would be dead if my friend and I hadn't put him back together. That's more than a kink."

"I'm working every day to make the boards safer. In the meantime, every board is going to come with an emergency kit. See?"

She led me over to a worktable containing a long wooden box. Inside, there was a clear bin containing coal, buttons, and a plastic carrot nestled next to a collapsible shovel.

"A powderized snowman can't fix himself," I pointed out.

"But Santaland's a friendly place. Folks help out. Like you did yesterday."

"What's the shovel for?"

"Road clearance." Even though it was only us in the room, she lowered her voice. "In case—heaven forbid—the worst happens."

I shook my head. "This isn't a solution."

Since the crash emergency kit wasn't working on me the way she'd hoped, she dragged my attention back to the Snomaneuver itself. "I'm also fine-tuning the acceleration and deceleration functions so that the boards can't make sudden movements. It just takes some training."

"Who's going to provide that?" I asked.

"Every Snomaneuver comes with detailed instructions, and hopefully the businesses that employ the snowmen will provide the training."

"Have you *met* Walnut? He doesn't waste time on things that won't result in a sale."

"But these will," she insisted. "Think of the freedom we're unlocking for a whole population here. And then imagine the convenience of having your pesky errands taken care of by someone gliding down the streets. It's a green form of delivery! The boards run on solar-powered batteries. Picture clean streets as opposed to reindeer pooping everywhere. Christmastown will save loads in street cleaning."

Just what Santaland needed—another reason for reindeer to get their antlers in a twist.

Holly took my arm. "Try it for yourself. While you're here, you should at least get a sense of what you're talking about."

"I shouldn't. I'm accident prone."

"Nonsense." She guided me onto the board. "This indoor demo has wheels on the skids, but it'll give an approximate simulation of how it glides on snow."

I felt anxious stepping on the board. It was comfortably wide and stable feeling, however. "How do I make it go?"

"Press forward on the green panel at the front. One press turns it on, and the next press accelerates it."

Reluctantly, I pressed twice and felt my heart skip as the board glided forward. Now I understood why she kept the room so spare: the place doubled as a track. Shifting my weight as she commanded me, I did a careful loop around the workshop, then couldn't resist taking another turn at a slightly faster pace. I might even have let out a whoop. It really was fun—it felt much more controllable than a skateboard, and certainly more than a regular snowboard.

But of course, I had human reflexes. And I was in a building, not out in the streets.

"How do I stop this thing?" I asked after my third go-round. I was turning a little too fast and could envision myself taking out a wall of shelves.

"Center yourself!"

I did my best—and to my surprise, it worked.

When I stepped off, Holly beamed at me and handed me that mug of peppermint tea she'd promised. "Now wasn't that fun? Think how useful they'd be on a big estate like Castle Kringle. Getting to outbuildings in inclement weather would be a snap. And if you wanted to use snowmen to relay messages—"

I raised my free hand to put a halt to the hard sell. "I'm really not in the market for one of these. But I am interested in hearing a little more about your dealings with the Brightlow brothers."

Disappointment was written all over her face. "What about them?"

"What did you think of Blinky and Dabbs?"

She considered this for a second. "They were fine. We just didn't share the same vision."

"I was wondering about the drone-deer strike and who could have caused it."

She bit her lip, thinking. "Someone who owned a drone-deer, I guess."

"Do *you* own one?"

"I never bought one, no," she said.

"But you wouldn't have any trouble operating one."

"Gosh no, any fool could." She frowned. "Wait just a minute. Are the Brightlows fingering *me* for what happened at Peppermint Pond?" She tossed her hands up in the air. "Great! That's all I need—to have that cloud hovering over my head while I'm trying to get my fledgling business off the ground."

"No one's accused you. But naturally the constabulary will want to follow all leads."

She crossed her arms. "I'm not a lead, and you're not Constable Crinkles."

She had me there.

"When the Brightlows let you go—"

"They didn't fire me," she insisted. "I left on my own before they had a chance. It's like they think they won't even need elves anymore."

"Any particular animus toward any particular Brightlow or Brightlow employee?"

She chewed her lip. "I was a little disappointed in Virgil."

I hoped I hid the spike in my curiosity. "The accountant?"

She nodded. "When I worked there, I thought he liked me. And then to find out that his cost-benefit report torpedoed my pet project? That stung. But of course I try not to take it personally. Lots of corporations are short-sighted, but I was raised to see each obstacle as a challenge—an opportunity to prove my capability."

She certainly proved herself capable at turning snowmen into powder. Although when I looked at the Snomaneuver again, I couldn't forget how fun it was to ride. Maybe they *would* be useful to have around Castle Kringle . . .

Holly picked up on the gleam that must have been shining in my eyes. "I can send you home with one today," she said in a snake-tempting-Adam tone. "We have a no-risk thirty-day return policy."

The word *home* landed in my ears with a jolt, shaking me out of my Snomaneuver seduction. I needed to get back to the castle to ferry people over to Mildred's dessert potluck. I set my tea down on her worktable.

"I'll think about it," I promised. And I would also think about what she said about the Brightlows. Despite her denials, I sensed there was something more there.

As I was hurrying down Sparkletoe Lane toward my sleigh, I glimpsed the figure of an elf coming from the opposite direction. Though his head was down, brow furrowed beneath the band of his tasseled cap, I recognized him at once: Virgil.

When he was about ten feet away, he looked up as if he sensed my eyes on him. His own brown eyes went saucer wide in surprise, and he stopped in his tracks. A heartbeat later, he did an about-face and scurried off in the direction he'd come from.

"Wait!" I called out. Did he know I'd tried to telephone him?

Maybe that was why he was fleeing.

At the sound of my voice calling after him, his short legs pumped faster as he jaywalked across the street and ducked down an alley.

I stopped, puzzling over his appearance here on Sparkletoe Lane. Where had he been heading?

I looked back at the door to Holly Silverpick's. Was that where Virgil had been going? His destination could have been any other shop on Sparkletoe Lane. But seeing me had derailed whatever he'd had in mind.

Unfortunately, I was already too late starting back to the castle to pursue him. I could call him again later. At the moment I didn't have time to go haring after nervous elves.

Chapter 8

When I sped up to the castle, Claire was waiting for me at the front portico, clutching her ice cream in a silver canister. She wore her blue coat and had a long, colorful print silk scarf draped around her neck.

"I discovered a great thing about Santaland," she said, all enthusiasm as she hopped into the sleigh. "I never have to worry about ice cream melting."

She looked perkier than I ever did after a morning cooped up with Pamela. While we waited, I made a mental note to try harder to get along with my mother-in-law. Although I don't know how well she would look upon me when I fessed up to my knitting procrastination. The closer we came to the Kringle Heights Ladies' Guild craft bazaar, the louder the drumbeat of panic in my head became over those unknit tea cozies.

Claire fixed me with a look of concern. "April? Is the sleigh out of juice or something? Shouldn't we get going?"

I snapped out of my craft panic. "I'm waiting for Pamela."

"Oh, she left already. An elf who works around here— Salty, I think his name was?—picked her up in his oxcart a half hour ago and drove her over."

Pamela preferred to be driven in a utility wagon pulled by

musk ox than risk going with me? "For Pete's sake. I wasn't late."

She hesitated a tick before explaining, "I think she was afraid about her dessert."

My resolution to forge a better relationship with my mother-in-law was already faltering. "Nothing like a show of trust from one's family."

"I can tell Pamela really likes you," Claire said. "She told me you've shaken the castle up."

"I don't think she meant that in a good way." I pressed my foot on the accelerator and turned us back down the mountain.

"Wait till you see the dessert she made. A peppermint pavlova. It's gorgeous."

"It'll be amazing if I'm allowed in the same room with it at the party."

She laughed. "What did you find out from Holly?"

I filled her in on my trip to town, including Holly's protestation of innocence over the drone-deer incident.

When I was done, Claire said, "So she said she bore no grudges, then pointed the finger at Virgil."

"Not really, but it was clear she blames him for the company not taking up her brilliant invention. And I definitely don't think getting squeezed out of Brightlow Enterprises was the blessing in disguise Holly was trying to make it out to be."

It didn't take us long to reach Mildred's. For a Claus dwelling, it was very modest. It was also very old and borderline creepy both inside and out. The house was positioned on a small ridge at the bottom of Kringle Heights, close to the funicular stop, and always seemed to me to bear an alarming resemblance in silhouette to Norman Bates's house in *Psycho*, except this place had been built in dark gray stone.

Mildred inherited the home from her father, who'd been notable among his generation of Claus relations in that he actually worked for his stipend, overseeing the Candy Cane Factory until he died a decade before. Now, because of an edict from Nick, all adult Clauses were required to do *something* to earn their keep. Mildred, who really was good-hearted, manned the Christmastown Depression Center and Hotline, which was allotted a closet of a room in City Hall. Elves aren't prone to depression, so it was a lonely job. The one time I'd dropped in to say hello, it had just been Mildred at a desk with a silent phone and a plate of stale cookies. The whole setup seemed a little . . . depressing.

Another sign of Mildred's goodness was that she had given over one of her many spare rooms to Elspeth Claus, who, as far as I could see, didn't do much to repay Mildred's kindness.

The lights outlining Château Mildred and its windows in an attempt to adorn its gloomy bones were the old chunky bulbs no one had made in the past fifty years. An inadequately inflated Santa's sleigh scene wobbled on the rooftop.

I hadn't baked anything, but as a surprise for Mildred, I'd lined up an elf barbershop quartet called the Santaland Serenaders to perform as the guests arrived. They were singing "Jolly Old Saint Nicholas" as Claire and I parked. We stopped to listen to a chorus before going in, and I gave them a thumbs-up.

Mildred greeted us wearing a dark burgundy sack dress that was a slightly fancier version of the ones she wore every day.

"Weren't you *so nice* to send those singers to entertain us, April," she said, practically twittering with excitement.

"It was the least I could do." I handed her the bottle of bearberry wine I'd brought, and pointed to Claire's offering. "Claire's specialty back home is ice cream. She made some this morning for your potluck."

You'd have thought Claire was presenting Mildred with the crown jewels. "How marvelous! I'll have Olive pop it into the freezer room."

Olive was Mildred's longtime housekeeper, and older than Mildred by at least three decades. A rattling sound alerted us to her, a wizened old elf with a dowager's hump. She was out-fitted in a black-and-white maid's dress like something out of an old movie, and pushed a serving trolley with a wonky, squeaky wheel. I half suspected the cart was holding her up. She took the ice cream with quavery arms, put it on her cart, and slowly rolled away.

"That was Olive," I said to Claire.

"I thought maybe someone had put Yoda in a maid's uni-form," she whispered back.

"Olive's been working here at the château since I was a little girl," Mildred explained. "I don't know what I'd do without her. She did all the decorations you see—even the ones outside."

In the silence that followed, both Claire and I imagined ancient Olive scrabbling over the sloped roof to string lights and secure a giant inflated sleigh and reindeer.

"I wish you'd called the castle about your decorations," I said. "We could have sent someone to help."

Mildred dismissed that idea with a wave. "Nonsense. Olive loves to do it. And she harnessed herself to the chimney so she wouldn't fall off—at least too far. Of course, that ice storm last weekend slowed her down a little, but she was de-termined to get it all done in plenty of time for the party."

"Couldn't Elspeth have helped?" Elspeth was a few years older than me, but half a century younger than Olive.

Mildred lowered her voice. "Oh dear, no. Elspeth's been so busy working on her crafts for the Kringle Heights Ladies' Guild Holiday Crafts Bazaar this week, I haven't wanted to bother her. She *really* wants to make this a success, especially after *last* year."

Another moment of silence ticked by for the ear-sock debacle. Elspeth might not be my favorite Claus, but I sympathized with anyone who had seen her best-laid plans go wildly awry.

"Of course, Pamela tells me you're busy, busy, busy with your project, too," Mildred said.

I thought of the unknit tea cozies, currently in the giant ball-of-wool pupa stage in the corner of my bedroom. I really needed to get a few of those done tonight. Trouble was, there wasn't much time left. I'd have to knit five a night just to have ten to sell. Ten wasn't many, but maybe if I spread them out on the table it would look like more.

I peered into the main room, eager to change the subject. "Is Lucia here?"

Mildred's party face vanished, and she lowered her voice. "When I told her Quasar wasn't invited, she didn't take it well. I felt terrible, but you remember what happened the last time he was here."

"He ate the mantel swags," I explained to Claire. "But he felt really bad about that."

"I know it," Mildred said. She'd obviously agonized over this. "But Olive works so hard at decorating for me. It seems unfair to invite a guest over who'll chew up all her work in one afternoon."

Other guests' arrivals pressed us farther into the house, so Claire and I ditched our coats in the vestibule and continued into the main parlor. It was more crowded than I'd expected. I introduced Claire to as many elves and people as I knew, although there were a few guests whom I'd never met, including one peculiar-looking but obviously very well-to-do elf woman installed on a settee next to Pamela.

"This is fantastic!" Claire gazed around the room in all its gloomy glory. Like the old keep at Castle Kringle, Château Mildred's walls had a layer of accumulated soot from centuries of fireplace use. The furniture was threadbare, ancient, and sparse, leaving all but the oldest guests milling awkwardly around the room.

The brightest thing about the room was the long table along one wall covered in a festive white tablecloth embroidered with holly leaves and berries, on top of which stood the vast assortment of desserts everyone had brought. At the very center, on an impressive crystal pedestal, stood Pamela's peppermint pavlova, a mountain of baked meringue topped with pink whipped cream and sprinkled with crushed peppermint. It was a work of art.

I glanced over at my mother-in-law, who was giving me a warning side-eye not to get too close to the pavlova. A sigh caught in my throat. Trust had to be earned; I made a resolution to be extra careful this afternoon. Olive squeaked by with drinks on her cart, and both Claire and I grabbed flutes of sparkling cider.

I found myself next to Constable Crinkles, who was standing on his own, in full uniform except for his hat, and holding an empty buffet plate.

"Armed and ready, Constable?" I said.

He chuckled. "You know how it gets at the dessert potluck. You have to strategize or you'll miss all the good stuff." He narrowed his gaze on the buffet table, eyeing it with the same intensity with which Eisenhower probably studied maps of Omaha Beach before D-Day. "I'm going in between the iced plum cake and the ginger-cranberry trifle."

"Where's Ollie?" I asked.

"I left him in charge at the constabulary. He sent over that chocolate bundt cake. It's delicious—he made an extra for the constabulary."

"I'll have to try a piece," I said.

Alarm flashed in Crinkles's eyes. "Mayor Firlog's getting a

touch too close to the plum cake for my comfort." He sidled closer to his target.

"And I thought *I* took sweets seriously," Claire murmured. "This is next-level."

Amory swaggered over, grinning. He was dressed in a holiday sweater I knew had been given to him by Pamela some year. Sweaters were her forte, along with baking. This one featured smiling Christmas trees.

"I've got a treat for you," he said. He poked the elf at his side, who spun around, ending with a bounce on his heels. The young fellow had cheeks that were as round as the rest of him, a thick mop of dark blond hair with a pronounced cowlick in front, and bright blue eyes that were lit up with pleasure. He radiated so much energy, it was like standing before a Fourth of July sparkler in elf form.

"This," Amory announced with as much pride as if he'd been introducing a visiting dignitary, "is Butterbean."

That explained his bright green tunic with a scarlet *B* on the front. Also, hanging off his cap in place of a pom-pom was another shiny red *B*.

The elf hopped forward, took my hand, and bowed over it. "Honored, Mrs. Claus! I can't believe I'm finally getting to meet you!"

It was hard not to feel flattered by so much enthusiasm. "I've heard a lot about you, too."

"And who is your beautiful elf friend?" Butterbean asked.

"I'm not an elf," Claire said.

"Ears, Butterbean," Amory admonished.

"Oh, sorry!" Nervous laughter spilled out of him. "I'm just so excited to be here, I'm not thinking properly."

"Don't let him fool you," Amory stage whispered to us. "Butterbean is the most tack-sharp elf in Santaland. Wait till you see the brilliant fireworks show he has planned."

The elf burst with such pride for his creation that he made a jazz-hand gesture as he assured us, "It'll be spectacular!"

"I'm sorry I missed the one last summer," I said.

"That one was small-time," Amory assured us. "This one will knock your socks off."

Butterbean lifted on his toes and attempted to pull off a modest shrug. "I try never to do the same thing twice."

Amory took my arm, his face turning serious. "Now tell me, do we have the symphony?"

I'd forgotten to break the news to him. "I'm afraid there was a *Nutcracker* conflict, but I got you the Santaland Concert Band."

Disappointment flickered across his face. "And the choir?"

"I'm sorry. We're going to play the *1812 Overture.*"

"For *Christmas?*" Amory exclaimed.

"That's terrific!" Butterbean said, hopping in excitement. He was like a living, breathing shot of B12. "Perfect!"

Amory looked at him doubtfully. "Really? I wanted a 'Hallelujah Chorus.'"

"This will be even better!" Nothing could dampen Butterbean's enthusiasm. He was the happiest soul in the room. Probably in any room. "In fact, I think we can work with that— maybe make a few adjustments here and there to really make the whole thing pop. It'll be stupendous! This could be the beginning of a new Christmas week tradition here in Santaland—the Fireworks Spectacular."

"Butterbean's a peculiar name for a fireworks designer," Claire said.

"My parents were kitchen elves. They had their hopes that I would follow in their footsteps, but I had my own dreams." Butterbean thought for a moment and added with a chuckle, "Also, I accidentally burned down a dining room when a flambé of roast boar went a little haywire. But it propelled me out of the kitchen to follow my own destiny."

"His sister, Lettuce, works at the lodge kitchen," Amory explained. "It was she who brought Butterbean to my attention."

As if Butterbean needed a publicist. The guy was a walking billboard for himself.

"Leaping lemmings! I can't believe I'm at a party with all these illustrious people." He gazed around the room like a movie fan behind the rope, watching stars on the red carpet at the Oscars. "Mrs. Pamela Claus is right over there!"

"I could introduce you," I said.

"That's okay." Amory put a protective hand on his protégé's shoulder. "I'll take Butterbean over myself."

The elf made a little bow. "It was wonderful talking to you, Mrs. Claus—and meeting you, Miss Claire!"

"Likewise," Claire said. When they were gone, she turned to me. "I can't decide if he's adorable or excruciating."

"He certainly has pep."

The rest of the guests were growing restive. Everyone was migrating toward the dessert bar, and Claire and I joined the herd. From the corner of my eye, I could see Butterbean doing what looked like an imitation of a Roman candle for my perplexed mother-in-law. Finally, Olive and her trolley squeaked over to the table with the ice cream, and Mildred announced, "You may all serve yourselves now."

The feeding frenzy began. Everyone muscled in to load their plate with a selection of cream puffs, pies, ice cream, cake, and of course, Pamela's peppermint pavlova, which I very carefully carved a slice of, along with an assortment of the other offerings, including a scoop of Claire's ice cream. I tucked into the latter right away. "You have no idea how much I miss this," I told her after savoring my first bite.

She laughed. "Right—you're in sweets central, with the best chocolates, scones, muffins, and everything else on earth. And you miss ice cream?"

"Yes I do."

"I'll make you a few tubs before I go. That freezer room of yours has plenty of space."

The castle's freezer was a side room off the kitchen where a window was kept open year-round. Her offer was like being handed the best Christmas present ever. "You're right. There's tons of room there—enough for a year supply."

"Whoa. I wasn't expecting this to be a busman's holiday."

I tried to temper my ice cream greed. "Maybe a gallon or two?"

"Just tell me what flavors."

My mind harkened back to all my favorites that were written on the chalkboard at her Cloudberry Bay store. I had a lot of favorites. Mocha ripple. White chocolate Cloudberry. Coconut pineapple. Even as I started mentally cataloguing and ranking them all, a brittle voice broke through my thoughts.

". . . and the goings-on around here have been *terrible*. The constable isn't doing nearly enough! And now look at him—he's over there shoveling down cream puffs."

Any criticism of Constable Crinkles usually met with my approval, so I looked over to see who was doing the grousing. It was the old elf lady I'd noticed earlier. She'd loaded up a plate and resumed her perch on the settee, her expensively bootied feet not touching the floor. The dress she wore was a fanciful concoction of deep blue velvet that seemed planned to match the blue rinse of her updo. In lieu of an elf cap, a fascinator poked out of her hair—a spray of red with a small wooden cardinal perched on the end. The bird was decorated with dyed red feathers.

"There's an elf woman harassing my son, and when I called the constabulary, Crinkles refused to do a thing about it unless he heard from Blinky directly. As if a genius like Blinky Brightlow doesn't have more important things to do than deal with a crazed librarian."

My heart did a somersault. This had to be the mother of Blinky and Dabbs—and she was trash talking Juniper.

"That's slander," I said.

The elf lady tilted a look up at me. "I don't believe we've met."

"I'm April Claus. And you must be Mrs. Brightlow."

Her eyes gave me a cool up-and-down rake. "Yes, I must be."

Pamela swooped in to warn me off antagonizing the old elf. "Mrs. Brightlow donates generously to so many causes in Santaland, April."

"Didn't I hear you accuse Juniper of harassing Blinky?" I asked.

Her thin lips twisted in distaste. "If that's the librarian's name. She claims they're an item, but my Blinky would never involve himself with—" Her voice faltered before she concluded, "Well. There are all sorts of stories around town about that one."

Oh, for heaven's sake. "Juniper is hardworking and honest," I said, "and all I've heard from her is that she's concerned for Blinky's safety."

Mrs. Brightlow sniffed. "Blinky doesn't need her concern or her interference. He's a genius, and needs time alone to concentrate. He doesn't need a demented elf woman pestering him night and day." The old woman thumped her cane. "Honestly, one has to question her motives."

My blood approached a rolling boil. Pamela wrapped a hand with clawlike strength around my arm to steady me.

"Motives for expressing concern?" I asked.

"For trying to link her name with my son's. I doubt they pay much at the library."

For a moment I thought Pamela was going to have to bar me physically from attacking the old termagant. Imagine implying that Juniper was a gold digger!

"Juniper's heart is as big as Santaland," I said.

She lifted her chin. "The list of men she's left in her wake is also that big, I've heard."

I was moments away from telling the woman to step outside when I caught myself. I wouldn't stoop to her level. I wouldn't. I was Mrs. Claus. I would be the bigger Santalander.

I lifted my chin. "That's a terrible thing to say about someone, especially one who's served the public at the library her whole adult life, like Juniper."

"Not for much longer, if I have anything to say in the matter," the woman said. "I wrote letters to the library board and the Christmastown City Council warning them about what an unstable man-eater they're employing."

"I'm sorry, Mrs. Brightlow, *you're* the one who sounds unstable."

She hopped off the settee and stumped toward me with her cane. "I didn't come here to be insulted!"

"Of course you didn't," Pamela said fretfully. "April didn't mean—"

"Oh yes I did."

Without warning, the woman hauled back with her plate and sent a whole selection of Santaland's tastiest homemade treats flying toward me. They made a direct hit on my bolero jacket. I stood, vibrating in my boots. *I will be the bigger Santalander. I will be the bigger Santalander.*

Mrs. Brightlow puffed up like a cartoon pigeon. "You Clauses can't cover up crimes."

"Cover up?" I asked, astounded. Had the lady flipped her lid?

"What crimes have we covered up?" Pamela asked.

"I take threats to my boys seriously. Don't be so sure you Clauses won't get knocked off your pedestal someday! Mark my words—change is coming to Santaland."

Change was apparently closer than anyone anticipated. While Mrs. Brightlow raved, Pamela strolled over to her peppermint pavlova, picked it up stand and all, and crossed back to dump the whole thing right on the old elf's head.

For a moment, the shocked silence in the room was broken only by the gentle splat of crème dripping off Mrs. Brightlow's person. No one had ever seen my mother-in-law lose her cool before. I was as stunned as everyone else, although inside I was doing high fives and back handsprings.

"Oh, I'm so sorry," Pamela said sweetly. "My peppermint pavlova got knocked off its pedestal somehow."

Chapter 9

"Can you believe that old woman, smearing Juniper like that?" Claire and I had escaped to the castle, where I changed into non-icing-coated clothes.

"I can't believe Pamela weaponized her peppermint pavlova," Claire said.

"Dowager food fight at the dessert potluck was definitely not on my bingo card this week." I know it was the threat against the Clauses that had caused Pamela to act out, but at the time it had felt as if she was striking a blow for me and maybe even Juniper, too. "Pamela couldn't have picked a better target. That old elf has an incredible arm. She could be the Nolan Ryan of dessert tossers."

"She's even better at throwing insults around," Claire said.

I reached for my phone. I still hadn't received a call back from Virgil. I texted Juniper. **Claire and I going to We 3 Beans. Will swing by library to see if you can join us.**

Soon the dots were blinking. **Bad Day. Can't make it.**

I turned the screen so Claire could read it. Her eyes mirrored my own worries. "Do you think the powers that be have already said something to her about Mrs. Brightlow's poisonous letters?" she asked.

"No telling." I frowned at the screen. "She's not very

forthcoming." She didn't include a word of regret for not being able to join us, either. Not even a crying snowman emoji. "Well, if Juniper won't go to the coffee shop . . ."

We would take the coffee shop to Juniper. On the way, Claire stared out at the snow and evergreens gliding by and let out a sigh. "It really is beautiful here, April."

"I know. I still get bowled over by the scenery."

She crossed her arms. "I know I was a little freaked out when I first got here . . ."

"You should have seen me last year. Learning I was going to be Mrs. Claus? Talk about freaked out."

"But I can see why you love Nick, and why you love this place. It suits you. It's full of strangeness."

I laughed. "Thanks."

"Of course I'm still *slightly* skeptical about the whole Santa bit—the big Christmas Eve thing. But after I've seen talking snowmen and irascible elves, I guess I'll keep an open mind."

"Just wait till Christmas Eve—it's amazing."

She pulled out her phone. "Anyway, to get into the April Claus spirit of things, I decided to do a little sleuthing myself today. Remember what Dabbs said about customers writing negative things about Brightlow Enterprises? I looked on Yelf! and surfed the reviews."

"Did you find anything?" I'd forgotten about Yelf!

Within seconds, Claire had the site up on her screen and was scrolling through the reviews. "There aren't many comments about Brightlow Enterprises, but several are written by someone bearing the handle ArgentoTheGreat. Here's the worst: *'The drone-deer is a faulty piece of junk. No quality control. Silly design over function. It's only a matter of time before someone gets hurt!'* "

"Do you think that last line was a warning," I asked, "or a threat?"

"Hard to say. Could be someone with a grudge, though. Maybe they crashed a drone-deer to draw bad publicity to Brightlow Enterprises."

I considered that. "But if somebody thought drone-deer really were pieces of junk, would they trust that they would be able to precision crash one onto the neck of an ice reindeer?"

"Good point," said Claire.

Still, I thought about that review for the rest of the drive into town. Someone in this town had been harboring strong feelings about drone-deer for at least a month.

The old library building sat in a large plaza in downtown Christmastown. The arched stone entrance featured whimsical carvings of old Santaland tales and elves reading books. Claire and I bustled inside with three large coffees and a scone, hoping to lure Juniper into taking a break, even if it was just ten minutes in the library conference room.

She wasn't at the front desk, though, and Candy, the librarian stationed there, shook her head both at our chances of getting past her with our coffees and at my question about Juniper.

"She left about ten minutes ago." She narrowed her eyes at the coffees. "Are those lids secure?"

"Of course." I frowned. "Where did she go?"

The receptionist's brow scrunched. "I don't know. I was right next to her when she got a call about ten minutes ago. It seemed to agitate her—she wrote down an address and then turned to me and said she had to leave. I haven't seen her since. It was pretty odd behavior from Juniper, but she'd been acting strangely all day. She got a reprimand from the head librarian for misfiling some medical books."

"Anyone can make a mistake," I said.

"She filed them on a children's shelf. A mother found her toddler leafing through pictures of skin diseases."

Oh dear. Poor Juniper. I could see now why she felt she couldn't have coffee. But then why did she jump up and leave *after* that?

"She didn't give any clue whom she was talking to on the phone?" I asked.

"No, but I noticed she sounded . . . worried, maybe? And the next thing I knew she was saying she would meet the person in fifteen minutes, tops."

Juniper would be on foot. "It must be somewhere close, then."

Claire looked down at the empty chair next to the one Candy was sitting at. "Juniper was sitting here?"

The librarian nodded.

Claire picked up the pad. "Mind if we borrow this for a second?" She barely waited for Candy's head shake before borrowing a pencil out of the cup on the desk, too.

"What are you doing?" I asked.

"The old pencil-rubbing trick."

Candy sucked in a breath and leaned in. "Just like Nancy Drew!"

Claire rubbed the flat of the pencil lead against the top sheet of paper, and soon an address was visible in Juniper's distinct, round script:

390 Wonderland Lane.

1st floor.

Claire ripped the sheet from the pad and handed the paper to me, then she put the pad back on the desk. "Thanks."

"If you see Juniper," Candy said, "tell her someone from the town council was calling for her."

"I will," I lied. If Juniper was already having a bad day, the last thing she needed to hear was Mrs. Brightlow's poisonous gossip.

* * *

Wonderland Lane was five streets back from Festival Boule-vard, Christmastown's main traffic artery. My sleigh got us there quickly. Except for a café and a couple of other small businesses at the corner, the block where 390 was located was solidly residential. The cottages here were slightly separated from one another and set back just a few feet from the side-walk, which allowed for small evergreen hedges to grow. These were strung with lights, and wreaths were displayed on almost all the doors. Number 390 was no exception. Its pine wreath was decorated with nuts and ribbons, and had tiny foil-wrapped presents dotting it. I was curious to see who lived here. From the faint glow behind the windows, it ap-peared someone was home. Yet there was a stillness around us, as if the house was holding its breath.

I rang the bell. While we waited for an answer, Claire pointed a gloved hand toward the snow at our feet. From the sidewalk to the porch there was a mass of crossing bootprints along the walkway, but a single set of footprints led off the side of the porch and disappeared around the side of the house. Someone else had been here recently, and they'd walked around to the back.

"Small feet," Claire observed.

"An elf."

No one was going to answer the bell, it soon became clear. I eyed those footprints. "I'm going around back. Maybe they can't hear the bell back there."

The truth was, the stillness and those footprints gave me a bad feeling. Claire followed me to the little alleyway that led to the back of the house, but we were soon stopped by a fig-ure running toward us. It was Juniper, her short legs pumping like pistons.

"He's dead!" she shouted, skidding to a stop. She was too discombobulated to register surprise at our being there.

I put my hands on her shoulders to steady her. She was shivering. "Who's dead?" I asked.

She heaved a breath. "Virgil."

"This is his house?"

Her head bobbed frantically. "When I got here, he didn't answer the door. I peered in the window and saw a light on in back, so I went around. I just had an odd feeling, you know?"

"I had the same odd feeling just now."

"Is he outside?" Claire asked.

"No, he's in the kitchen, on the floor. I could see his feet, and . . ." She shuddered. "He's gone."

I already had my phone out and was dialing Constable Crinkles. The emergency services were all filtered through the constabulary.

Two rings later, Ollie's voice chirped at me. "This is the Christmastown Constabulary wishing you a happy holiday week—and don't forget iceball season will soon be upon us. How may I help you?"

"Ollie, there's been an incident. I'm at 390 Wonderland Lane."

A sigh issued from my phone's speaker. "Not those two again. Can't you just tell them to cut it out?"

I frowned at the ground. "What are you talking about?"

"Goldie and what's-his-name." A second of silence followed before he asked, confused, "What are *you* talking about?"

"Ollie, Virgil is dead."

"Holy doodle! Are you sure?"

"Well, *I* haven't seen him, but I'm at his house and Juniper assures me he is. He's lying on the floor of his kitchen."

"What should we do?" Ollie asked.

"Get over here, maybe? And call the coroner. Crinkles will know the drill."

"Unc's taking a nap. He said he overindulged at the dessert potluck."

Great. We had an emergency here, and our constable was in a sugar coma.

"Well, wake him up. We'll stay here until one of you arrives," I said.

"Thanks, that'll be a big help. I guess my uncle might want to talk to you."

"I'm pretty sure he will."

"I mean about the body you found. Of course, he always enjoys visiting with you. He doesn't always—"

"Just wake him," I interrupted. "We'll see you soon." I ended the call and turned back to the questioning looks of Juniper and Claire. "The Keystone Cops will be here any year now."

Juniper leaned against the side of the house, shaking. "I can't believe he's dead."

"You're really sure he is?"

At my question, a faint hope kindled in her eyes. "I mean, I just looked. I didn't want to . . . touch him."

"We should make certain—in case there's something we can do for him."

She pushed herself off the wall and sucked in a breath. "I'll take you to him."

We started to go, but I noticed Claire was still planted firmly where she was. She jutted her head in the other direction. "I'll wait out front for the constable."

She was in no hurry to witness the carnage firsthand, and I couldn't blame her. Some vacation this was turning out to be.

"Doc Honeytree, our coroner, might actually get here first," I told her. "He's very old. Coke-bottle glasses. He might have trouble finding the place."

The back porch of Virgil's house was just as tidy as the front. Even the garbage pails gleamed. The door was slightly ajar, and the door's window panel had been broken.

"Did you do this?" I asked Juniper, nodding to the glass.

She shook her head. "I didn't do anything, I swear. It was all like this when I showed up."

"So you actually went inside?"

"Yes. The door was open, just like it is now."

Gingerly, I pushed the door open farther with my gloved hand. The creak of the hinges made my insides clench, as did a sweet, strange smell. In the next moment, I took in what Juniper must have first seen through the window—two curly-toed slippers and striped socks poking out from behind the kitchen island. I tried to swallow, but my mouth was dry as desert sand.

Get a grip. This isn't the first time you've seen a dead body. It still seemed terrible, though, and when I stepped forward, the blood spattering the cabinets and tile floor made me freeze. A long metal object lay on the floor nearby; it was so out of place in the kitchen that it took me a moment to recognize it as a fireplace poker. The pointed tip had clearly been used to attack Virgil. There was nothing natural about this death. He'd been murdered.

I looked away from the weapon and focused on Virgil. He was facedown and still in the clothes I'd seen him in earlier— salt-and-pepper wool with a velvet collar and piping—but he'd put on a pair of house slippers. Also around him was more shattered glass, as well as some kind of liquid.

"What is that?"

"Eggnog," Juniper said. "He must have been making some for both of us." She nodded to the extra glass that was sitting on the counter.

That was the weird smell—burning milk. I looked at the

saucepan, which was filled with curdled eggnog. The bottom was clearly burned, although the burners were unlit.

"Did you turn off the stove?" I asked.

"No. Virgil must have, or else—"

The murderer. Apparently he was a conscientious killer. I forced myself to step forward, tiptoeing to avoid stepping on eggnog, glass, or blood. I bent down and touched Virgil's neck. It felt stiff, lifeless.

Who had done this terrible thing?

"So it was Virgil who called you at the library?"

She nodded. "Yes. I know I'd told you to call, but I'd also left a few messages at Brightlow Enterprises today."

"What exactly did he say to you over the phone?"

Her brows scrunched in thought. "He sounded worried—his voice was breathy, as if he'd been running. He said there was something urgent he had to tell me."

"That's it?"

She bit her lip. "Just one other thing—he said that with my connections, maybe I could help."

"Connections with whom?"

She shrugged. "I never found that out, but I got the sense that he was calling about Blinky."

She had Blinky on the brain. "You think that was the connection he meant—you and Blinky?"

"What other connections do I have? The library?"

"It just seems like he would have told you more." Or maybe it was that I wished he'd told her more.

Juniper looked me straight in the eye. "I didn't kill him."

"Of course you didn't." This kind of violence just wasn't in Juniper. I was shocked that it could be in anyone—especially in anyone I might know.

"You might start thinking it, though," she said.

"No I won't. Why should I?"

She didn't answer that. Instead, she asked, "Do *you* think this has anything to do with Blinky?"

"I'm not sure we can—"

"Shhh!" Juniper held a finger to her lips. Then, with her free hand, she pointed toward the interior door. Footsteps came from within the house. Very soft ones.

My heart slammed against my ribs. Was the murderer still here?

Holding our breaths, we eased toward the inside door. Juniper's hand clamped around my arm as we prepared to peek into what was probably the living room. I wondered if she could feel me shaking. I wasn't a coward, but I wasn't a fool, either. I didn't want us to wind up like Virgil.

We both craned our heads around the doorjamb.

A figure loomed, and both Juniper and I shrieked in terror. In response, the intruder screamed, too.

Once my heart started beating normally again, I collapsed against the doorjamb. The intruder was Claire.

"We thought you were the murderer," Juniper said.

Claire's eyes widened. "Virgil was murdered? Are you sure?"

"I'm sure," I said. "Unless he decided to beat himself over the head with a fireplace poker."

Claire looked ready to turn back and leave the house the way she came in, which was probably the sane response.

"Wait," I said, confused. "How did you get into the house? Is the constable here already?"

She shook her head. "While I was standing out there, I got bored and tried the doorknob. The front door wasn't locked."

"Oh." Come to think of it, I hadn't actually tried to open the door.

"Maybe he left it unlocked for me, but I didn't know it

was open," Juniper said. "I went around the back. He was dead when I got here, I swear."

Her voice grew more agitated as she spoke, as if she expected me to doubt her word. This was the second time she'd proclaimed her innocence to me. "You don't have to swear. I believe you."

Now that my heart had stopped its fight-or-flight racing, I took a moment to look around Virgil's living room. It looked comfortable, if on the bare side. The corner nearest the kitchen had been set aside for a small dining table with four chairs. The fire behind the grate was mostly ashes now. The living room furniture was arranged in a semicircle around the hearth—a couch flanked by two chairs, with a low table in front of the couch. A library book lay on it: *The Humanoids*. Sci-fi seemed a little out there for an elf's Christmas week reading, but I supposed it was as good a way as any to unwind. But that was the only book in view. Virgil hadn't bothered with homey touches. There were no throw pillows or blankets strewn about, no pictures and knickknacks, no bookshelves.

A wave of sadness hit me at the finality of it. You'd think seeing a corpse would be the worst part of death, but to me it was looking at Virgil's house and realizing that, for him, there was no more time. No more opportunity. Whatever dreams he'd had for himself would never be realized. They'd been stolen by some maniac with a fireplace poker. Or maybe it hadn't been a maniac; just someone who, for whatever evil, selfish reasons, thought their desires trumped someone else's right to live.

But who? I already had a suspect in mind.

"April?" Juniper's face pinched with worry. "We probably shouldn't be standing in here."

She was right. The house was a crime scene. I turned off

the light and we trooped outside to wait for the constable. Claire seemed happy to avoid a trip to the kitchen.

While we stood on the front porch, a middle-aged elf woman walking a dog that came up to her shoulder marched up the walkway. "What's going on?"

Recognition hit me, and both Juniper and I said, "Goldie?"

Goldie played baritone saxophone in our concert band.

"What are you doing here?" I asked.

"I live here. What are *you* doing here? Was there a rehearsal I didn't know about?" she asked with a husky laugh. Her jovial expression slid away in confusion when she caught our uncomfortable reactions.

"You live with Virgil?" I asked.

Her eyes widened. "Golly, no. I'm on the second floor." She nodded to a door on the right side of the house. "Not that Mr. Persnickety down here wouldn't love to pitch me out. But I'VE GOT A LEASE, MISTER!"

She yelled the last words so loudly at Virgil's front window that her dog let out a surprised bark. The three of us on the porch jumped.

"You and Virgil didn't get on very well?" I guessed.

"Like walruses on a too-small ice floe," she said, before doing a double take. "What do you mean, *didn't*? Where's he gone to?"

"He's dead," Juniper said.

Goldie absorbed this information with surprising matter-of-factness. "What happened to him?"

"Someone killed him," I said. "We're waiting for Constable Crinkles to arrive."

"Killed? Right here?" Her gaze scanned the surrounding area, as if she would be able to detect where in the neighborhood the violence had crept in. "How could that have happened?"

More to the point, how could it have happened without Goldie knowing?

"What's your dog's name?" I asked.

"Phil."

"You didn't hear anything happening in Virgil's place this evening? Phil didn't bark?"

"No, we must have been out already."

"How long were you gone?"

Her gaze turned skyward as she calculated. "About two hours, I'd guess."

Two hours!

"That's a long walk," Juniper said.

"It's usual for us. We circled Peppermint Pond and then watched the sledding at Toboggan Hill."

"Did anyone see you?"

Goldie drew back. "How should I know? Probably, but I didn't foresee that someone was going to up and murder Virgil and I'd need an alibi."

Ollie's reaction to hearing the address made sense now. At some point the constable and his deputy had been called out to maintain the peace between Virgil and Goldie. Which indicated that their spats had gone beyond the usual neighborly resentments.

"Why didn't you and Virgil get along?"

"I got along fine with him—I've got no problems with anybody. But his highness down here is—was—bothered by every little noise. The dog's barking bothered him. The sound of the dog walking bothered him. I had to put down carpet. He also complained about the sax."

To be fair, a bari sax wasn't exactly something easy to ignore.

"I have the same problem with my neighbors," Juniper lamented.

Only I doubt her neighbors had ever called Constable Crinkles because she was practicing euphonium. Juniper wasn't Goldie. Goldie wasn't one to play nice or back down from an argument, and I could see her whacking someone's skull with a fireplace poker. Not with the intent to kill, maybe—she didn't strike me as an evil elf—but if her temper got the better of her . . .

"I'm going inside," she announced. "Phil needs his dinner."

"Don't you want to wait for Crinkles?" Juniper asked.

"Crinkles knows where to find me."

After Goldie's door closed, Claire looked searchingly at both Juniper and me and asked, "Do you think she did it?"

"No," I had to confess. "I wish she'd been home, though. Maybe she would have seen or heard something."

The sounds of the two constabulary snowmobiles coming down the street grabbed our attention. Crinkles pulled up first, followed by Ollie with Doc Honeytree riding in the sidecar. It took a moment to extricate the old doctor from the vehicle and set him on his pins again. He grabbed his black doctor's bag and followed the lawmen up the walkway.

"Sorry it took us so long," Crinkles said to us as he huffed up the porch steps. "We had to give Doc Honeytree a lift."

"Even the doctor's reindeer are on strike?" I asked, shocked.

"Oh no," Doc Honeytree said. "They told the herd council that they're essential, but I gave them the night off." He shook his head. "I should have known better. There are always shenanigans during Christmas week."

"What the Fig Newtons has happened here?" Crinkles said.

"Something worse than shenanigans," I warned them.

For some reason, the three men seemed doubtful of my claim as they tromped through Virgil's house. Crinkles led the way through to the kitchen, then slammed to a stop, throwing

his arms out to his sides as if to stop us from stepping any farther. "He's dead!"

The doctor ducked under his arm, crouched, and checked
for a pulse on Virgil's neck as I had done earlier. "Definitely
deceased," he confirmed.

The constable gaped in bewilderment. "This is terrible.
What are we going to do about this?"

The doctor snapped his bag closed. "There's nothing *I* can
do except call the undertaker. When do you think you'll be
finished here?"

Crinkles tilted his head. "Finished with what?"

Crinkles often needed to be prodded to get moving on the
basics. "Finding out who did this," I said. "Investigating."

"I bet it was that woman upstairs," Ollie said. "Goldie?
She was always getting into fights with Virgil. He called us out
here once because she'd brought elf cloggers over to annoy
him. We had to break it up."

I couldn't help but take my hat off to Goldie. Weaponiz-
ing elf cloggers was a creative way to escalate hostilities with
one's neighbors.

But I still didn't believe Goldie could do something this
awful. "You might want to speak to an elf named Holly Silverpick," I said. "I was just talking to her yesterday. I think
she had some issues with Virgil, as well."

Crinkles brows rose with interest. "Is that so? Well! This is
getting complicated, isn't it?" He buried his hands in his
pockets. "I don't like complicated. I mean, Goldie lives right
upstairs."

"You can't collar someone for a crime just because they're
a neighbor," I said.

Ollie let out a cry and bent down. He'd discovered the
murder weapon. "I bet whoever did it used this." He frowned
at the poker. "It's got blood on it, and little bits of—"

"Shush with the gruesome details, Ollie," his uncle said, cutting him off. "We've got ladies here."

"The ladies are the ones who found Virgil," I pointed out. "And we've already seen the fireplace poker."

I couldn't help noticing that Juniper had gone a whiter shade of pale at the mention of the murder weapon.

"I guess that Goldie—or whoever the killer was—interrupted Virgil while he was making his after-work eggnog," Crinkles said.

They hadn't noticed that there were two eggnog glasses yet—one on the counter and the one that had shattered on the kitchen tiles. At some point we would have to tell him that Juniper was meeting Virgil. Although I worried it might sound incriminating, since she was at the scene of the murder so soon after he was killed.

Then again, Crinkles was already off to the races with his theory that Goldie was the guilty party. ". . . and maybe they argued, and Gold—er, the killer—whacked him on the head with his fireplace poker," he said, thinking aloud.

Ollie stepped forward. "Hey, Unc, all we have to do is go see if Goldie's fireplace poker is missing."

Crinkles practically hopped with excitement. "That's right. Doc, tell the undertaker he can come over right away. No need to do anything more here. Once we locate the owner of that fireplace poker, we'll have our killer."

"No, you won't," Juniper said.

Everyone turned to her. She looked like she was going to faint.

"Why not?" Crinkles asked.

Belatedly, I shot another glance at the poker in Ollie's hand. I should have noticed it right away. I'd been distracted by the business end of the thing—the sharp end that had been used to do the damage to Virgil and the blood on it. My brain had glossed over the fact that I'd seen the handle before. It was a brass snowman.

My chest clenched. Too late, I began to warn my friend. "Juniper, don't say anyth—"

"It's mine," she blurted out, tears in her eyes. "My fireplace poker killed Virgil."

Chapter 10

"*I* didn't kill him, though," Juniper swore. "I didn't even touch him."

"Why'd you bring your fireplace poker over, then?" Crinkles asked.

"I didn't." She related the conversation she'd had with Virgil over the phone. "I came directly here from the library."

The constable scratched his chin. "You might have had it at work with you."

"You don't think someone would have noticed a librarian walking around the stacks with a fireplace poker?" I asked.

Claire frowned. "For that matter, how do we even know the poker is Juniper's?"

"The snowman handle," Juniper said. Despite my frantic facial contortions of warning, she apparently didn't grasp the concept of not incriminating herself. "My parents gave me the set when I moved into my own apartment. They had it made special by a metalworker friend of my dad's."

"That doesn't mean it's the only one in existence," I said. "If this elf made one for your parents to give you, he might have made one for somebody else. Or dozens of them."

"That's right," Claire said. "We should at least check."

"Okay." Crinkles turned to his nephew. "Run over to Juniper's place and see if her fireplace poker's there."

Juniper hitched her purse on her shoulder. "I'd better go with you, Ollie. It's locked."

"Just give him the keys," Crinkles said. "I might have more questions for you."

She looked almost frightened, though I wasn't sure if it was at the prospect of further interrogation from Crinkles or the idea of Deputy Ollie going into her apartment.

"I'll go with him," I said.

The suggestion of my leaving seemed to alarm Juniper even more. Claire leapt in. "I'll go," she offered. "You stay here with Juniper."

That was probably the best solution. Crinkles wasn't the Grand Inquisitor, but Juniper didn't look up to a lot of questions at the moment.

Claire and Ollie set out, leaving just Crinkles, Doc Honeytree, Juniper, and me.

"So why were you here?" Crinkles asked Juniper.

"I told you—I got a call from Virgil. We knew each other from a long time ago. Yesterday I saw him at Brightlow Enterprises when I went to ask about Blinky again."

"I was with her," I said. "Virgil was acting odd while we were there. He seemed uncomfortable."

"Uncomfortable seeing Juniper?" Crinkles asked.

Too late, I realized that observation didn't exactly help Juniper. I wondered if I should mention that the last time I'd seen him, he practically ran in terror at the sight of me.

That probably wasn't a good thing to mention, either.

I shrugged. "He just seemed anxious."

Crinkles bobbed on his toes. "And what are *you* doing here? The last time I saw you, it was during that food fight with Mrs. Brightlow."

Juniper rounded on me. "What happened?"

"Just a small incident," I said.

Crinkles tsked. "Shame. I never got to sample the peppermint pavlova before it landed all over Mrs. Brightlow."

Juniper leveled her professional look of consternation and disappointment on me. "Did you do that?"

"No, Pamela did."

Juniper gasped. "Old Mrs. Claus?"

"Mrs. Brightlow's a battle-ax." I still felt bitter over the things she'd said. At least none of her slurs seemed to have reached Juniper yet.

Crinkles frowned at me. "You still haven't explained why you're here."

His persistence was impressive. He seemed to have brought his A game this evening. Who knew Crinkles even possessed an A game? Maybe sugar overload chased with a nap had tapped dormant investigative powers in his brain.

"Claire and I wanted to see Juniper, so we went around to the library. Claire and I figured out she'd come here and followed to find out what was going on."

"Because you were worried about her?"

"Yes, but not that she might kill Virgil—or anyone else."

Juniper's face scrunched into a puzzled frown. "What were you worried about?"

Damn. Me and my big mouth. "It was nothing. You've just been so preoccupied lately."

There. I gave myself a mental pat on the back for finessing my answer.

"Well, I guess I'd have been worried about her, too, after the way Mrs. Brightlow was badmouthing her at that party," Crinkles allowed. "Whoo-ee!"

Juniper looked crushed. "Mrs. Brightlow was saying bad things about me? At the dessert potluck?"

"Nothing too bad," I lied.

Crinkles shook his head. "But she sure doesn't want you involved with her son."

Juniper's face fell. "Oh."

Doc Honeytree stepped forward and patted her kindly on the shoulder. "Don't worry. No one else thinks you're a gold-digging man-eater."

"*What?*" Her eyes bugged. "You were there, too, Doc?"

He scratched his chin. "No, I heard it from a patient of mine, whose cousin was there."

She moaned.

Thanks, guys. "Mrs. Brightlow is horrible," I told Juniper. "I wish the entire Brightlow family would disappear."

"Cheese and Crackers!" Crinkles exclaimed. "Don't say that. I've got enough to deal with, with one of them AWOL. And now a murder to deal with!"

Juniper bit her lip. "Maybe they're connected."

I doubted spouting off conspiracies about Blinky's absence being linked to Virgil's death would help Juniper's predicament any. Did elves have the right to remain silent?

Crinkles's phone rang with a "Holly Jolly Christmas" ring tone, and he fumbled in his pocket to retrieve it. "Uh-huh," he said, after picking up and listening for a moment. He mouthed "Ollie" at the rest of us. "Well, that's that, then. Yes, you'd better come back here and wait with Doc for the undertaker. You'll need to give him a ride home."

He ended the call and turned to Juniper. "Your poker's missing."

She nodded grimly, as if she hadn't expected any other outcome.

He took her arm. "You'd better come with me to the constabulary."

"No!" Was he arresting her? I was horrified. "This is a

mistake. Juniper did not do this. You need to stay and look for clues. And aren't you going to interview Goldie?"

"It'll all get sorted out," he assured me. "And in the meantime, we've got fresh flannel sheets on the cell bed at the constabulary, and Ollie made that chocolate cake this morning. Juniper will be snug as a bug."

"This is madness," I insisted. "I *saw* Juniper right after she discovered Virgil's body, and she was running in terror. If she'd just killed Virgil with her own fireplace poker that she, for some reason, had been carrying around with her all day, why would she leave it lying there next to his body?"

"Because she was panicked? You said she looked panicked."

"Terrified," I corrected. "When I saw Virgil's slippers sticking out from behind the kitchen island, I wanted to run, too."

"But you didn't. You called me. That's what a cool-headed, innocent person would do."

Juniper looked dazed. She'd probably thought she was coming to Virgil's to help solve one mystery, and then next thing she knew she was plunged into another, nastier one—this time as the prime suspect.

But she wasn't the only suspect. "I can think of several other people who might have killed him. Holly Silverpick was telling me that she blamed him for her being squeezed out of Brightlow Enterprises. Why don't you talk to her?"

"Because the fireplace poker doesn't belong to Holly Silverpick," Crinkles said. "If it did, I'd be taking Holly to the constabulary, not Juniper."

I tossed up my hands. Of all the times for Crinkles to start using logic, it would have to be now.

He lowered his voice. "I just can't let a murder suspect go, April. Even if she is your friend."

"But—"

Juniper shook her head. "It's okay, April. They can't find me guilty if I didn't do it, can they?"

I didn't even know where to begin with that kind of thinking. She obviously hadn't been reading the same newspapers I had my whole life. Of course she hadn't. She'd spent her whole life in Santaland. The crime blotter in the *Christmastown Herald* usually featured double-parked sleighs and candy cane smuggling. Not murder.

"Just keep trying to find out what happened to Blinky," she said. "I'm more worried about him than ever."

Blinky? Was she serious? She was a suspect in a murder investigation.

Still, as Crinkles hustled Juniper off the porch and toward the constabulary snowmobile, I couldn't bring myself to argue with her. "I'll be looking into everything," I promised her. "We'll prove you didn't do this."

She nodded, and then followed Crinkles.

"Don't you worry," the doctor consoled me after the constabulary snowmobile had disappeared from view. "Everyone will know that Juniper's innocent."

"How? She'll be sitting in a jail cell, unable to prove it."

"*You'll* prove it. You've done it before."

Doc had a lot more confidence in my sleuthing abilities than I did. I knew nothing about Virgil, or who might hold such a grudge against him that they'd subject him to death by fireplace poker.

Claire and Ollie returned after the undertaker and his assistants arrived and were taking Virgil away. We watched them in silence. There was something awful about seeing someone being hauled out of their home on a stretcher, draped by a sheet. By this time, half the elves in the neighborhood were on their porches, watching.

"Don't worry about giving me a lift home," Doc told

Ollie. "I'll ride with the undertaker. They go right past my house."

That just left Ollie, Claire, and me. We lingered as the deputy made sure the fire was out and patched the back window with duct tape and cardboard. "I guess I should get back to the constabulary," he said when he was done.

"Shouldn't you go over the crime scene more?" I asked. "Fingerprints? Photos?"

He considered the question for a moment and then shrugged in dismissal. "It'll be fine. Unc and I got a really good look."

I must not have disguised my disapproval.

"You want to go back to the constabulary to tell my uncle his job?" he asked.

"No, but I might go see Juniper, if she needs me."

I was already texting her, knowing that Crinkles would allow her to keep her phone. **Would you like company?**

She wrote back, **Thanks, but my parents are coming. Mom might spend the night. It's already going to be crowded in here.**

Let me know if you need anything.

Thanks. Don't forget about Blinky!

Blinky again. Being arrested was affecting her reason. How could she still care about what was going on with Blinky?

"That's it, then," Ollie said. "I guess I'll be seeing you if you come by to visit Juniper."

We watched him drive away, and then I turned on my heel and went straight back into Virgil's house. With my phone, I took pictures of everything—the crime scene, the house, the contents of drawers, Virgil's medicine cabinet . . . Anything that might remotely help in an investigation, I snapped photos of.

Claire went along patiently with the time-consuming exercise, although she finally gave up, flopped on the couch, and picked up *The Humanoids* and desultorily leafed through a few pages before tossing it back on the table. For good measure, I photographed it, too. I noticed the library stamp on the cover. Virgil had checked the book out from the library. Had he seen Juniper there? Had they spoken? Did the book have anything to do with anything? There were so many unknowns.

But it gave me something to ask Juniper about.

"It's disappointing," Claire said when I was finally done. "I've been watching crime scene investigation shows for over a decade, and now here I am at my first crime scene and I don't see anything that could be an 'aha' clue."

I didn't, either. And yet, I suspected that somewhere in that apartment, or in all the pictures I'd taken, was a detail that would point straight to the guilty party. And there was. I just didn't know what I was seeing—or where to look.

But I knew someone who might. I picked up my phone again and scrolled through my contacts.

"Who are you calling?" Claire asked.

"A detective. A real one."

Chapter 11

The next morning I was up early and dressed in my band uniform for the Little Gliders ice recital. Sunrise was still a few hours off, so I still had plenty of time to savor a coffee. Unfortunately, Jingles hadn't arrived with it yet.

I glanced over at the pile of wool balls in a basket by the fireplace. I'd knit half a cozy last night. I should have gotten more done, but my head was buzzing from all the unknowns around me. How could I prove Juniper's innocence when so many circumstances pointed to her guilt? Would Jake Frost, the detective I messaged, show up today? The private detective was a strange, enigmatic figure who hailed from the Farthest Frozen Reaches.

Nick was doing up the buttons of his best Santa Suit—he'd promised to stop by the Little Gliders show, and he liked to pull out all the stops when making an appearance for children.

"I'm worried about Jake," I said. "Do you think he'll arrive today?"

"If he said he'll be here, he will," Nick assured me.

The detective had sent a three-word reply to my SOS: **On my way.**

But on his way from where? The Farthest Frozen Reaches

was a massive place. If he was on the top of Mount Myrrh, or on the other side of it, it might take him a while to reach Christmastown.

"If he does arrive today, I hope he can find us."

Nick shot an amazed look at me. "We're not exactly traveling around Santaland incognito."

I laughed. It was true. We were Santa and Mrs. Claus, and though *I* wasn't running around in a red suit, I would spend part of my morning sporting what looked like a drum majorette's shako hat. I was the opposite of inconspicuous.

"Besides, Jake knows all he has to do to find you is ask Jingles."

Where *was* Jingles? He usually arrived with my coffee tray by now.

Nick donned his Santa hat, so I guessed he was getting ready to leave the castle. But it was still too early for the Little Gliders event. "Where are you off to?" I asked.

"I thought I'd stop by Brightlow Enterprises," he said.

My antennae were fully extended. "Are you going to question them about Virgil's murder?"

His brows drew together. "That's the constable's business."

I folded my arms. "While Juniper's in the clink, it's our business, too. Last night I developed a theory about this killing."

"You mean you dreamt something up?"

"Dreaming never entered into it. How could I sleep when Juniper's in jail?" True, she was in a cozy room in the constabulary, tucked into flannel sheets and probably being plied with baked goods. Still, even 24/7 chocolate cake access doesn't take the sting out of being branded a murderess.

"Okay, what's this theory?" Nick asked.

"Blinky did it."

He looked warier than ever. "I thought Blinky was missing."

"And isn't *that* a useful bit of coincidence? Leaving town

just before someone is murdered. Also, Virgil and Juniper had some kind of puppy love thing in school, and for all I know Virgil was still carrying a torch for her. So when she and Blinky started dating, it created a deadly love triangle."

Nick frowned. "In that scenario, wouldn't *Virgil* have been the one who wanted to kill Blinky?"

That was . . . logical. Which was the problem with thoughts that occurred at two a.m.: they rarely held up to the cold light of morning.

"Also, you were saying that you thought Blinky and Juniper didn't actually have much of a relationship," Nick pointed out.

"But Juniper was obviously concerned about Blinky. She was telling me to keep looking for him even as Crinkles dragged her off to the hoosegow."

"Again, jealousy would have been a reason for Virgil to feel murderous, not Blinky."

I sighed. I hoped Jake got here soon. Maybe he could make some sense of this. "So why *are* you going to Brightlow Enterprises?" I asked.

"I still have the reindeer strike to worry about. I'm going to ask Brightlow to consider renaming the drone-deer, and to take the antlers off the design. That might appease the reindeer somewhat."

A knock sounded at the door. Nick, who was closest, pulled it open, and a second later Jingleini whirred in with the coffee tray.

"Good morning, Mrs. Claus," his mechanical voice greeted me.

I didn't know if I had the patience to deal with a Selfy this morning. "Where is Jingles?"

Jingleini halted abruptly, rattling the contents of his tray. Coffee sloshed out of the coffee cup. "Good morning, Mrs. Claus."

Nick laughed.

I spoke loudly and clearly at what I presumed to be the Selfy's ear, or speaker, or whatever that grill was on the side of its head. "Tell your elfman overlord that I've got juicy gossip to relate to him."

The words "juicy gossip" worked their magic. Quicker than a fox chasing a snowshoe hare, Jingles appeared in the doorway. "Anything I can help you with, Mrs. Claus?"

Nick gave me a hug—a very satisfying gesture when the giver of the hug is wearing a fuzzy velvet suit. "I'll see you later, at Peppermint Pond." As he passed Jingles on his way out, he said, "April really doesn't need caffeine. She's got a murder keeping her brain ticking."

In a flash, Jingles was at my side. "The death in Christmastown last night? That really was a murder?"

"Unless Virgil clunked himself on the head with a fireplace poker." I took the tray from Jingleini.

"Good morning, Mrs. Claus," he bleeped again.

Was I imagining it, or was he starting to sound forlorn?

Jingles scowled and flipped the switch on what would have been the nape of Jingleini's neck. Then he followed me over to the dressing table where I was stirring milk into my coffee. "What do we know so far?" he asked.

"It's only been twelve hours since we found Virgil," I said. "The gist of the situation is that Virgil was killed, and the constable thinks Juniper did it."

Jingles drew back, aghast. "*Our* Juniper?"

"Her fireplace poker was the murder weapon."

Jingles put his hands on his hips. "That's ridiculous. If I was going to bludgeon someone, I certainly wouldn't use my own fireplace poker."

"That's what I told the constable."

"Great minds . . ." Jingles let out a sigh. "How are we going to crack this case?"

"I've summoned Jake Frost."

He worked his jaw back and forth in thought. "Do you really think we need him?"

"With Juniper's life on the line, I want all the help we can get."

"Well, I suppose you do have a lot on your plate this week."

"Nothing more important than clearing Juniper's name."

He looked pointedly at my uniform, and I understood what he meant. Juniper might be in jail, but I was still going to the Little Gliders skating recital. There was no stopping Christmas week and all its festivities. I also had Claire to consider.

"Between murder and being put to work making ice cream, poor Claire is probably wondering why she came here on vacation."

"Oh, I doubt that," Jingles said. "I saw her in the kitchen yesterday. She was having the time of her life teaching the other kitchen elves 'I'm Gonna Lasso Santa Claus.' The other elves were having a ball, too. Even Felice the cook joined in."

That mental image made me smile. Claire might look like a pint-sized femme fatale, but she still had a little glee club geek in her. "What was Pamela doing?"

"Singing," he said.

Hard to imagine. Pamela was so conscious of setting a dignified Mrs. Claus example, she rarely let her hair down. At least, not in front of me. It was like trying to envision Queen Elizabeth pole dancing.

Jingles sighed. "I'm not sure Jingleini is going to work out. Not if I have to spend so much time looking after him that I'm missing important gos—information."

"I want your life to be easier," I said, "but Jingleini is a poor substitute for you."

For a moment, it looked as if Jingles might cry. He hitched his throat, straightened, and said, "How can I help you prove Juniper's innocence?"

I'd thought about this. "For now, keep your ear to the ground and your eyes open around the castle elves. There must be someone else in Virgil's life who wanted him gone."

Assignment received, he practically saluted. "You're right. There's bound to be someone around here who knows him."

He powered Jingleini back up. "Come along, you big-brained garbage can."

After he left, my phone pinged with a text. It was a text from Juniper.

Could you swing by to feed Dave today?

I replied, **Of course! Not a problem.**

Also, if you go by Virgil's again, you might grab that book on his coffee table. It needs to go back to the library?

I smiled. Being arrested for murder couldn't dull Juniper's librarian instinct.

Claire and I took the funicular down to town, she bundled in her stylish peacock blue wool swing coat, me huddled in my heaviest black coat over my band uniform. I looked like a festively hatted Cossack.

The newly renovated funicular ran up and down the lower part of Sugarplum Mountain, offering spectacular views of Christmastown and beyond—all the way to Mount Myrrh in the Farthest Frozen Reaches. Though I harbored some bad memories of the funicular crashing a few months ago, I thought Claire would appreciate the scenery—and besides, I'd lent my sleigh to Nick.

My friend's mind seemed more focused on the puzzle of Virgil's murder than on the scenery, though. "That bludgeoning was violent. And personal. On cop shows they always say that overkill is a sign of the perpetrator having a personal relationship to the victim."

"Or maybe they just wanted to make sure he was really dead." I frowned. "Or . . . they wanted everyone else to think it was a crime of passion."

"Exactly. This is a crafty murderer, April. Someone who knew framing Juniper would be the best way to deflect blame. Or someone who wanted, more than merely killing Virgil, to punish Juniper. Is there anyone who's in love with Juniper?"

Of course there was. I would be standing right next to him at the Little Gliders concert this morning. But Smudge wasn't a murderer. He was just a moody percussionist. He certainly wouldn't want Juniper in jail. Would he?

It was horrible to contemplate. Smudge wasn't my favorite elf in the world, but we'd finally achieved a level of camaraderie.

"April?"

I forced myself to smile. "You shouldn't have to think about murder. You're here on vacation."

"Actually, it's been exciting—aside from being horrible. So different from my usual thing. You know my usual pattern—the vacation fling I regret the moment I get home. No chance of that here."

"You mean you weren't tempted by Walnut?"

She laughed. "He's very colorful, I'll give him that."

"He's one of the richest elves in Santaland. Quite a catch, really."

She leveled a look at me. "Are you trying to encourage me? You usually think I go a little too crazy on vacation."

"No, no—I'm not recommending a Christmas fling with Walnut or anyone. I just don't want you to get bored."

"Are you kidding? I'm in a winter wonderland. It's a novelty to be staying out of trouble for once."

After we arrived at Peppermint Pond and I'd deposited

Claire in her seat and climbed the bandstand, I ran into Goldie, rolling her saxophone case on a little red wagon.

"I heard they arrested your friend," she said by way of greeting.

My gaze strayed to Juniper's empty chair. "Juniper's innocent." I retreated to the back of the stage, where all the percussion was waiting. Maybe that's why Smudge looked extra taciturn today. He'd done all the setup already.

"I thought I got here in plenty of time to help put our equipment out," I said in apology for all the work he must have done on his own.

"It's okay. I got the morning off from the factory and didn't have anything else to do." He ducked his head.

"You took the morning off? During Christmas week?"

His face darkened. "I didn't feel like making candy canes."

Now that I got a closer look at him, his face looked drawn, tired.

"Are you worried about Juniper?" I asked. Or was it guilt that had kept him awake?

"What do you think?"

I wasn't sure. I assumed I would have known if I'd been playing percussion alongside a diabolical psychopath who would kill for love and then let his ex take the rap.

And why would he have thought Virgil and Juniper were an item? Smudge hadn't been there at Brightlow Enterprises to see the way Virgil reacted to Juniper. Smudge would have to have followed Juniper, or known ahead of time that she was going to meet Virgil.

Or maybe it was Smudge who'd called the library, to set her up . . .

But Juniper would have recognized Smudge's voice.

As we made our last preparations for the concert to begin, I looked out over the audience. Nick had arrived in my sleigh, and he was surrounded by children. He released a blast of ho-

ho-ho's, delighting his pint-sized audience. He wasn't always comfortable being in Santaland's showy top job, but he genuinely loved being around kids, and seeing their excited reaction to his costume. If he didn't have weightier matters to attend to, he would have let them yank on his beard all day long.

I surveyed the rest of the crowd. Claire was checking her phone messages as all the seats filled in around her. A scan of the entire audience area told me that Jake Frost had not arrived.

Soon I had to concentrate on the music, which wasn't easy. There's nothing more distracting than four- to seven-year-old elves wobbling around on the ice in adorable getups. My sister-in-law, Tiffany, did a great job with costumes. One grouping of toddlers skated in puffy white blobs to "A Marshmallow World." They were followed by slightly older children in reindeer antlers and bells doing a crack-the-whip on ice to "Sleigh Ride." The program wrapped up with older children performing an interpretive skate to a long medley from *The Nutcracker*. My first *Nutcracker* of the week—it wouldn't be my last. When the children were done and taking their bows with Tiffany standing proudly behind them, I scanned the audience again and spied a familiar figure in black in the back of the crowd, with his dark fedora brim tilted across his brow. Jake. He'd made it.

I was tossing the small percussion instruments into their storage box when I heard the rapping of Luther's baton against his stand. The sound struck a regular Pavlov's dog response in me, and I straightened to attention, ready for the conductor's instructions, as did the rest of the band. The audience—the part not consisting of parents—had already started heading back toward town.

"As most of you know," Luther began, "one of our own, Juniper, was arrested last night."

Murmurs broke out among the band members, and I cut a glance over to the drum kit to check Smudge's reaction. Smudge wasn't there. In confusion, I looked around and caught sight of him walking toward Luther. He stopped and stood solemnly with his hands behind his back.

"This was not just a blow to our low brass section, but also a gross miscarriage of justice," Luther continued. "To show our support, Smudge has suggested that those of you who wish to can join in a cheering serenade this evening at the constabulary to lift Juniper's spirits."

Band members jumped to their feet, clapping. My heart swelled. At least the band had Juniper's back.

When the announcement was over, I approached Smudge. "You thought of this?" And here I'd toyed with the idea that he'd killed Virgil and had set Juniper up to take the blame.

He shrugged. "I don't want her to feel abandoned."

It was a wonderful gesture. "I wonder what the constable will make of our serenade."

"Crinkles?" Smudge expelled a cynical laugh. "He knows. He and Ollie are planning to sell cookies and turn it into a fundraiser-recruitment opportunity for the Christmastown Twinklers."

"*Seriously?*"

He shrugged. "They need a new forward."

As soon as I could put my percussion instruments away, I made my way over to Jake.

"How long have you been here?" I asked without pre-amble.

It was okay. Jake wasn't one to concern himself with niceties. He appreciated matter-of-factness. "Long enough. I stopped by the constabulary and talked to Crinkles."

"Does he still think Juniper killed Virgil?"

"I don't think he wants to believe it, but circumstances do point to her."

"Only superficially."

His black brows rose in sharp, inverted *V*s. "The murder weapon?"

I scoffed. "Obviously stolen from her place and planted at the murder scene."

"We'll have to see about that."

That "we" came as a relief. Jake could be sniffy about amateurs muscling in on his sleuthing. "I'm glad you're including me in your plans," I told him.

"Who said I was?"

"Who else would you mean by 'we'?"

He jerked his head in the direction of Gert's Pretzels cart, which was parked on a nearby street to take advantage of the recital traffic. "My assistant, the one you set me up with, came with me."

Quince, an orphaned elf who'd dreamed of adventure, had joined the private detective in the Farthest Frozen Reaches, along with his snowman friend, Pocket. Quince had made Pocket when he was small, so the snowman was on the diminutive side, but he seemed to have weathered the Farthest Frozen Reaches well so far. He'd apparently been given one of Jake's cast-off hats, so even he had a Sam Spade aura now.

I was glad to see them again—we needed all the help we could get—but I had no intention of being sidelined.

"I'm not going to stand by and do nothing," I said. "It's Juniper."

I expected an argument, but Jake probably sensed that resistance was futile. "The more the merrier." His tone was about as merry as a funeral, though.

"Don't worry that I'll be in your way," I told him. "I have my own assistant."

"Who?"

I looked around for Claire in the audience. Then I felt a tug at my coat sleeve. My friend was standing just to the side and behind me, in my blind spot. Her bright eyes were glued on Jake Frost, and the look in them made me very uncomfortable. I'd seen that look before. The air around her practically crackled with interest.

"Jake, this is my friend Claire from Cloudberry Bay. Claire, this is—"

"Holiday trouble," she said, interrupting. Her intense, hungry gaze was pinned on the detective.

"Jake Frost." His lips twisted as he touched the brim of his fedora. "Hopefully the solver of holiday trouble."

She smiled. "That's what I meant, of course."

That was *not* what she meant.

Chapter 12

Our first stop was to revisit the scene of the crime. Pocket, being a snowman, couldn't come into the house, and Quince had decided to stay with him on the sidewalk while Jake viewed Virgil's kitchen. So it was just Jake, Claire, and me going in. It wasn't locked, but even if it had been, I doubted Crinkles would have minded our breaking in. In the past he'd given Jake Frost generous leeway to poke around cases.

Jake pushed the back door open and frowned at the floor, taking in the shattered glass pieces and the smear of blood. I sucked in a breath, dreading going in and seeing the scene of that horrible crime again. Claire was right next to Jake. She hadn't taken her eyes off the detective since we'd left Peppermint Pond.

"See anything?" she asked him.

His gaze was pinned to the floor. "Mm."

Poor Claire. I should have warned her that Jake wasn't exactly a great communicator. Not that it would have mattered. She was hanging on his every monosyllable.

I picked my way across broken glass. I knew from experience how to get Jake talking. "From the way Virgil was lying on the floor, facedown, I'd say he was hit from behind. He'd obviously been in the middle of pouring himself an eggnog when someone sneaked up on him."

Jake's head whipped toward me, his light gray eyes sharp. "*Sneaked?*" I couldn't tell which his tone conveyed more of: withering contempt or disappointment. "Even an elf with a fanatical love of eggnog would have been able to hear the window glass shattering a few feet away." I smiled, and he shook his head. "Were you just trying to wind me up?"

"I got you talking, at least."

"Maybe the killer broke in earlier and hid himself," Claire suggested.

Jake gestured to the floor. "And Virgil wouldn't have noticed glass everywhere?"

I hiked my muffler a little higher on my face, both against the cold and the slightly sour smell. In this case, death had the tang of spoiled eggnog. "Not to mention the cold air that would have been rushing through the broken pane." I shook my head. "The other thing that seems odd is that Juniper specifically said that Virgil sounded anxious and breathy on the phone, almost as if he'd been running, but he was here in his slippers making eggnog, looking as if he was having a quiet evening at home."

"You've noticed a lot," Jake said. "Why am I here, exactly?"

"Because I know Juniper had nothing to do with this, but everything we've observed here so far makes her look guilty. Virgil was expecting Juniper, after all. He'd probably even left the front door unlocked for her, though she didn't know that."

"She says," Jake murmured, hesitant to take anyone's word at face value.

"She didn't know," I insisted. "When Claire and I arrived last night, we saw her footprints going around to the back. And then she was running toward us from the same direction."

I could tell he was picturing the scene in his mind's eye. "So we're left with an assailant who came armed with Juniper's fireplace poker, and who—by coincidence?—arrived just before she did, killed Virgil while he was making eggnog, and then escaped just before Juniper arrived."

"Yes." Stated so baldly, the bare facts made it sound like Juniper should start packing her bags now for the Farthest Frozen Reaches penal colony. But I would never stop believing in my friend's innocence. "The killer must have been someone else Virgil knew."

"And who also knew Juniper," Claire said, "and that she had a distinctive fireplace poker."

"Why was the door's glass pane broken, though?" Jake wondered aloud, staring at the door. "And look at the glass on the floor. If someone had broken in from the outside, the shattered glass would be around the door—maybe even a little on the porch. But the glass fell well inside the kitchen." He stepped over and pulled the door open, stopping its arc over where most of the glass shards lay on the floor. It was open about a foot. "Right about here. That's how far it was open when the killer broke the glass pane."

"So the killer just wanted to make it look like a break-in." Claire beamed at him. "Aren't you clever."

He shrugged modestly. "It's pretty obvious."

I should have seen it. "So we're looking for an incompetent murderer." Or a murderer who was counting on incompetent investigators. Then again, Christmastown was Constable Crinkles's patch, so . . .

"The killer was very competent at murder," Jake said. "It was the cover-up he botched."

The pieces still didn't seem to fit together. "But if they were framing Juniper, why the broken window? Virgil invited Juniper here, and was waiting for her."

"Maybe his killer didn't know that," Jake guessed.

A coincidence? I wished we knew what Virgil had wanted to talk to Juniper about. Could he have wanted to tell her he'd seen me on the street?

Claire crossed her arms. "Detective Frost, do you think we're searching for an enemy of Virgil, or Juniper?"

"Not sure." He almost smiled. "And I don't carry a badge. Just call me Jake."

"All right." She looked up at him like a snake mesmerized by a mongoose. "Jake." She cast her gaze to the ceiling and lowered her voice. "That elf woman from upstairs had a motive, and she knows Juniper."

He glanced at us curiously. "Crinkles said the woman upstairs had an alibi for the time of the murder."

Claire didn't look impressed. "That business about walking her dog was pretty flimsy, if you ask me."

"Goldie's odd," I allowed, "but a killer? And I seriously doubt she'd set Juniper up. In band, they've always been cordial—well, as much as Goldie is cordial with anyone. Besides, what would connect Goldie to the drone-deer crash?"

"What makes you think the murder and the crash are connected?" Claire asked.

"Nothing . . . yet." I just didn't like to think that two separate threads of violence were happening concurrently in Christmastown.

Jake leaned back against the kitchen counter and crossed his arms. He ignored my drone-deer/murder linkage. "I want to look around Juniper's apartment. See if the killer left a trace of himself when he stole that poker."

"I have to go there anyway," I said. "I promised to look after Dave, her pet rabbit."

"Good," Jake said. "We can see if any of her neighbors caught sight of a fireplace poker thief, if there was one."

Did he *still* doubt Juniper? "There was," I said.

His expression told me he preferred to wait for evidence

than to take my word. It was frustrating, but I supposed a good detective couldn't just accept a character reference at face value even if it was coming from a source as trustworthy as yours truly.

For that matter, maybe I shouldn't have believed Goldie's alibi, either. And what about Lucia? She'd said menacing things about the Brightlows' drone-deer and the Brightlows themselves, but I couldn't believe she'd harm an elf like Virgil, or set up Juniper.

Who else was there? Holly Silverpick? Dabbs? Or what about Blinky?

"When was the last time *you* saw Virgil?" Jake asked me.

The question startled me. Was I a suspect? "I glimpsed him after I'd stopped by Holly Silverpick's business to talk to her. He looked nervous—almost afraid—and ran off."

"Afraid of you?"

"I'm not sure. I don't see why he would be."

"He looked nervous when we saw him at Brightlow's, too," Claire said. "Maybe he always looked that way."

Jake nodded. "I'll send Quince over to make some inquiries at Holly Silverpick's."

"Do you think Quince is the right one for this job?" I asked him. I didn't want to cast aspersions, but Quince was just eighteen and relatively new to the detection racket.

"He's perfect," Jake said. "Most people in Christmastown know I'm a detective, and they know you're Juniper's friend." He arched a brow. "Also, you're Mrs. Claus. But a kid like Quince can get people talking before they realize who they're talking to, and how much they've said."

I trusted his instincts.

While Jake took a quick turn through the house. I darted into the living room and picked up the library book from the coffee table. Jake eyed the cover of *The Humanoids* curiously.

"It's a library book," I said. "It needs to go back—it's probably late already."

"Hopefully the library will accept death as an excuse," Jake said.

Claire laughed. "I don't know. I've known some pretty ruthless librarians in my time."

When we went outside and I saw the eagerness with which Quince received his marching orders, I felt more confident about Jake's game plan. Our two teams went separate ways—Quince and Pocket to Holly Silverpick's, and Jake, Claire, and I to Juniper's. We took Jake's snowmobile, which had a sidecar and a small wagon in the back. I guessed the wagon was how Pocket traveled with the detective and his assistant. Now, though, I was the one climbing into the back of the wagon. Claire jumped happily into the sidecar next to Jake. I felt a little like Quasar must feel when he drove around with Lucia in the custom-built sleigh she'd had made so that he could tag along with her everywhere.

As we headed for Juniper's, I focused on two problems. First, there was the fact that the murderer had tried to throw us off his scent with the muddled misdirection of the broken window. Why?

Second, Claire had her eye on Jake, who was from the Farthest Frozen Reaches. And to think that just days ago Claire was completely freaked out by Castle Kringle, and Christmastown. Now she looked like she was gearing up for a walk on the wild side with a guy who was from a place that took "wild side" to a whole new level. If she thought snowmen were freaky, what would she think of snow monsters? How could this possibly end well?

A few streets over, a crowd had gathered. My heart sank when I saw what they were standing around: a pile of snow next to a Snomaneuver. A band of dread constricted around my chest. "Stop!" I said.

As soon as Jake double-parked the snowmobile, I hopped off and ran slipping and sliding over to the gathering.

"Who was it?" I asked the elf standing closest to me.

"We think it's Ebenezer, but it's hard to tell. He hit a mailbox and disintegrated on impact."

"We think we can see a purple top hat under the snow, though," someone else piped up. "Ebenezer always had a quirky sense of style."

Another elf explained, "I saw him coming down that hill over there a few minutes ago—he was whooping up a storm, having the time of his life."

His now foreshortened life. I felt sick.

Jake and Claire came up behind me. "Another Snomaneuver crash?" Claire asked. "I was just telling Jake about the one we saw yesterday."

"This looks fatal." I got out my phone and was going to call Holly Silverpick. Something really needed to be done about those Snomaneuvers before they decimated Santaland's snowman population.

Holly Silverpick wasn't answering her phone—Quince might be there already. I hung up and was going to redial when I heard a piercing klaxon growing closer. A vehicle roared toward us, then stopped, its emergency light still flashing like a hysterical beacon. The snowmobile had a truck cab behind it and bore the letters *WSR*. An elf in a white uniform that looked vaguely medical hopped out and placed orange-and-white candy-striped traffic cones around the scene of the accident. Then, eyeing the pile of snow, he retrieved a large insulated container and a shovel from the back of his vehicle.

"You can move along, folks," the man in the white suit announced. "This is all under control."

I put my hands on my hips. "Who are you?"

He nodded to his vehicle. "Walnut's Snowman Repair."

Walnut is in the snowman repair business now?

Of course he was.

"I don't know if Ebenezer can be repaired," I said. "He's been"—I almost used the word *totaled*—"very badly hurt."

"Not a problem," the elf said confidently as he shoveled his patient into a garbage bag. "We'll have him as good as new in no time."

The crowd started to dissipate as the man continued his work. "Come on, April," Jake said. "Nothing more you can do here."

We settled back into our places in Jake's vehicle. I drooped over the wagon's partition like angsty cargo. I had so many questions. Snowmen were created with love and magic by the elves and people who crafted them. Were snowmen who got patched up "just as good as new" the same as they were before? A reconstituted snowman seemed like it would be a completely different being. What would Santaland be like in a few weeks, populated with reanimated zombie snowmen?

"I'd hoped Santaland would be one place that wouldn't succumb to modern changes," I said over the buzz of Jake's motor.

He shook his head, incredulous. "You just moved to Santaland last year. You expect that we're going to be frozen in time up here for your benefit?"

"Well . . ." I guess that did sound a little arrogant, like I wanted the denizens of Santaland to present a falsely preserved world—like the model pioneer village my school used to visit on field trips. Then again, there was a lot about quaint, old-fashioned Santaland to love. Why did everyone have to join the twenty-first century?

I directed Jake to Juniper's apartment. I'd never been in it without her. It made me sad to see all her things there without her being there to laugh with us and offer tea or some of her dad's homemade bearberry wine. Even Dave looked forlorn when he realized Juniper wasn't coming through the door after us. Okay—maybe I was projecting my own feelings on the rabbit just a little bit. But in my opinion that bunny looked a little down. I hoped he wasn't sick; the last thing Juniper needed at this moment was a pet emergency.

He perked up a little when I tipped some rabbit pellets into his feed bowl.

"Do you see anything out of place?" Jake asked, looking around.

I shook my head. "It all seems the same as it did when Claire and I were here yesterday morning." Except that Ollie or Crinkles, in a bizarre attempt to appear official, had come back and strung yellow crime scene tape around Juniper's fireplace utensil holder. The spot where the missing poker had once hung made me shiver.

"The tape wasn't there last night when Ollie and I left," Claire said.

Jake nodded. "Crinkles said he was going to recheck the place today."

"He *would* decide to be thorough when it's Juniper's neck on the line," I grumbled.

"If she's innocent, the thoroughness will work in her favor," he said.

Footsteps sounded on the landing outside, causing us all to tense. The door pushed open behind us and a stooped elf with iron-gray hair and whiskers appeared.

"Who are you?" Jake asked, all alertness.

"Name's Otto Henberry. I'm the landlord here. I might ask you the same question."

"We know Juniper," I explained, "and came to look at the apartment."

"Oh! Well, then you should know that if she's sentenced to exile in the Farthest Frozen Reaches, it's within my rights to rent this apartment again. I'm warning you, though, I can get a lot more for it now that it's got an infamous tenant who lived here."

He thought we were taking advantage of Juniper's situation to get a good deal on her apartment? "We're not checking the place out," I said. "Juniper is innocent. She'll be back soon."

Otto Henberry looked unconvinced. "I'll probably start a waiting list just in case, if you want to put your name down."

I was ready to pick a fight with the man, but Claire insinuated herself between us and gave the landlord her sultriest smile. "You certainly have a nice building, Mr. Henberry."

The elf straightened his cap, blazing with pride. "Thanks. It's one of the newest apartment houses in Christmastown. My grandfather built it sixty years ago."

While the old elf was still preening, Jake asked him, "Were you here yesterday evening?"

"Of course. I'm always here."

"Then maybe you saw someone strange come in . . . someone who's not a resident?"

"'Course I did," the landlord said. "I saw that Deputy Ollie come in with some woman."

"You didn't recognize her?" I asked.

"I don't know every elf in Santaland," he said crankily.

"Maybe she wasn't an elf," Claire said.

"Sure looked like one to me," Henberry said.

That put Claire's back up. Before she could set the man straight, Jake asked, "You didn't see anyone *before* the deputy came here?"

He shook his head. "Nope—but I heard someone clattering down the stairs about an hour before that."

"Clattering?" I asked.

"Yeah, tippy-tapping down those stairs like they were in a real big hurry."

"You didn't see them, though?"

He shook his head. "I didn't think to look out. I just assumed it was Juniper or one of the other tenants."

"And you're sure it was an hour before the deputy was here that you heard someone clattering down the stairs?"

He rubbed his jaw. "Well now, if you want exactly the time, I can't say. After all, it was just loud footsteps—not really a reason to look up at the clock. If I'd suspected one of my tenants was a notorious murderer . . ."

I was ready to shift into full-throttle defense mode, but Jake stepped between us. "Do you remember anything else, sir?"

"Just from when Deputy Ollie was here with that woman. I saw the deputy in the hallway and asked if he needed a key. He said he had one, but—"

"He didn't use it," Claire finished for him.

The landlord blinked as if she'd just put the *Claire* in clairvoyant. "How'd you know?"

"Lucky guess," she said modestly.

Juniper had expected the apartment to be locked—that's why she'd given Crinkles and Ollie the key. "Was the door ajar?" I asked.

"Nope, just unlocked."

Juniper wouldn't have left it that way. She was not a lax elf. So how had the thief who'd taken the poker entered the apartment? They either stole a key or picked the lock. I edged toward the door, eyeing the keyhole for . . . what, exactly? I wasn't an expert on lock picking, but this lock didn't look like it would take an expert to pick. It wasn't a deadbolt, but the old kind with the keyhole you could peek through.

After the landlord was gone, Jake sighed. "Well, at least we have one clue—there might have been a stranger in the apartment an hour before the murder."

"If Henberry can be a reliable witness," I pointed out.

"Why wouldn't he be?" Jake asked.

Claire and I exchanged smiles. "I'm the woman who was here with Deputy Ollie," she said. "Henberry didn't even recognize me."

"So what now?" I asked.

"We knock on doors here and ask if anyone heard the person on the stairs—or *was* the individual on the stairs," Jake said. "Then I want to pay a visit to Dabbs Brightlow and see if his list of drone-deer purchases raises any flags."

"So you *do* think the drone-deer strike and Virgil's killing are connected?" I asked.

He shook his head. "I doubt it, but Virgil did work over there. Getting that drone-deer list is at least a good pretext for poking around his workplace a little."

Chapter 13

A note on the outer door of Brightlow Enterprises informed visitors that, for the company Christmas party, business hours ended at three o'clock. The building was open, but this time when we entered, there was no Cookie the security guard to stop us or call for a handler to take us up to the executive floor.

In the vestibule, the sounds of Christmas music filtered through the glass doors. Claire, Jake, and I followed the sound.

The main workshop floor had been cleared. Tables were pushed against the wall, draped in red and green swags, and loaded down with goodies. Brenda Lee was belting out "Rockin' Around the Christmas Tree" over the loudspeakers. In the back of the room, a ginormous tree had been fabricated out of what looked like spare parts and decorated with home-made ornaments and flashing lights. I thought about what Holly had told me about firings. There were surprisingly few revelers here, although every elf present seemed to be singing, dancing, or both. From the glassy look in some eyes, I had a feeling there was some potent punch on hand somewhere in the room. Before we could escape to the third-floor offices, an elf grabbed Claire and reeled her off onto the makeshift dance floor.

Claire yipped in alarm, then glee.

"She likes to dance," I told Jake.

"Evidently." For a moment he was so mesmerized watching her that he seemed to forget why we were there.

I tapped him on the arm and his gaze snapped back to mine, startled, as if he'd forgotten me, too. "Dabbs?" I reminded him.

I hadn't seen Dabbs among the partiers, so I assumed he was in his office.

Jake nodded, but he hesitated to follow me. He jabbed his thumb in the direction of the dance floor where Claire was spinning between two elves. "Should we . . . ?"

"Claire's on vacation," I said. "Besides, she knows the way."

After we got off the elevator on the third floor, the clicking of fingers on a keyboard sounded from a nearby office. The rest of the corridor was so quiet, I couldn't help poking my head in to see who was still working. An elf perched at her desk, a pile of papers at her side. She was obviously working on some kind of data entry project, and seemed irritated about it. Had she been forced to work instead of attending the party?

She looked up with red-rimmed blue eyes. "Are you lost?" she asked.

"We've come to talk to Dabbs Brightlow," Jake said.

"End of the hall," she answered shortly.

As we headed toward Dabbs's office, I heard the elf we'd just left blowing her nose loudly. Maybe she was getting over a cold.

Dabbs's secretary must have been downstairs. When we tapped on his door and opened it, we discovered the head of Brightlow Enterprises and a female elf in a passionate clinch across his executive desk. Dabbs was wearing a Santa hat, which might have offended me if I hadn't been trying so hard not to laugh.

I cleared my throat, and when the arms and legs untangled, I recognized the other elf as Velvet Sprucebud, Bright-low's public relations manager. The two sprang apart, red with embarrassment. Within moments, however, Dabbs recovered his composure enough to be annoyed.

"Mrs. Claus," he said with only a cursory attempt at warmth in his tone. "What can I do for you today?"

He was speaking to me, but his gaze was locked on Jake. Jake Frost was known by many in Santaland, and from the displeasure that crossed Dabbs's face, I guessed he was one of those who was aware that Jake was a detective.

"I'm sorry," I said, "we seem to be interrupting you at a festive moment."

I meant the company Christmas party, but he took the comment to be a barb aimed at him and Velvet. "We're engaged," he said defensively.

Readjusting her clothes, Velvet flushed to her blond hairline.

"Why are you here, exactly?" Dabbs asked us.

I gestured to Jake. 'My friend Jake Frost is here to investigate all the things that have been happening in Santaland these past few days, including the drone-deer accident and Virgil's death."

Dabbs sputtered. "I don't see how one thing has anything to do with the other."

"Don't you?"

"I certainly do not. One was simply an unfortunate accident—no one was hurt—while the other . . ." He swallowed. "We're all very upset about Virgil. He was a great asset to Brightlow Enterprises."

I lowered myself into one of the two guest chairs that Dabbs had failed to invite us to sit in.

"I've already spoken to Constable Crinkles about Virgil," Dabbs said. "I don't know what more I can tell you—or why I should tell you anything at all."

"Actually, we came here to see if you had that list of drone-deer buyers you were going to draw up," Jake said.

Dabbs looked confused. "We sent that to the constabulary."

"Not according to Crinkles," Jake said.

Dabbs pivoted toward Velvet again. "Didn't we?"

Her brow wrinkled ever-so-slightly. "I'll check. Maybe the fax didn't go through."

I couldn't hide my surprise. *"Fax?"*

Velvet's mouth twisted. "I offered to email it, but Constable Crinkles says he has trouble with attachments."

For Pete's sake. Forget the twenty-first century. The Christmastown Constabulary was still struggling with the twentieth.

"I'll track down that list for you," Velvet said, and left the room.

Dabbs didn't seem happy to be left alone with Jake and me. Especially not when he heard my next question.

"Where were you last night between six and seven o'clock?"

He drew back in his chair defensively. "I was here, of course. I'm here most evenings."

"Were others with you?" Jake asked.

"Certainly. I know Velvet was here, at least. And I'm sure Cookie must have seen us once or twice."

"What did Blinky say when he heard about Virgil's murder?"

Dabbs shifted uncomfortably. "I, um, haven't told him."

"Because you still don't know where he is?" I guessed.

"I don't want to upset him right now. He liked Virgil, and when he learns he was killed by this elf he'd been seeing . . ."

"Juniper had nothing to do with that horrid murder," I said.

"The evidence indicates otherwise."

"You've never heard of planted evidence?" I asked. "Juniper is innocent."

Dabbs smirked. "I'll see what's keeping Velvet."

As soon as he was gone, I declared, "I don't like that guy." Jake collapsed into the club chair next to mine. "Me neither. But it would have been better to keep him talking than to chase him away."

"I suspect most of his talk is lies anyway. For all we know, *he* killed Virgil. Having Velvet as his alibi is pretty flimsy. And who knows what's happened to Blinky. Maybe he intends to pin his brother's murder on Juniper, too."

"Whoa there." Jake shook his head. "That brain of yours is making more leaps than a reindeer at the yearling hop."

Maybe so, but I couldn't help feeling uneasy. "Did you notice he didn't answer when I asked about Blinky's whereabouts again? How can an elf just disappear?"

"These inventor types are eccentric."

"Eccentric, or heartless? Virgil was killed last night, and everyone's having a party." Except for one lone, sick elf.

"It's Christmas week," Jake pointed out. "We don't know what went on before we arrived."

I saw his point. I was being judgy. The trouble was, I couldn't help seeing all this from Juniper's point of view. She would never have been downstairs drinking and laughing while one coworker was missing and another was dead.

A few seconds later, Claire breezed in, flushed. "That eggnog in the water cooler downstairs is ninety proof."

"Did you see Cookie the doorman?" I asked.

"The very drunk doorman?"

Jake and I exchanged glances. Probably not a great time to double-check an alibi with him.

Claire hiked a hip onto the corner of Dabbs's desk. "What are we doing?"

"Waiting for Dabbs and Velvet to come back with the list of drone-deer purchasers," I said.

"Ah." Claire absently spun a keychain around her finger. I narrowed my gaze on the thing. "What's that?"

She handed it over. "There was a bowlful of them downstairs. Christmas Party favors."

The top part of the keychain was a figurine of a Selfy. It looked like Jingles's creature, without the personalizing touches he'd bestowed on Jingleini. The Selfy was standing on a plastic base, around which were written the words, *Brightlow Enterprises "Santaland's tomorrow, today!"*

Velvet returned carrying a legal-sized sheet of paper. "Sorry—it's been so hectic around here lately, it took me a while to remember where to find the document I was looking for."

She folded up the paper and was about to put it into my eagerly outstretched palm. At the last moment she handed it over to Jake instead.

"Has Stew the sculptor threatened to sue you over his Blitzen the First being destroyed?" I asked.

"No . . ." Confusion crossed her face before she said, as if to someone very thick, "To be honest, we've been preoccupied with a more serious crime today. Virgil was part of our Brightlow family."

His murder hadn't seemed to be preoccupying her and Dabbs when we'd walked in.

"Do you have any ideas about who killed Virgil?" Jake asked.

She gave him a slow blink, as if he were particularly dense, too. "Well, of course. The librarian did it. Everyone knows that she and Virgil were an item back in the day, and that she's guilty, guilty, guilty. And if this homicidal librarian is on a tear, killing all the elves she's dated, who's to say she won't go after Blinky next? His family's worried sick."

"Juniper wouldn't harm a fly." I was beginning to wish I had Crinkles's bullhorn so I could just yell it from the top of Sugarplum Mountain instead of repeating it to everyone. "She certainly wouldn't kill Virgil. Or harm Blinky."

"All the same," Dabbs said, strolling back into the room, "my family's not going to take any chances. It's a very sensitive time here for us at Brightlow Enterprises. We can't afford for anything else to go wrong."

Go wrong was a bizarre way to refer to a colleague's brutal murder, but I was beginning to suspect everyone connected to the Brightlows was a taco shy of a full combo plate.

"We're already worried enough about the constable possibly letting Juniper go," Velvet said.

"She had nothing to do with Virgil's murder," I repeated.

"But the evidence—"

I interrupted her, not bothering to hide my irritation. "No murderer would carry her own fireplace poker in order to kill a guy she's barely thought of in the past decade, and then, once the nefarious deed was done, conveniently drop it next to the body for the constable to find."

"I wasn't referring to the fireplace poker," Dabbs said. "I'm talking about that letter they found in Juniper's apartment."

His words brought me up short. "What letter?"

"The one Blinky sent her, begging her to leave him alone."

Jake, Claire, and I exchanged surprised looks. "Juniper never told me about any letter."

"She wouldn't, would she?" Velvet leveled a scornful gaze on me. "We wondered why Blinky wanted to get away— now we know. We can only guess that he realized how unhinged that librarian is."

I hopped to my feet. "This is outrageous. Juniper was the

only one who cared when Blinky first seemed to be missing. She was nearly—" I shut my mouth before the words *out of her mind with worry* could come out. "She was very upset."

"That letter they found speaks volumes," Dabbs said. "I tell you, when I heard what Blinky had written, it gave me chills."

"What did it say?" Jake asked.

"He asks her in no uncertain terms to leave him alone." Velvet crossed her arms. "Until we locate him, we've asked the constable not to release Juniper."

I wanted to bang my head against the wall. How could this be happening?

Jake frowned. "What measures have been taken to look for Blinky?"

"We've searched the grounds around both the family chalet and fishing cabin," Dabbs said. "He's not in either of those places."

I turned to Jake and Claire. "Come on. Let's go."

I wanted to see that letter for myself.

When we stepped outside, Jake's phone rang. I was already speeding toward the sleigh, but he held up a hand in the universal I've-got-to-take-this-call gesture. He mumbled a few words into his phone and then asked, surprised, "Already? Okay we'll wait here." He hung up. "That was Quince."

I was in no mood to wait on anyone. "Are we going to have to stand around here half the day for them to make it out here from Holly Silverpick's place?"

"They won't be long. Quince says they're nearly here."

"Oh sure, a guy and a snowman—"

Oh no. They were coming from Holly Silverpick's. Just as a terrible thought occurred to me, I heard the sounds of whooping approaching. Quince and Pocket appeared, both perched on a single Snomaneuver as they careened down the sleigh path at daredevil speed. I held my breath as they fishtailed into the parking lot. Then they hit a bump, sending them both up in the air.

I squeezed my eyes shut and braced for the worst. A moment later, though, I heard the machine swoosh toward us and then stop. When I dared open my eyes again, the two were just a few feet away, and Quince was hopping off, his cheeks red from the thrill ride. I'd never seen a snowman looking flushed before, but I could almost swear that Pocket's snowy face was flushed, too.

"Have you ever seen anything so awesome?" Quince asked.

Claire shook her head. "It's a miracle you didn't end up in a pile in the parking lot."

The pair laughed at our killjoy expressions. If Pocket's stick arms could have moved faster, they would have exchanged a high five.

"Pocket and I will be able to get things done twice as fast now," Quince told Jake.

"Don't be a fool on that thing," the detective told him. "We just saw a snowman being scooped up after a crash this morning."

"We'll be careful," Quince said unconvincingly. I wondered if we were going to have to produce some educational Snomaneuver scare films like the ones they showed us in Driver's Ed.

I took my mittens from my pockets and pulled them on over my gloves. Evening was drawing in, making double-gloving a must. "So while Holly was giving you the hard sell on Snomaneuvers, did you manage to get anything from her?"

Quince nodded. "Sure—we talked her way down on the price. I gave her my sob story about being raised at the orphanage." He seemed very pleased with himself. "Works every time."

"I meant did you get any information about how she felt

about Virgil when they worked here at Brightlow Enterprises?"

"Oh yeah. She was full of opinions about the murder."

"Does she have any idea who did it?" Claire asked.

"Sure—Juniper."

For heaven's sake. "Does she even know Juniper?"

"Know her?" Quince and Pocket looked at each other again and laughed. "She *hates* her."

I drew back. How was that possible? Hating Juniper would be like hating ice cream. "Everybody likes Juniper."

"Holly Silverpick sure doesn't. She said that it was just like Juniper to be treacherous, and that the murder didn't surprise her at all. I asked her why she thought Juniper was so terrible, and she said—" He broke off and looked at Pocket. "What was that word she used?"

"Gobbledygook."

Quince snapped his fingers. "That was it. Gobbledygook."

Frowning, I looked at the others to see if this made any sense to them, but Claire and Jake looked as perplexed as I felt.

"You're sure that's the word she used?" I asked Pocket.

"Oh yes," the snowman said. "I heard her with my own head."

"*You* were in the showroom?"

Quince blurted out a laugh. "Of course not. But you don't think I'm going to make a major purchase like a Snomaneuver without taking it for a test drive, do you? Holly came outside to talk to us about it."

Gobbledygook. What could it mean? "She didn't say any more than that?"

"I don't think she *could* say more," Quince said. "Just that one word choked her with anger. I had to change the subject for fear she'd decide to call off the sale."

I climbed back onto the snowmobile. "Let's go."

Claire followed me, but Jake held back to give Quince and Pocket more instructions. He handed over the list that Velvet had given us and told them to copy it, then joined Claire and me.

"Where are we going now?" Claire asked.

"The constabulary." First I wanted to see the letter Velvet had told us about. Then I needed to talk to Juniper and find out what had happened between her and Holly to cause Holly to call Juniper a murderer.

Chapter 14

On the way, I texted Nick. **Claire and I might be late. We're headed to the constabulary.**

He replied a moment later. **You'll be there just in time for dinner.**

He wasn't wrong. Ollie greeted us at the door with a *Mister Good Lookin' Is Cookin'* apron tied neatly over his uniform. "Hey there—you're just in time! I just put the main course on the table for everybody."

Everybody?

He led us through to the dining room, where Crinkles was presiding over a table heaped with platters of food. In the center of it all was a soup tureen decorated in a mistletoe pattern. Around the table were Juniper, her parents—Mr. and Mrs. Greenleaf—and her cousin Sparkle.

Juniper jumped up and introduced Claire and Jake to her family as if she were hostessing a dinner party. If she was aware of her growing reputation as Santaland's notorious librarian love killer, she didn't show it.

"You're just in time for some delicious snailfish chowder!" Crinkles called out from the head of the table. "When Juniper mentioned that she had a freezer full of chowder, well, it seemed a shame to let it just sit there."

I looked at the people gathered and apologized in advance for taking the constable away from his meal. "I hate to bother you while you're eating, Constable Crinkles, but Jake and I have a few important questions to ask you."

"Of course." Crinkles rose officiously, his collar like a bib. "We can go into my office."

I checked to see if Claire wanted to join Crinkles and me, but she smiled and lowered herself into a free chair next to Mrs. Greenleaf. "I want to try this chowder," she said.

I remembered guiltily that we'd skipped lunch. I wasn't being a very good host.

Ollie, by contrast, wasted no time bringing her a place setting.

Crinkles's office was only slightly more official looking than the rest of the constabulary. Between two Currier and Ives scenes there hung a pennant in red with TWINKLERS in block yellow letters. Crinkles at least had a desk—an antique roll-top in dark walnut. He settled into his office chair, and Jake and I pulled up wooden Queen Anne side chairs.

Crinkles pushed a bowl of licorice allsorts toward us. "Candy?"

"No thanks." I was determined to stick to business. "We heard about the—"

"Say, I bet you'd make a dilly of an iceball forward," he said to Jake.

Jake shook his head curtly. "Not my thing. Besides, I'm a Destroyers fan."

I cleared my throat and belatedly finished my sentence. "The letter?"

The constable popped a colorful licorice into his mouth. "What letter?"

"Someone at Brightlow Enterprises said you'd unearthed a letter Blinky sent to Juniper."

"Oh, *that* letter!" He chuckled as if he had hundreds of

letters in evidence to keep track of. "It's a piece of a letter, actually. It was in her fireplace."

"May we look at it?" Jake asked.

The constable produced a piece of plain white paper, the
top of which had been torn away. It was clearly just half a
sheet of paper, and unfortunately the top half appeared to have
contained most of the message. There was only one line of
writing left on the scrap of stationery—one complete sentence
and a fragment:

> *it's finished. Now I'm begging you to leave me alone!*
> *Blinky*

I squinted at the paper as I reread the line, which was written in a clear but not fussy hand. Black ink. There was only
one smudge of soot on the paper. "This was in the fireplace?"

"Ollie ran across it this morning when he went to retrieve
the chowder. He was taping off the utensils, and it was right
there on the top log." He tilted his head and looked from Jake
to me. "Sure you won't have a bowl of chowder? I could have
Ollie bring some in on a tray."

Jake and I shook our heads.

"If Juniper was trying to destroy that letter in a fire, why
would there just be this one scrap?" Jake asked.

Crinkles leaned back in his chair. "Maybe she already
burned the rest?"

"And kept this one incriminating scrap to burn later?" I
asked.

Jake added, "If this just happened to escape a previous fire,
why wasn't it charred?"

Crinkles's wattles quivered. He clearly felt we were gang-
ing up on him with logic.

I felt sorry for him, but I couldn't help asking, "How do
we know that's Blinky's handwriting?" I asked. "Has someone
identified it?"

"Dabbs Brightlow did."

How reliable was Dabbs?

"It's still just a fragment of a letter," Jake said. "We can't even be sure Blinky—or whoever purportedly wrote that letter—was even addressing Juniper."

"Then why was it found in her apartment?" Crinkles asked.

"It could have been planted there," I said.

Crinkles's brows rose. "Yesterday you were saying that somebody took her fireplace poker and planted *that* over at Virgil's house."

"They did."

Crinkles looked flummoxed. "Well, whatever it's proof of—or not proof of—this scrap of paper has caused the Brightlows to ask me not to release Juniper. They're worried about Blinky."

I rolled my eyes. "*Now* they're worried. Two days ago Juniper was the only one in town who seemed to care about where he was."

"The Brightlows think that's suspicious, too," Crinkles said. 'They're putting it out that she was acting unbalanced about Blinky the day of the drone-deer crash."

"Because *she was worried*." I huffed in exasperation. "Do the Brightlows run this town now?"

Crinkles frowned. "No . . . but they've got a lot of clout."

I stood. "So do the Clauses." I hated to play the Claus card, but sometimes you had to fight fire with fire. "One way or another, I'm going to get Juniper out of here."

"Her family thinks she's better off here. So does Juniper."

My jaw dropped. "Why?"

"They worry *she's* in danger."

Why would Juniper be in danger? "That doesn't even make sense."

"Things falling out of the sky, people getting killed—everyone's jumpy," Crinkles said. "At least with Juniper here, I can keep an eye on her."

"May I speak to Juniper alone?" I needed to know if she actually wanted to stay at the constabulary, or if she felt pressured to.

"Sure." Crinkles cocked his head, listening to the clinking of cutlery against china. "But wouldn't you like to join us for dessert first?"

"I don't think—"

"It's Ollie's ginger-pear tart."

"Oh."

No harm in a little dessert. Detecting worked up an appetite. And we had skipped lunch.

Ollie's ginger-pear tart was awfully good. He made it with a shortbread crust, and served it with a delicious dollop of brandy whipped cream. I was tempted to have two helpings, but I really was eager to talk to Juniper. After we were done, Juniper and I went back to her so-called cell and sat down opposite each other on the twin beds covered in cheery double-wedding ring quilts. Mine had a duffel bag on it, which I guessed held Sparkle's overnight things.

"Crinkles said you want to stay here," I said.

"My parents think it's safer."

"But you're not in any danger," I said. "*You're* the one being set up."

"That's true . . ." Juniper considered this and then shrugged. "But it's okay. I promised Sparkle she could stay here tonight." She lowered her voice. "I think she's sweet on Ollie. It's sort of cute."

"You shouldn't stay in jail just because your cousin has a crush on the deputy."

"I know, but this way if anyone else turns up dead, no one can point the finger at me."

Should I tell her that she was already suspected in the possible murder of Blinky, even when no one was sure if he was alive or dead? I didn't want to upset her, but the subject of Blinky couldn't be avoided entirely.

"When did you receive that letter from Blinky?" I asked.

"That scrap of paper Ollie found?" She shook her head. "I'd never seen it before. I can't even say for sure if that's Blinky's handwriting. He never wrote me anything besides texts."

"I don't guess you've heard from him since you've been here," I said.

"No." She released a sigh. "I have this feeling that the Brightlows have poisoned him against me."

And how. "Can you think of anyone"—anyone besides the entire Brightlow clan, I meant—"who might have planted something like that in your apartment? Do you have any enemies?"

The possibility clearly disturbed her, but she gave it some thought. "Sometimes people get mad about the late fees on overdue books . . ."

"I think this is more personal than a library fine." And I spoke as one whose late fees had probably done more to fund libraries since Andrew Carnegie.

Juniper's face contorted as she racked her brain to think of a name of someone who hated her enough to see her exiled to the Farthest Frozen Reaches for a murder she didn't commit. She tossed her hands in the air. "I just don't know."

"Holly Silverpick?" I prompted.

Her brow creased. "I know her—I mean, I know of her—but I've never had much to do with her."

"Gobbledygook," I said.

I'd meant the word as a hint, but she took it as an expression of disbelief.

"I'm not lying, April."

"I know. Quince was talking to Holly Silverpick earlier today, and when your name came up she reacted very strongly. And when Quince asked why, she said, 'Gobbledygook.'"

Juniper blinked, and then her eyes widened in understanding. "But it's been twenty years!"

"Since what?"

"Since the Santaland Regional Spelling Bee, junior division. I was eleven years old, and Holly and I were in the final round. She misspelled gobbledygook, and I won."

"Seriously?"

"I know, right? That shouldn't even have been a final-round word, it was so easy." Juniper snorted. "She spelled it with 'de' instead of 'dy.'"

"I meant, twenty years is a long time to hold a grudge over a misspelled word."

"Have you ever been in a spelling bee? The pressure is brutal."

Even so . . . "I find it hard to believe she would murder Virgil to set you up to take the rap, all over a misspelled word."

"Me too," Juniper said.

But she was the closest thing to an enemy of Juniper I'd turned up so far. I tilted my head. "Are you sure it was Virgil who called you at the library?"

She blinked in surprise. "He said he was."

"You're sure it was a he?" I asked. "You said the voice sounded breathless."

"But male." She frowned. "Unless there's a woman out there who can do a good Virgil impression."

Or a man who could.

"How's Dave?" Juniper asked me.

"Fine. I'd take him with me to the castle, but Lynxie . . ."

Lucia's lynx-housecat mix was unpredictable. His presence hadn't done much to control the woolly ice rat problem in the castle's old keep, but he was very good at attacking my calves and taking little chunks out of them. I doubted he'd be intimidated by Dave the bunny.

"It's okay," Juniper said. "Ollie said he would look in on him for me and feed him."

Poor Dave. "I don't mind feeding him," I insisted.

She shook her head. "You've got company this week, and I'm already taking up enough of your time with this murder thing. How is Claire enjoying Santaland?"

"A lot more since Jake Frost arrived."

Juniper's face lit with interest. She loved a romance. "Does Jake like her, too?"

"We're mostly focused on getting you out of here. I don't want you spending Christmas in jail."

"I'll be fine," she said with surprising cheer. "Sparkle's here tonight, and I have plenty of books to read."

"I know, but—"

A knock sounded at the door, and Ollie poked his head in. "Can I bring you another piece of tart, Juniper? There's one left."

"That's okay, Ollie. I'm stuffed. You should wrap it up for April, though. She loves your pear tart."

Before I could put up a feeble protest, he gave her a thumbs-up and darted away.

"One last thing," I said. "Your door was unlocked when Claire and Ollie went by to see if the poker was there. Could you have left your apartment unlocked?"

"I don't think so. Was the door damaged?"

"Not that I could tell. Who has keys to your place?"

"You, and Mr. Henberry."

"No one else?" I asked.

"My parents, but *they* didn't kill Virgil." Her eyes teared up. "I feel so bad about him, April. He was really great to me back in school. I remember he used to give me the ginger-bread men from his lunchbox. They were delicious, too."

"So you gave Ollie your key?" I asked, doing my Joe Friday best to bring us back to just facts.

She nodded. "I won't need to borrow yours anymore."

I frowned. Could it have been *my* key that had been taken to let someone into Juniper's apartment and steal the poker? I always kept the key in my bedside table, except if I knew that I would need it, as I had today. Could someone from the castle have taken it?

I could think of only one suspect living in Castle Kringle: Lucia. Even the possibility of someone so close to me being involved in a murder and harming Juniper made me ill.

From outside, the ringing of a bell preceded the startling sound of the Santaland Concert Band playing "Winter Wonderland."

"Holy smokes," I said. "I forgot all about the band serenading you tonight." I'd been so busy all day, it had completely slipped my mind. At least I still had my hat.

"It's for me?" Juniper asked, eyes wide.

We got up and sped to the front of the constabulary, where everyone had gathered in the doorway to listen. On the way, I told Juniper, "Smudge was the one who thought of this."

She released a wistful sigh. "Of all my ex-boyfriends, he really is the least awful."

I hurried outside to join the band. Smudge had brought the wooden box with all the small instruments I played—the triangle, the bells, the blocks that made the horse hoof clip-clop sounds. Luckily he'd also brought the key that opened it. I'd completely forgotten I'd need it. We played our hearts out for thirty minutes, and we even drew more of a crowd to the constabulary. Besides the group standing in the doorway, little clusters of elves appeared from other buildings. I noticed one elf standing by herself in a red hat. She looked vaguely familiar, but I couldn't place her. She wasn't watching the band. Her gaze was locked on the constabulary.

After the serenade ended, I looked for her again, but the elf in the red hat had disappeared.

I turned to Smudge to give credit where it was due. "Thanks for thinking of this serenade. Juniper was really touched."

"She didn't kill anyone," he said. "She shouldn't be in jail."

"I know. But apparently now the Greenleafs have decided she's safer here than on her own."

"You mean she *wants* to be here?"

"It's complicated." Although given the pampering and food being bestowed on her by Crinkles and Ollie, I was beginning to think the constabulary wouldn't be bad as a retreat . . . if not for the small inconvenience of that murder rap hanging over her head.

"She needs protection," he said. "How do we know that whoever killed Virgil won't try to kill Juniper?"

I was about to go into my spiel about Juniper being safe, since she was the scapegoat—after all, someone had gone to a lot of trouble to set her up—but then the memory of that elf in the red hat flashed through my mind again, and a little of Smudge's unease snaked through me.

Where had I seen that elf before?

Chapter 15

When Jake dropped us off at Castle Kringle that evening, we found Pamela sitting in the drawing room by the Christmas tree, a roaring fire by the hearth, knitting up a storm. Her industriousness reminded me of all those tea cozies I still hadn't knitted. The countdown clock to the craft bazaar was ticking. Somehow, I felt even worse for letting her down about the cozies after she'd stood up for me, Juniper, and the Clauses at the dessert potluck.

Pamela dealt with the fallout from the potluck much as she handled most unpleasant things: by not speaking of it. She glanced up at us over her bifocals. "I didn't delay dinner for you. Nick and I dined alone."

"Didn't Nick tell you I wasn't going to make it this evening?"

"He did—once we were sitting at an empty table."

I almost felt jealous of someone sitting at an empty table with Nick. Not that I wasn't enjoying having Claire here, but I was seeing so little of Nick this week. And when we did have time together—before going to bed and early in the morning—he seemed distracted by Christmas week worries, especially the reindeer strike.

"Is Nick in his office?" I asked. Santa's big night required prodigious planning. All through December, Nick could often be found in his office, staring at his wall map of the world to double-check his route.

"After dinner he headed up to Kringle Lodge," Pamela said. "He's talking to Amory about alternate transportation on Christmas Eve."

"Why? Does Amory have an airplane parked some-where?"

"No, but an elf named Butterbean has a line on an army surplus helicopter."

Hearing the name Butterbean combined with heavy trans-port aircraft unnerved me. I sank onto the couch. "Where does Butterbean think he can find this helicopter?"

Her needles never stopped clicking. "When Nick was on the phone with Amory, I heard him mention something about a boneyard."

A shudder went through me. How could she sit there knitting and maintain her queen mother coolness while dis-cussing her son possibly spending a night flying around in something plucked from an aviation boneyard? Of course, this was a woman who for the past forty years had watched her husband and then sons fly around the world in an open sleigh. I was just beginning to come to terms with that. Maybe it was a sign of my Clausification that I was now calmer about sleigh travel than helicopters.

A helicopter from a boneyard, though, procured by Butter-bean? That terrified me.

"April, you're looking peaky." Pamela put her knitting aside and went to the bell pull. "I'll order some tea for you now. Has Claire eaten?"

Claire laughed. "Not for an hour and a half. That has to be a Santaland record."

"Felice made dinner for you both, which we sent out to Salty and some of his grounds workers so it wouldn't go to waste." She shook her head. "And that's not the only reason she was put out."

Uh-oh. Felice was temperamental, but she was also the best cook in all of Santaland. I was trying to think what else I could have done to offend her, when Jingles appeared at the door.

"Tea, please, Jingles," Pamela said. "April and Claire just arrived."

Jingles bowed, shooting me a meaningful glance before he retreated.

Pamela waited until the steward had closed the door before she pivoted toward me and said, "You need to speak to Jingles. He's under the delusion that he's Santaland's answer to Hercule Poirot and can just bully all the elves until one of them confesses to murder."

Jingles could get a little overzealous sometimes. "I'll have a talk with him."

"I would have spoken to him on the matter myself, but you two seem thick as thieves whenever it comes to these little investigations of yours. How you have time to racket about looking into murders during Christmas week is beyond me. Especially when you have company."

"I don't mind." Claire smiled at me. "I'm finding it fascinating."

Pamela sucked in a breath. "That reminds me—I need to talk to Felice about luncheon tomorrow."

She bustled out the door, and I collapsed on the couch, hugging a throw pillow embroidered with snowflakes. "Pamela's right. I've been running you ragged, and you're on vacation."

"Are you kidding? This was the best day yet." She caught my look and amended, "I mean, apart from the murder and Juniper being in jail. That's all terrible."

"Uh-huh." I'd seen that spark in her eyes before. It usually preceded what she later called a romantic misadventure.

"You have to admit, Jake's a very good-looking—" Her face collapsed into a pensive frown. "Is he an elf? I can't tell from looking at him. Even his ears are inscrutable."

I wasn't sure, either. "No one knows if he's an elf, a human, or some kind of weird hybrid ice being. He's a distant relation to Jack Frost, so I suspect there's something supernatural going on there. I can tell you"—*warn you,* I meant—"that he comes from a place full of misfits, renegade hunters, and snow monsters. I'm talking literal monsters that can flatten cities. I don't think you'd like it there."

She laughed. "I'm not talking about marrying the guy and setting up housekeeping next to snow monsters." Her smile dissolved as a possibility occurred to her. "He isn't married, is he?"

"I don't think he likes to get involved with anyone."

She steepled her fingertips. "A challenge."

I groaned. "Nothing I've said has discouraged you, has it?"

She shook her head. "No, but keep trying."

Jingles returned, rolling the tea trolley right over to the couch Claire and I were sitting on. He shot me a look that was just short of a conspiratorial wink. Maybe his playing Grand Inquisitor with the servants today had turned up some information. "If I might have a word with you before you retire, ma'am," he said to me.

He always put on a Jeeves persona when there were other people around.

"Should I leave the room?" Claire joked.

"It's not you, ma'am." Jingles's gaze darted toward the door. "The walls have ears."

This must be some primo castle gossip he squeezed out of somebody.

"Of course. I'll go upstairs after tea. I'm bushed."

As he left the room, he passed Lucia coming in. Quasar clopped in behind her.

"Just who I've been looking for," I told her as I poured out two cups of tea for Claire and me.

Lucia swooped in and nabbed two jam tarts from the cart. "You could have fooled me. It looks like you're ensconced on that couch like two ticks on a musk-ox hide."

Lovely. "It's about Juniper," I said. "She asked me for the key to her apartment. Have you seen it?"

Claire's confused stare burned into me. She knew I was lying, but she kept mum.

"How would I know?" Lucia asked. "Where do you usually keep it?"

"In my room. I was wondering if you might have seen it lying around."

"Not likely, if you keep it in your room," she said through a mouthful of tart. "I never go in there."

"Y-yes you do," Quasar interrupted. "You were in there yesterday, remember?"

She shot him an annoyed look. "Only because I was looking for Lynxie."

"Why would Lynxie be in my room?" I asked.

She shrugged. "Kittens get into all sorts of places they shouldn't."

I sputtered. "Calling that creature a kitten is like calling Godzilla a gecko."

"He's just working out his growing pains."

"I wish he wouldn't work them out by sinking his teeth into my leg."

Lucia dismissed my complaint with a roll of her eyes. "One little nip and you act as if you were mauled by a snow leopard." Before I could respond, she said, "Anyway, Lynxie *wasn't* in your room. And I have no idea where your keys are, so you can cool your jets."

"Just thought I'd ask." I wanted to ask what she'd *really* been doing in my room, but I knew she wasn't going to change her story now.

Lucia grabbed another handful of tarts and stalked out, looking disgruntled and defensive. There was something she wasn't telling me. I just wasn't sure if it had anything to do with Juniper's key.

"What was *that* about?" Claire asked when Lucia and Quasar were out of earshot.

"I wanted to see if she'd admit to knowing where I hid my key. Someone managed to get into Juniper's apartment—maybe twice—and mine is one of the few spare keys."

"You don't suspect Lucia, do you?"

"She's being furtive about something."

Up in my bedroom after Claire and I said good night, I checked under my bed for housecat-lynx hybrids.

A knock sounded and I called, "Come in!"

Jingles found me half under the bed. "Did you lose an earring, or is this some kind of weird emergency drill?"

I crawled out from under the bed. *All clear.* "Lucia said she came in looking for Lynxie sometime recently. She swore he wasn't ever in here, but I'm not sure I believe her."

He nodded. "It's best not to take any chances. Lynxie can get into all sorts of places. Salty thought the poultry houses were secure, too."

"Oh no."

His lips turned down. "Luckily, Lynxie was found right away and only managed to wound one rooster. It suffered a punctured trachea. You might have noticed that the cock-a-doodle-dooing has been much more subdued lately."

I sank onto the edge of the bed. "Pamela said you were interrogating elves today. Did you discover anything?"

"Didn't I just." He rubbed his hands together. "Ruby the
dairy girl said a friend of hers told her that she has a spinster
cousin at Brightlow Enterprises who was in love with Virgil.
Unrequited, apparently—and now sadly unrequited for all
time. Ruby said that when they told the poor elf about Virgil's murder, she let out a wail you could hear all across Santaland. Her family had to call Doc Honeytree to prescribe a
sedative to mix into her eggnog."

"What's this elf's name?"

"Prunella."

"She works at Brightlow?" I thought about the elf I'd seen
typing today—the one with the red-rimmed eyes. "Brown
hair?"

Jingles frowned. "Ruby called her mousy."

I nodded. If Prunella was the elf I'd seen, the description
fit. She looked very upset. In fact—

I gasped.

Jingles tilted his head. "What?"

"There was an elf woman in a red hat standing by herself
by the constabulary tonight, glaring at us while we were serenading Juniper. I saw her earlier today at Brightlow Enterprises, red-eyed over her keyboard while the rest of the office
was having a party."

"Well, I can understand her not feeling like celebrating."

"I wonder if there was something more to it. The way
Virgil died—it was a violent attack."

Jingles's eyes widened. "You mean it could have been a
crime of unrequited passion?"

"It's not impossible."

He straightened, his expression a mix of amazement and
satisfaction. "I've done it again!"

I frowned. "What?"

"Solved another crime." He sniffed, practically dusting his hands in gloating triumph. "You see? We didn't need Jake Frost for this one at all."

"It's not like Prunella's confessed to the crime," I pointed out. "It's just a theory."

"Mark my words—it's her."

I wasn't going to count my chickens before they hatched. There were still too many loose ends dangling. I wanted Juniper out of jail, but pointing the finger of blame at the wrong elf could leave a vicious killer still at large in Santaland during Christmas week.

Chapter 16

Nick's astonished concern at seeing me up bright and early the next morning made me laugh. If anything, his being up at this unholy hour was even more miraculous: the meeting at Kringle Lodge had lasted until the wee small hours. I'd long since nodded off over *The Humanoids* and a pile of unknit wool when I'd felt his side of the mattress sink under his exhausted weight.

"Why are *you* up so early?" I asked. "Please tell me it doesn't have anything to do with helicopters."

He drew back. "No one's supposed to know about that."

"Your mom announced it to me and Claire."

"Well, keep it under your hat. If word gets out now that we're making alternate arrangements, it will ensure the reindeer won't show up on Christmas Eve."

"You're not actually considering Butterbean's helicopter idea, are you?"

"I still believe the reindeer will rally. But just in case . . ."

Was he insane? "You don't know how to fly a helicopter."

"No worries there. Butterbean's a pilot."

I crossed my arms. "Self taught?"

He frowned. "I didn't ask to see his license."

"You should." That flambé incident leapt to mind. "Did you know that as a sous-chef he nearly burned down a château?"

"I don't see what one thing has to do with the other," Nick said. "Besides, we're in a tight spot."

"No, being in a tight spot would be flying around the earth in a used boneyard helicopter with Captain Butterbean."

He laughed. "Hopefully it won't come to that. The reindeer are having a dawn relay. I'm meeting Lucia there—I'm hoping a show of support will sway them. And Felice cooked up a whole batch of her special lichen bars for me to take."

"Pastry diplomacy is always a good idea," I said. "Could you drive me into town?"

He cast a pointed look at the clock on his bedside table. I didn't usually go to Christmastown this early.

"I need to talk to Tiffany about Christopher's gift—someplace where Christopher won't overhear us." Christopher was second only to Jingles for having the sharpest ear for gossip in the castle. "Conferring at the tea shop seems wiser." I added, "And this way, you and I have an excuse to take a quiet morning drive on our own."

"I like the sound of that, but what about Claire?"

"She asked me to let her sleep in. Especially since tonight promises to be another late one."

"Why?" Nick asked.

"Don't tell me you forgot *The Nutcracker,*" I said, secretly pleased that I wasn't the only one.

Nick groaned. He wasn't a fan of ballet, elf or otherwise, but *The Nutcracker* was an unmissable annual event, especially for Santaland's most prominent citizen. "I'll be there," he promised.

I bundled up in my warmest, puffiest coat and we headed out. It was a gorgeous morning. Still full dark, of course, but trees had been decorated along the sleigh path, and the various houses and châteaux that dotted Kringle Heights had all upped their lights-and-decorations game in the run-up to Christmas.

Nick stopped the sleigh at an overlook that afforded the best view of the lights of Christmastown, aside from the one atop the old tower of Castle Kringle. Unlike the one at the castle, this view had the added advantage of not requiring a climb up an ancient stone staircase to appreciate it.

I scooted closer to him on the bench seat. "Let me guess. This was your inspiration point when you were all teenagers."

He waggled his brows. "Feeling inspired?"

I smiled. "Persuadable."

He pulled me closer. "Just wanted to see if the magic still works."

It did.

Twenty minutes later, he was letting me off in front of Tea-piphany. I waved good-bye to him, and, calculating that I had a few minutes to spare, I went inside. Tiffany was just setting to work on baking her heavenly scones.

"What are you doing here at this hour?" she asked, surprised. Then her eyes narrowed. "And why is your lipstick smudged?"

I grabbed a poinsettia-bordered napkin off the nearest table and did some cosmetic cleanup. "I wanted to talk to you about Christopher's present. I'm pretty sure I can get you a deal on a Selfy, slightly used."

She heaved a sigh. "That's good. I kept hoping he'd mention something else, but he hasn't."

"I also wanted to run another idea past you. For Christopher's present from Nick and me, I was thinking of a Snomaneuver . . ." I was about to add, *"if that's okay with you,"* but she was gaping at me as if I'd taken leave of my senses, so I concluded it was very far from okay.

"You mean like the thing Ebenezer wiped out on yesterday?" she asked.

"Well, yes. But Christopher isn't a snowman. He already snowboards."

"Right, and he's already broken his arm."

"I tried one of those Snomaneuvers. It was more controllable than a snowboard. At least, for someone who isn't made of snow. I managed not to crash on it."

"Really?"

Her astonishment didn't speak well for what she thought of my dexterity. But Tiffany had been a competitive ice skater. She could do backflips on ice. Everyone was a klutz next to her.

Her background in sports also made her realize the futility of trying to keep a child wrapped in cotton wool. She shook her head. "Someday Christopher's going to be a grown man who's resigned to opening boxes containing shirts and ties on Christmas morning, and I'll miss these years, right?"

I laughed, and glanced at the teapot clock on the wall. "So you're okay with the Snomaneuver idea?"

She studied me. "You didn't really come all the way into town at oh-lordy-o'clock just to ask me about Christopher's Christmas gift, did you?"

"I need to shadow someone," I admitted. "I want to catch them on their way to work."

She poured steaming tea into a to-go cup and handed it to me. "I know tea isn't your usual eye opener, but you need something warm if you're going to be creeping around town on a morning like this."

I felt so grateful. Tiffany understood my susceptibility to cold. Like me, she was a transplant from "the south." In Santaland, a southerner was anyone who lived outside the Arctic Circle. I thanked her and, armed with my tea cup as a hand warmer, headed back out into the cold.

According to Jingle's castle source, Prunella lived with her family in a row house in Christmastown, on Frankincense

Street. I headed that way at a quick clip, hoping to catch Prunella before she left the house.

I parked myself outside the house Ruby had named, keeping my eye glued on the front door. I was wearing a warm but not conspicuous coat this morning—my shadowing coat, I called it. I stood so long that I feared I'd missed Prunella altogether. I began to regret not just hanging out at Tea-piphany until Tiffany's scones came out of the oven.

"Mrs. Claus?"

I'd been so focused on Prunella's doorway that the loud voice behind me made me jump. When I turned, a female elf with a large bag hiked over her shoulder was looking up at me with keen interest. She wore a quilted tunic coat in a patchwork pattern. Hippie elf—it was a style you didn't see that often.

"You *are* Mrs. Claus, aren't you?"

So much for trying to go incognito. "Yes, I am."

"My name's Sherry. I make hats." She smiled expectantly.

I returned her smile, although I wished she wasn't quite so loud a hatmaker. Her voice echoed on the empty street. "Oh?"

"How would you like to buy a hat this morning, Mrs. Claus?"

I looked around. Prunella's door was still closed. *"Here?"* I said, just above a whisper, hoping she'd take the hint.

"Your patronage would mean the world to me. Just imagine—everyone at Castle Kringle wearing *my* hats!" She opened her bag, revealing a jumble of craft materials. On closer inspection, that jumble *was* her inventory. She plopped one on her fist to model it.

I couldn't imagine anyone at Castle Kringle wearing these hats. Not even Lucia. They were shaped like sawed-off triangles, as if Sherry hadn't taken into account the shape of an actual head, human or elven. She had sewn them in a variety of clashing colors with no consideration for the eyeball. Some

were two- and three-toned, and all of them had been decorated in a completely haphazard way, some with pom-poms
sewn on all over, some with tinsel-colored thread zigzagging
across them. Others looked like a toddler had been set loose
with glitter and a glue gun.

"They're very"—I strained for a compliment—"unique."

She nodded eagerly. "No two hats are alike."

"You sell them on the street?"

"You gotta start somewhere, right? It's a new business for
me. I used to work at Brightlow Enterprises, but I quit to follow my millinery dreams."

"Oh—" I almost said "oh no," but stopped myself just in
time. Following one's dreams was usually considered a good
thing, but in this case . . .

"That was very brave of you."

"Well, *technically* I was let go, but you know how it is over
there. I was never meant to be a cog in a machine. And in fact
that's why they let me go. I did piecework, riveting, things
like that. They said a Selfy could do my job."

"That's awful." Just before Christmas, too. Outrage
swelled in my breast. "And now you're hawking hats on the
street?" That sounded grim. Was this the "Santaland's tomorrow, today" that Brightlow's stupid slogan promised?

She waved off my outrage. "I always wanted to do something more creative. This seemed like my chance."

From what I'd seen of Jingleini, replacing elves with Selfies wouldn't be a very sound business strategy. But maybe the
company was worse off than they were letting on. Could that
have anything to do with what happened to Virgil?

"Interesting," I said.

She took that as encouragement and held up another of
her hats—a brown-and-orange one with a hodgepodge of
decorative sequins, streaks of glitter, and a green pom-pom at
the top. On one hand, the inside was lined with fleece and it

appeared very warm. On the other, it was hideous. I cast an anxious glance at the doorway down the street. I didn't need a hat, but I needed to get away from the hat lady before Prunella appeared.

I hadn't said anything, but already Sherry looked dejected. "You don't want it."

Her forlorn tone pierced me. "Of course I do. I'll take this one." I held up the hat in my hand and then was distracted by movement at the house. Had I detected the front curtain twitching?

"Never mind," Sherry said. "You shouldn't feel obliged to buy it." She began to tug the hat back from me.

I held fast and dragged my gaze away from the house. "No, I mean it. I'll take it."

She shook her head. "I'll just head downtown. The Depression Center will be opening soon."

The Depression Center? Oh no. I imagined her spending the morning with Mildred and her stale cookies. And these hats.

Maybe it was in my power to give this one depressed elf a boost.

"In fact, just give me all of them," I said, taking the bag from her.

Her jaw dropped in amazement. "Really?"

"Of course." It was easier to keep my voice chipper if I didn't look at what I was buying. I opened my purse and pulled out handfuls of bills. "I'm always losing hats. Now I'll have a ready supply."

She frowned. "But they're not all your size."

My mind frantically searched for a justification for buying wrong-sized hats. "Stocking stuffers."

She beamed. "This must be my lucky day!"

I just hoped the money would help tide her over until she could find another position.

Her face was ecstatic, and I felt hopeful that I'd helped her until she exclaimed, "I'd better get back home and start making more hats! Once everyone at Castle Kringle starts wearing them, I'm bound to get rush orders!"

She hurried away, almost as if she were afraid I'd want to give the hats back.

Her departure was timed well. As Sherry turned the corner at the end of the block, Prunella's door opened. I jumped back behind a fir tree ringed in garlands and let her get a good head start. The elf had on her red hat again, so she was easy to track, even though her short legs moved with quick, purposeful steps toward downtown.

When she reached Festival Boulevard, instead of turning left and heading farther out of town toward Brightlow Enterprises, she went in the other direction, deeper into the downtown area. A few more elves were bustling down the street now, and business owners were opening up their shops for the day, sweeping the night's accumulated flurries off the meticulously cleared sidewalks. To my delight I saw that Prunella was heading toward my favorite place in Christmastown, the We Three Beans coffeehouse.

I dropped my tea into a nearby trash bin, hung back, and watched her go inside. Then I followed her in, pushing through the front door to the cheery tinkling of the bell attached to it. The aroma of roasting coffee beans hit me like a shot of adrenaline. Juniper and I spent so many hours here, the coffeehouse with its low coved ceilings was like a second home.

The owner, Trumpet, greeted me. "How are you doin', April?"

Prunella flicked a glance at me. Her mouth was turned down. She'd already ordered and was standing back, waiting. I placed mine to go and stood next to her.

Most of the tables were still empty at this time of day, but elves seated around the room were already singing along to music piped through speakers. I hummed along to "Winter Wonderland" for a few bars until my double latte arrived in a to-go cup emblazoned with We Three Beans' logo and the motto "A caffeinated elf is a happy elf."

But Prunella didn't get hers to go. Instead, when her order was ready she took her mug and found a table near the fireplace. I followed and settled myself in an empty spot across from her. She wasn't singing along with the other elves. In fact, a very unelflike irritation radiated from her.

I smiled at her and lifted my coffee cup. "I needed this."

I meant it as a friendly conversation opener. It opened her up, all right.

"You don't have to pretend." Her voice had an edge. "I know who you are."

I smiled nervously and—I hoped—placatingly. "It's hard for Mrs. Claus to escape notice in this town."

"I don't care if you're Mrs. Claus or the man in the moon. To me, you're the friend of a murderess."

So much for placating. The word *murderess* raised my hackles. "Juniper didn't kill Virgil."

"Who did, then?"

"I was wondering if you had any ideas about that."

"Is that why you followed me from my home to here?" As heat crept into my face, she shook her head. "You thought I couldn't spot Mrs. Claus hiding behind a tree? Not to mention buying hats right there on my street."

Something about buying a bag of hats I didn't want or need embarrassed me more than being seen ducking behind the tree like a burglar. "I wanted an opportunity to talk to you."

"Really? You saw me yesterday at work and didn't say anything. Then I was at that nauseating display of murderess coddling last night at the constabulary, and you didn't say a word to me there, either, even though I know you saw me."

"I didn't put together until later that you were the same elf I'd seen at Brightlow Enterprises. You were the only one there who seemed to care that Virgil was gone."

She slapped the table in frustration. "I *am* the only one who cares. He was so kind, so unassuming, most people at that place treated him like part of the furniture. But I tried to get to know him. If we were in the lunchroom together, I'd ask him about what he'd done the night before, and what he was reading. He was big on reading." Her brow furrowed. "I guess that's where he met his killer."

"Juniper didn't kill him," I repeated. "And they met in school. She says they barely knew each other as adults, really, except for the few times when she saw him at the library."

"*I* knew him." Prunella sniffed and looked down at her nutmeg mochaccino. "I knew the kind of sandwiches he liked, the yogurt he brought for his lunch. There's still a yogurt in our employee refrigerator with his name on it . . ." She sucked in a stuttering breath before she could go on. "Eggnog flavored. His favorite."

It took every fiber of restraint in me to keep from making a *blech* face. Eggnog *yogurt*? I couldn't think of anything more nauseating.

Still, Virgil's terrible taste in yogurt didn't make his death any less tragic, or less sad for Prunella, who had tears in her eyes. "I'm so sorry. I know how hard this must be for you."

"No you don't. If you didn't know him, you can't imagine what it was like to be around him day after day, exchanging little pleasantries, hoping he'd pay special attention to you."

"Did he?"

She stared into her mug again. "He was good at being a kindly office acquaintance, but it never went beyond that. Not with me, and I suspect not with anyone."

I frowned, remembering something Holly had said. She'd

also thought Virgil had liked her, and had been blindsided when his cost-benefit analysis had caused the Brightlows to nix her Snomaneuver.

But hours before he died, Virgil had been heading in Holly's direction. Had he really meant to go to her place of business—and if so, why? I wondered if my seeing him on the street had stopped him from visiting with Holly. What if that one coincidence had caused him to take some action that had led to his death?

"Where were you the night he was killed?"

Without hesitation, she replied, "Working late at Bright-low Enterprises."

"Did anyone see you there?"

She thought back. "I don't know. It's pretty quiet there nights lately."

Strange. Santa's Workshops ramped up to practically 24/7 operation this time of year.

"But I'm pretty sure Cookie was there," she said. "He always is."

Cookie—obviously not the brightest bulb on the tree—was a shaky alibi. "What about Dabbs?"

"I don't know. He might have been there."

"Did you ever witness any friction between him and Virgil?"

"Only work friction. Virgil thought Brightlow was over-investing in one project."

"The drone-deer?" I guessed.

She hiked her shoulders. "I'm not in the inner circle, but Virgil would grumble from time to time. Tensions have a way of seeping out of executive meetings."

Interesting. "Was there ever tension with Blinky?"

She gaped at me. "Blinky doesn't have conflicts with anyone. That elf is living in a different world from the rest of us—the world of his own brain."

"Do you ever remember him going missing for this long?"

"You think *he* killed Virgil?" she asked, as if the idea were outlandish.

"Would he have had a reason to? Maybe if Virgil was standing in the way of the realization of one of Blinky's pet projects?"

She shook her head. "Virgil didn't control anything at Brightlow. And Blinky generally gets whatever he wants. He's in his thirties, but they still treat him like the boy genius, especially that crazy mother of theirs." Her expression collapsed into a scowl. "I'll tell you one person who might have had it in for Virgil. Holly Silverpick."

I scooted forward in my chair. "What about her?"

"That thing she's selling—that was all Virgil's idea."

"I thought Virgil was an accountant, not an inventor."

Prunella drew up, all sharp angles. "Virgil had a keen mind. I overheard them talking in the lunchroom before she left. He was telling her the idea had potential with places like Walnut's." Her brow arched. "And lo and behold, who was her first—and so far only—client?"

Walnut. Maybe that was why Virgil was going to see Holly that afternoon before he was killed—to ask her for a cut of the profits from the deal she'd struck with Walnut. What was a better motive for murder than money?

Chapter 17

The valued customer reception I'd first received at the Silverpick Industries headquarters was absent this time. When I crossed the threshold, Holly's expectant smile melted. "You're back."

"I need to ask you some questions about a few things."

"Such as?"

"Such as where you were the night Virgil was murdered."

Her arms went rigid at her sides. "I'm being blamed for that now, too? Calling me an ice sculpture destroyer wasn't enough?"

I'd come armed for that denial. I flashed my phone at her. On the screen was the Yelf! review by ArgentotheGreat, warning that someone would be hurt. "Argento is Italian for silver. Do you deny this is you?"

She didn't have to. Her face went scarlet, and her chin hiked up. "I was right, wasn't I? Thank goodness no one *was* hurt. Just a statue."

"The sculptor who saw his work destroyed was hurt," I reminded her.

"Not by me."

"So you still deny programming that drone-deer to crash."

"Most certainly I deny it. Yes, I wrote the review. I write lots of reviews. I trashed Merry Muffins, too." At my sharp intake of breath, she explained, "They tried to pass off a stale day-old as fresh."

"They wouldn't do that."

"*Now* they wouldn't. Not since I called them on it."

Her smug manner gave me an uneasy feeling. She clearly saw herself as a righter of wrongs—the crusader against stale muffins. How far would she go to get her way in other areas?

Her lips twisted. "Is there any other wrongdoing you'd like to accuse me of?"

"You still haven't said where you were the evening Virgil was murdered."

She paled. "You're joking. You really want to accuse me of murdering Virgil?"

"When I left here the other day, I nearly ran into him coming up Sparkletoe Lane."

"So?" She drummed her fingers together. "The whole street doesn't belong to me. He could have been going anywhere."

But the way she avoided my eye confirmed that this had been his destination. "Why did he look panicked when I came out of your door and saw him walking in this direction?" I asked.

"It sounds like he had some reason to avoid *you*. Maybe *you* killed him."

"I didn't steal his idea."

She stopped fidgeting. "Who told you that?"

"Never mind. I can tell by your reaction that there's some truth in it."

"No, there's not." She shook her head in frustration. "Crumb cakes, crumb cakes, crumb cakes! I told him it would never work."

"Told who?"

"Virgil." She sighed. "He was a partner in my business. My silent partner."

He was certainly silent now. "When I talked to you the other day, you made it sound as if you resented Virgil for shooting down your Snomaneuver idea at Brightlow Enterprises."

"That was for Virgil's benefit. He didn't want the Brightlows to find out that he was invested in a competitor's business. That's why we kept it secret. He was adamant that we had to do everything we could to prevent having anyone associate him with Silverpick Industries."

That would explain why he appeared horrified that I came seconds from seeing him enter this building. "You said Brightlow Enterprises turned your Snomaneuver idea down because it wasn't going to make enough money. Was that also a lie?"

"He actually told them it might make a modest amount of money if marketed strategically. But they're not interested in modest profits over there. Not these days. Virgil told me they've got something in the works that's trumping everything else."

"So Virgil was also a disgruntled employee?"

She thought for a moment before answering. "My guess is that he wanted to hedge his bets. Just before I quit, he approached me privately with a plan to pitch my idea to Walnut."

Not privately enough. So far Prunella's information was spot on. Was she also right about Holly being a likely murder suspect?

"So did you see Virgil the afternoon he was murdered?"

She shook her head. "When he saw you, he must have worried that his cover would be blown. Especially if he'd seen you at Brightlow before you came here."

He had. "He didn't call you?"

"No."

"Can you think of any reason he would have called Juniper to meet him?"

"The librarian?" Her mouth set in a tight line. "I have nothing to do with her."

"I know you hate her. It's ridiculous. You were *ten.*"

Her face reddened. "I had to spell the word first! Do you think she could have spelled gobbledygook right if I hadn't spelled it wrong? I mean, there are only so many ways to screw that word up. Not that I actually got it *wrong,* except with those persnickety judges. *E* instead of *y* is an acceptable variant! Even Webster's says so."

"You've got to let it go."

"I have!" she yelled, then took a deep breath and made a tamping-down motion with her hands. "I really have. And I didn't even know she knew Virgil until she was arrested for his murder. To be honest, Virgil and I didn't talk that much about anything besides the Snomaneuver. I don't know what was going on with him the day he died."

"Do you have an alibi for that night?"

"You *still* think I killed him?"

"An alibi would help eliminate you as a potential suspect."

I expected her to question who I was to make demands for alibis, but she thought the request over and obviously saw the logic of it. "I know where I was, and there was a roomful of witnesses. I was at the Christmastown Symphony Orchestra's *Nutcracker* rehearsal. I play baritone."

It was my turn to be astounded. I was Santaland's musical events coordinator. I knew there had been a rehearsal that evening—I didn't know that Holly was in the orchestra.

She folded her arms. "Any more accusations? You haven't called me a snowman killer yet."

If the bootie fits . . . "I saw another crash yesterday. It was bad."

"I'm trying to make improvements, but getting Walnut to

pull the old models out of circulation is like trying to pry a candy cane away from a kid." She shook her head. "I feel like I've created a monster."

"I'm sorry." I knew something about unintended consequences. "I do have good news, though."

"What? You *don't* think I'm a murderer?"

I smiled. "I'm in the market for a Snomaneuver."

Her expression's instant transformation told me that she was more than willing for me to come over and accuse her of murder as long as she got a sale out it. Business was business.

On my way to visit Juniper, I circled back to We Three Beans and then swung by Puffy's All-Day Donuts. Bringing baked goods to the constabulary was a coals-to-Newcastle proposition if there ever was one, but as far as I knew, Ollie hadn't yet turned his hand to donut making.

Puffy's shelves were sagging with fresh-from-the-fryer donuts still shimmery with warm glaze. The sugar smell in the air was strong enough to give me a contact high. I'd meant to order a dozen, but looking at the mouthwatering variety of choices, I kept ordering until I had two dozen.

One street over from Puffy's, a crowd had gathered in front of the mayor's house. Fearing another snowman fatality, I hurried over. As I approached, I saw that the crowd's eyes were focused up, not down. And far from feeling tragic, this gathering had a flash-mob vibe about it. An elf across the street was playing "Jolly Old Saint Nicholas" on an accordion and I could hear some of the elves on the fringes singing along.

Clearing a trio of row houses, I stopped in my tracks, shocked. In a courtyard in front of the stately stone house where Mayor Firlog resided, a twenty-foot Christmas tree grew. Usually the tree was decorated within an inch of its life, a true showstopper. But today two elves on ladders were busily trying to unwind toilet paper from the branches, which had been both mummy-wrapped and festooned with strips hanging from branches like icicles. Someone had done a very thorough job of toilet papering the mayor's tree.

As a crowning touch, whoever it was who'd wrapped the tree had created a five-pointed star out of toilet paper rolls. I couldn't help smiling at that—and at the fact that the vandal had used red and green tinted paper.

I approached Mayor Firlog, who stood arms akimbo, trembling at the sight of his vandalized tree. His agitation wiped the smile off my face.

"I'm sorry," I told him. "It's a mess to clean up."

When I was a teenager, friends had TPed a tree in front of my house during the night after prom. My dad had rousted me out of bed at six a.m. to clean it up. I'd spent the entire morning crawling around the oak tree, picking Charmin out of branches. Fir needles would make the job even more diffi-cult, I reckoned now with an experienced eye.

Firlog bobbed on the stacked heels of his booties. "The hoodlum who did it was bold as brass. Why, I found him standing by his disgusting handiwork almost as if he *wanted* to be caught. I didn't even bother calling Crinkles. I escorted him to the constabulary myself."

"Couldn't you just have told him to clean it up?"

He drew back, disgusted. "I have servants for that. Crimi-nals belong in jail."

"He's in *jail*?"

Mayor Firlog eyed me as if I were a hopeless bleeding heart. "We have to set an example. Elves can't run around desecrating Christmas trees in Christmastown, during Christ-mas week!"

I held my tongue. I was still a relative newcomer here. My perspective wasn't always the same as an elf's.

But not all elves shared the mayor's outrage. The accordionist started playing a lively version of "O Christmas Tree," and all around us elves started singing. The mayor twitched. "Is that supposed to be funny?"

"I hope whoever did this wasn't anyone bearing a personal grudge," I said, trying to turn his attention away from the singing.

Firlog looked astonished at the suggestion. "I'd never even met this elf—a disreputable-looking fellow named Smudge."

My jaw practically hit the pavement. *"Smudge?"*

Firlog and I could have won first prize in a gaping contest. "You *know* that reprobate?"

"He's in the concert band." I took a step back. "I'm on my way to the constabulary right now. I'll see if I can get to the bottom of this."

"I caught him red-handed," the mayor called after me. "I've pressed charges!"

Charges of what? Tree papering?

At the constabulary, Crinkles was strutting around as if he'd personally collared Public Enemy Number One. He didn't even wait for me to get through the door before he started regaling me with the tale of the toilet paper caper. Except, of course, there was no caper. Smudge had stood by the tree, waiting to be caught.

The constable was so full of braggadocio, it was a full minute before he noticed the box in my hands. "Puffy's donuts?"

Some things knew no international borders, like cops and donuts.

I opened the box. "I brought two dozen. I figured Juniper might have visitors, but I didn't know you had two prisoners in custody."

He snatched a cherry-filled glazed with sprinkles. "They'll be much appreciated, I'm sure."

I hoped there would be some left by the time Crinkles and Ollie got through with their first pass. I looked around. "Where's Ollie?"

"Talking to Nippy Goldmitt. He wanted to get permission to tape *The Nutcracker* tonight for the prisoners." He finished the cherry donut in a gulp before reaching for a cinnamon sugar. "Just because elves perpetrate heinous acts, that doesn't mean they shouldn't enjoy the ballet."

No one would ever accuse the Christmastown Constabulary of being inhumane. One thing puzzled me, though. The jail only had one room—er, cell. "Where are you keeping Smudge?"

"In the cell." At my surprise, he licked a sugary finger and added quickly, "He'll stay at Ollie's place at night, of course. Nothing improper going on here, I assure you."

He said it with the certainty that improprieties never occurred during daylight hours.

"How long do you expect to hold him?"

"That'll be up to Judge Merrybutton. A few months, maybe?"

"Months?" I might have to take back my assessment of inhumane treatment.

"It was a Christmas tree," Crinkles said, wattles shaking.

"I know, but . . ." I tried to think of mitigating circumstances. All I could come up with was, "He used holiday-appropriate tinted bathroom tissue."

"We can't have lawlessness like that, especially during Christmas week." I was about to point out that we'd had a murder during Christmas week, but decided that maybe for Juniper's sake it wasn't politic to dwell on the gravity of the crime she was accused of. Anyway, Crinkles was already going on about the sanctity of protected trees in Santaland.

I held up the box, interrupting. "The chocolate éclairs are to die for."

Distracted, he picked one up. "Been so hectic here today, I forgot to eat lunch."

It wasn't noon yet, but okay. "Would it be all right if I took a few of these in to Juniper and Smudge now?"

The good constable struggled to hide his reluctance to let the box out of his sight. "Be my guest." He chuckled. "Maybe I shouldn't use that expression. We're already running out of room."

I smiled and closed the box—but too slowly to prevent Crinkles from nabbing a polar-bear claw.

When I opened the cell door—it wasn't locked—Juniper and Smudge were seated on the floor, a chessboard between them. The elf chess board had snowmen for pawns, various elf figures in the second tier, except for reindeer, which were knights, and Santa and Mrs. Claus for king and queen—very flattering, even if this queen resembled Pamela more than me.

Juniper hopped up. "April! It's so nice of you to visit."

"I brought donuts and a thermos of coffee from We Three Beans. Trumpet sends his regards."

"That's so nice of him. And two cups. Did he know Smudge was here?"

Actually, I'd grabbed that second go-cup for myself, but Smudge probably needed coffee more than I did. "I thought you might have company, but I didn't expect Smudge till I walked by the mayor's house."

He showed off a rare but not unattractive smile. "Impressive, wasn't it?"

Juniper wasn't happy. "You shouldn't have hurt a Christmas tree."

"I had to think of a surefire way to get myself arrested," he said, "and I didn't want to cause anyone bodily harm, or steal, or break a window."

"Why did you want to get arrested?" I asked.

"Because Juniper was here all alone."

As far as I could tell, the one thing Juniper *hadn't* been since being arrested was alone.

"What if she's in danger?" he said.

I'd wondered that, too, when I'd seen the red-hatted elf outside the constabulary. But after talking to Prunella, I didn't think she was a danger. Prunella might cheer were Juniper to be sent off to live out the rest of her natural life in the Farthest Frozen Reaches, but she wasn't violent herself.

Juniper tossed a snowman pawn at Smudge. "You gumdrop brain. What place could be more secure than the constabulary?"

"Anywhere," Smudge and I said in unison, and then exchanged astonished glances. It was probably the first time we'd agreed on anything.

"And what would you do now if the constabulary were attacked?" Juniper asked him. "You're in the same boat I'm in."

"Except no one has it in for me."

"The mayor," I reminded him.

"Luther Partridge isn't going to be too happy, either," Juniper added. "He's losing his first percussionist during Christmas week."

The blood drained from my face. She was right. I hadn't considered this aspect of Smudge's being locked up. "We're playing the *1812 Overture*. How's it going to sound with just me on percussion?"

"You can handle it," he said in a newfound show of confidence in my rhythmic abilities. A confidence I did not share.

"Maybe Crinkles will grant you a furlough for the fireworks," I said, grasping at straws.

"And leave Juniper here alone while everyone's at the top of Sugarplum Mountain?" He shook his head. "Not on your life."

I sank down and reached for a donut. Emotional eating, I know, but I was in distress.

Smudge leaned in to inspect the donut box. "Is that an eggnog cream–filled?"

That was the one I knew was Juniper's favorite. "I was saving that one for—"

Juniper jumped in before I could finish. "You can have it, Smudge."

Reading the situation, he withdrew his hand like the donut was a red-hot burner.

"Go ahead," Juniper insisted. "It's the best I can do to compensate you for so stupidly getting arrested on my behalf."

The donuts were forgotten. "Stupidly?" he bleated.

"I'll be out just as soon as April proves who killed Virgil," she said, showing an overinflated faith in my sleuthing abilities. "You, however, might be living here for months." She moved a piece. "Checkmate."

His gaze dropped down to the chessboard in dismay. "Already?" He sighed. "You want to play again? Winner gets the eggnog cream–filled."

Smiling, Juniper set the pieces back up again.

Chapter 18

One good thing about being Mrs. Claus: I got great *Nutcracker* seats. The Claus family's box hung over the stage-right side of the Christmastown Civic Theater, practically over the stage's apron. The box held six—two rows of three—so I let Claire have the front seat next to Pamela and Nick. Nick needed to be front and center, and he was dressed in his red velvet best for the occasion.

So was I, but I didn't mind taking a literal backseat to Pamela this evening. This let me focus on the spectacle instead of feeling like the spectacle. *The Nutcracker* isn't my favorite ballet, but it was the only one elves ever performed, and every year it was amazing. Elves aren't known for their grace—a low physical profile combined with a steady diet of carbs doesn't make for effortless jetés and pirouettes. Their ballet is more like interpretive dance in tutus than classic ballet, and they aren't above using ropes, wires, and other gimmicks to enhance their performances.

I was so mesmerized by the first act that I almost didn't notice a poke from Mildred, who was sitting next to me. When she had my attention she jabbed her finger toward the empty seat in the box that was supposed to be Lucia's. I lifted my shoulders. I didn't know where Lucia was.

"It's bad form to have empty seats in the Claus boxes," she hissed as the lights came up for intermission.

"If you want to give Lucia etiquette lessons, be my guest," I said, standing up. They always sold chocolate in the lobby during intermission, so I raced down there before the line got too long. I promised Claire I'd bring something back to the box.

In front of me in line, Carlotta and Clement, two distant cousins of Nick's, greeted me with enthusiasm, as if we hadn't just all met at Mildred's potluck. We'd also see each other again on Christmas Eve at Amory's fireworks show, and probably at the Ladies' Guild Holiday Craft Bazaar, too. That was how things rolled during Christmas week in Christmastown.

"Where's Lucia?" Clement asked. "Up on a roof, maybe?"

He and Carlotta exchanged amused glances.

Their joke went over my head. "Roof?"

"That's where we saw her during the ice sculpture contest," Carlotta said. "Hanging out on the City Hall roof like a pigeon, watching everyone."

What would Lucia have been doing on a roof?

"How did *you* see her?" I asked.

"Just by chance," Carlotta said. "When that drone appeared, I looked up and there was Lucia, up on the roof of City Hall."

Lucia hadn't mentioned she'd been anywhere near Peppermint Pond, never mind perched on the City Hall roof. I couldn't help remembering how she'd known how to manipulate the drone-deer. Could she have been on that rooftop so she could crash a drone-deer into the Blitzen statue by remote control? I didn't want to believe it, and yet . . .

It made sense. She hated drone-deer and was a tireless advocate for real reindeer.

Claire appeared at my side while Clement and Carlotta were

placing their orders. "I needed to stretch my legs," she said. "What are you getting? Please tell me it's alcoholic."

"You don't want chocolates?" I happened to know they were from Dash's Candy and Nut Shoppe, my favorite chocolate store.

"I can't believe it's me saying this," she said, "but I think I'm finally reaching my limit on chocolate. This place is like a Schick center for sweets."

I ordered two Proseccos and handed her one—but not without a backward glance of regret at the truffle tray. "Not enjoying the ballet?"

"Oh yes, I am." As she spoke, she scanned the crowd milling around the lobby. My gaze followed hers. Nick had been buttonholed by a host of young elves, which always happened at events like this. He ho-ho-hoed for them and pulled a few hard candies out of his pockets.

On the other side of the room, Ollie was holding out his phone—simulcasting the intermission for the jailbirds, I guessed. I waved, hoping Juniper would see me.

Claire took a sip of her drink. "It's a riot, actually. I've never seen trampolines used in ballet choreography before."

"Just for the jack-in-the-box and the dancing doll." I was launching into my explanation of elves' low gravity profile, when I noticed Claire wasn't listening.

"Hellooo."

All of a sudden, she stood up straighter. Jake Frost approached, clean-shaven and looking sharper than I'd ever seen him. He wore black tie, and also a black shirt.

He presented Claire a box of chocolate truffles in a Dash's box. "I brought these for you."

Claire squirmed with delight as she took the box, as if she hadn't declared just two minutes ago that she was chocolated out. "Thank you." She treated him to her most dazzling smile.

Feeling distinctly third wheelish, I began to back away. Jake stopped me. "I brought you something, too."

I hoped for fudge. No such luck.

He handed me a sheet of paper. "It's the list of all the people who bought drone-deer, and the ones who returned theirs."

I cast a glance over the first page. "Anyone who might carry over as a suspect in Virgil's murder?"

"Not sure." His hand rubbed his chin as if searching for whiskers no longer there. "One name in particular did jump out at me." He obviously expected me to find it on my own.

My eye skimmed down the list until it hit the name I was sure at once he'd been referring to.

AMORY CLAUS.

Amory? "He wouldn't have had a reason to crash a drone-deer. He certainly wouldn't have any reason to kill Virgil."

"There's something else," Jake said. "Since Virgil kept track of financial matters, I got Crinkles to convince Dabbs Brightlow to let me poke around Virgil's office. I found a list of investors. Turns out, Amory sank a lot of money into Brightlow Enterprises. Did you know that?"

"No, I didn't."

Jake shrugged. "Might be nothing, but . . ."

I folded the paper and handed it back to Jake. "I'll talk to Amory. I'm pretty sure he's too busy with his fireworks spectacular to get sidetracked with crashing drone-deer and killing elves."

Claire threaded her arm through his. "How about leaving off the investigation for a few minutes and getting another Prosecco?"

"Happy to," he said.

"You coming, April?" she asked.

I shook my head. "I need to visit the washroom before Act Two."

I left them and went to queue up for the washroom. The

elf in front of me was one of the musicians in the orchestra. I complimented her on the music. "You all sound great."

"It's a Christmas miracle," she said, laughing. "Most of us are running on fumes. I and several of the others work in Tinkertown at the Wrapping Works, and we've had two late-night rehearsals this week."

I frowned. "How late?"

"We started at nine to accommodate everyone's schedules."

Nine! That *was* late. In fact, it allowed Holly plenty of time to kill Virgil and then skip off to rehearsal. When she gave rehearsal as her alibi for the night of Virgil's death, she'd probably been counting on my not questioning the precise time the rehearsal had started.

So now I had to add her back to the suspect list, along with Amory. And maybe Lucia.

Instead of getting smaller, the list of possible wrongdoers had expanded by three in just the length of an intermission.

The lights blinked, giving the audience a five-minute warning.

As I returned to the box, I met Lucia in the lobby.

"I thought you weren't here," I blurted out.

Her lips twisted. "Would you like me to leave?"

"No, we'd just given up on you."

"I told Nick I'd be at the reindeer games most of the evening. Didn't he say anything to you?"

"No. Carlotta did, though."

Her brow lined in confusion. "I haven't seen Carlotta today."

"I know. She said the last time she saw you was during the ice sculpture contest."

"How did she know—?" Her words broke off and her face reddened. "Oh, okay. That was some kind of trap, I guess."

"What were you doing on the roof of City Hall?"

"What do you think? I was watching the ice sculpture contest."

"Why on a roof, though? And why deny being there?"

She crossed her arms. "You may not have noticed, but the reindeer have been boycotting Christmas events. *I* couldn't very well show up at the biggest event of the week. Not the biggest that the reindeer usually like to attend."

Tonight was different. Reindeer never came to the ballet. They didn't fit comfortably in the theater, and they were rather dismissive of the elves' lackluster leaping onstage.

"So you were hiding on the roof."

She didn't like that word *hiding*, even if that's exactly what she'd just confessed to doing. "You get a good view of Peppermint Pond from there."

"It would also be a great vantage point if you wanted to make a tactical drone-deer strike by remote control."

She scowled. "That's idiotic. If I wanted to ruin the contest, I certainly wouldn't have taken out the best sculpture there. The best sculpture ever, really."

"But why did you lie?"

"Because you were interrogating me at the all-herd meeting. I wasn't going to mention I'd been there around all those reindeer."

"You could have told me later."

"Frankly, I've had more important things on my mind. I've been working to get the reindeer involved in Christmas again."

Something tugged at my elbow and I turned to see Nick standing next to me, holding one hand behind his back. The lights flashed again.

Lucia sighed. "I might as well go in. Even though it's all downhill after the mice, in my opinion."

"I saved you a seat next to Mildred."

After she was gone, Nick presented me with a box of chocolates. The deluxe truffle tray. My heart bloomed at the sight. I kissed him. "Thank you."

"You should sit up with us for the second act."

"I don't want to displace Claire."

A shadow of discomfort crossed his face. "I think Claire's gone."

I peeked through the box door. Sure enough, Claire's seat was empty. "I saw her and Jake disappearing," Nick said.

Looked like Claire was going to have a holiday romance after all.

The tapping of the baton against the music stand alerted us to the first notes of the lead-in music to Act Two, and Nick and I hurried to our seats.

The second act transported us to the Land of the Sweets, and I enjoyed the spectacle of the various national dances and the Sugar Plum Fairy and the dewdrops or flowers or whatever they were supposed to be. The prince, aided by wires, performed some magnificent leaps that nearly brought the house down. Balanchine was probably spinning in his grave, but this crowd enjoyed it.

At the same time that I was absorbed in the spectacle, a distant corner of my mind was focused on tomorrow, which was going to be so busy. I was going to have to talk to Holly Silverpick *again*. She'd love that. I needed to question Amory. I would, of course, see him at the fireworks in the evening, along with practically all of Santaland.

But first I had to face the Kringle Heights Ladies' Guild Holiday Craft Bazaar, and I was still about ten tea cozies short.

Chapter 19

Jingles came into my room the next morning, sans Jingleini, coffee tray in hand, anxiety etched on his face. I tried not to let his panic transfer directly to my brain, at least not till I'd learned the crisis *du jour*.

I was dressed in my ultimate Mrs. Claus outfit—red wool with white trim, brass buttons shaped like bells, black belt and boots to match. I'd been contemplating coiling my red hair into a bun like Pamela's, but now I wanted to find out whatever it was Jingles knew that I didn't.

"What's the matter?" I asked.

He set the tray down on my dressing table. "I have a new mystery for you: the Case of the Missing Houseguest."

I let out my breath. Not a crisis, then. Not even a mystery. "Claire went out with Jake last night."

He sank onto the bed and reached absently for the croissant he'd just laid down. "My goodness. Do you think she and Jake are in love . . . or something?"

"Or something," I said.

His brow beetled as he swallowed down half my breakfast. "Have you told Claire about the Farthest Frozen Reaches, and that Jake's a"—his frown deepened—"whatever he is?"

"I've told her all that." I didn't mention that Claire had a history of holiday pickups that didn't last. "They're both adults. They might be star-crossed, but they're not Romeo and Juliet."

"Or Snowbell and Blurf."

"Who?"

"You've never heard of Snowbell and Blurf?" His eyes bugged in astonishment at my ignorance. "Snowbell was a privileged daughter of Christmastown, and Blurf was a hideous snow monster she happened across one day while gathering the buttercups that only peep out of the tundra for a few weeks in summer. He'd been wounded by a polar bear, and she stayed to nurse him back to health. There, in the harsh land where the wind blows across the barren tundra and the nights are pierced by the lonely howls of the arctic wolf, the flower of Christmastown and this hideous snow monster fell in love. But when Snowbell's wealthy father got wind of where his daughter had gone, he went berserk." He made a face. "Let's face it, nobody wants a snow monster for a son-in-law."

Jingles had a tendency toward snobbishness, but in this case I cut him some slack. I'd met a snow monster once, and I had to admit I wouldn't want to be sitting down with one at family dinners, either. The bad breath alone would put you off your dinner.

"Snowbell's father and several relatives pursued the lovers across the tundra," Jingles continued, "but as they were crossing a pond the thin summer ice cracked and they all fell in and died. Now, in the summer, when the ice melts in the center of Snowbell Pond, they say you can still see their bones through the water."

"Well. That's grim."

He arched a brow. "Grimmer than what happens in *Romeo and Juliet*?"

I took a breath and considered whether a double suicide

was worse than an entire clan and a snow monster entombed in an icy grave. But I was distracted by another detail in the story. "She was picking buttercups?"

He nodded. "That's what the legend says. It makes sense. Not much else grows out there."

Interesting. Juniper said Blinky had brought her dried buttercups. I wondered if she—or he—had been thinking of Snowbell and Blurf, and doomed love. But why would Blinky and Juniper be doomed? They were just two elves—there wasn't any impediment like Blinky being of a different species noted for potent halitosis and destroying villages.

"Where is Snowbell Pond?" I asked.

He waved a hand. "In the middle of nowhere near the border. Not a good place to hide your illicit snow-monster lover, actually. There's nothing out there for miles except the pond. The land is flat, and there's always a howling wind coming from the Farthest Frozen Reaches."

I shuddered. Christmastown was cold enough for me.

Jingles crossed his arms. "Well, I suppose as long as Claire and Jake's fling doesn't interfere with our investigation, it'll be fine."

I laughed. "I'll inform Claire that her affair has the Jingles seal of approval."

My stomach made a gnawing sound, causing him to frown. "What was *that*?"

"I haven't had breakfast yet," I reminded him.

"Then why don't you—" He glanced at the plate splattered with crumbs from the croissant he'd just devoured. "Oh dear. I can ask Felice to make you a real breakfast and you can eat it like a normal Claus, in the breakfast room with Pamela and Christopher."

"No thanks. The next time I see Pamela I'm going to have to admit that I never did get my tea cozies made. I'm a crafts bazaar failure."

"What's that, then?" He inclined his head toward a bag on top of my dresser.

"It's a bag of hats." I'd forgotten all about the hats that Sherry, the elf fired from Brightlow, had made. I'd tossed the bag there the other day and hadn't thought of it since.

Jingles edged closer to inspect the hats as cautiously as he would approach a king cobra. His nose wrinkled. "They remind me of the time when Lynxie was a kitten and got into Pamela's knitting craft bag and upchucked all afternoon."

I nodded, wondering how I was going to get everything done today. "I really need to talk to Holly Silverpick this morning. I'm not sure how I'll do that and deal with the crafts bazaar, too." I was going to have to beg forgiveness from Pamela, and apologize to Midge, the bazaar's chairwoman. Maybe I could help out at someone else's booth.

Jingles brightened. "*I'll* take care of the crafts bazaar situation. You go find the murderer—and maybe hunt down Claire and Jake, too. That's more important. You're Mrs. Claus. You have to learn to delegate."

"You would do that for me?"

"Of course."

It felt as though a weight had been lifted from my shoulders. I could have wept with relief. Maybe it was cowardly not to tell Pamela I'd failed, but if I caught a murderer, surely all would be forgiven.

"You're a lifesaver, Jingles."

He folded his hands over his slightly pot belly and rocked on his heels, pleased with himself. "I know."

I headed out directly to talk to Holly Silverpick. But at her shop in Sparkletoe Lane, I found a sign on her door announcing that she was closed until after Christmas. I frowned. What elf closed their business two days before Christmas?

I didn't have a home address for her, although surely if I

asked around I could find it. At the library, Juniper could have found it for me within thirty seconds.

Hands in my pockets, I headed back down Sparkletoe Lane and had to sidestep around someone exiting the hardware store with a loaded wagon of lumber and other materials. When I saw who it was, I stopped. "I was just looking for you!"

She frowned. "Was it about your canceled order?"

I put my hands on my hips. "You canceled my order?" Christopher would be disappointed.

"Well, maybe not forever." She struggled to keep her wagon steady under its unwieldy load.

"Let me help you."

We bumped the materials up the street, then into her building. Silverpick Industries was still Spartan looking on the inside, although a drafting table in the corner seemed to have gotten a lot of use in the past day. After dropping my end of the load, I wandered over to it. With an inventor's protectiveness for her creations, she scurried over to the drawings before I could get there.

She tapped a blueprint with a pencil eraser. "I'm scrapping the Snomaneuver."

The announcement shocked me. "What other product do you have?"

"I'm going to adapt them to be Elfmaneuvers—take off width, and get rid of the snowman mount," she explained. "I haven't given up entirely on snowman vehicles, but you were right. I visited Ebenezer last night."

"Did he die?" I asked.

"Not entirely. He was a complete re-roll, though, and they think it might have affected his personality. Word is he's rejecting his purple hat, and now he just stands outside the library yelling 'Humbug' at passersby."

"He's gone full-on Scrooge?" I asked. "That's terrible."

"It's all my fault," Holly lamented. "The Snomaneuvers

are too dangerous. I'm hoping I can get Walnut to take the ones I sold him out of circulation."

Good luck with that.

"Well, it's good of you to change direction for their sake. Maybe Dabbs was right."

"No, the Brightlows just cared about the bottom line. My invention didn't fit into whatever master plan they have."

"Santaland's Tomorrow, Today."

"Exactly." She laughed, but it faded quickly and those shrewd eyes focused on me. "Now why was it you were looking for me?"

I took a breath. I almost didn't want to broach the subject now. Would someone who'd put the well-being of snowmen before her own bottom line likely be a murderer?

Still, I couldn't think of any other reason to explain my being here except the truth. "You told me you were at rehearsal the night Virgil was killed."

"I was."

"You didn't mention that rehearsal started late that night."

She folded her arms over her chest. "So now you think I killed Virgil and then ran off to the *Nutcracker* rehearsal?"

"You would have had time to."

"But I didn't. I told you—I *liked* Virgil. He was my business partner. Virgil encouraged me even though he worked at Brightlow. Plus, he was the only person at that place with any ethical scruples."

I believed her—but I always believed her. And then there always turned out to be more than she was telling me. "You should have let me know about the late rehearsal before now."

"Oh right." She snorted. "Every time you come in here you accuse me of something under the weakest pretext—like old spelling bees."

"*You* were the one who brought up the spelling bee."

"Because it was unfair!" she said, irritated all over again. "But when you thought I would have murdered someone to frame an old spelling bee rival for murder, I certainly wasn't going to volunteer more ammunition to use against me."

Put that way, I could understand why she hadn't been more forthcoming. And she showed real remorse about the snowmen. Wasn't that indicative of an elf with a good heart?

After we were done, I made my way back up the mountain to put in an appearance at the bazaar, which was being held at the Kringle Heights Chalet—one of my favorite places in Santaland. Located near Calling Bird Cliff, the gothic pink-granite structure was the only public meeting house in Kringle Heights. During the winter, it hosted concerts and served as a place for parents to congregate while children raced down the surrounding sled hill. Once a year, the Kringle Heights Theatrical Society mounted a production of an old play.

Today, however, the place resounded with Christmas cheer. The vaulted ceiling was festooned with garland and lights, and the startling centerpiece of this architectural wonder, the thirty-foot living tree that had been planted when the structure was built, dripped with tinsel and heirloom ornaments donated by the families of Kringle Heights. The tree was over a hundred years old, and its crown now reached almost to the leaded glass skylights. Its size made sightlines during Theatrical Society performances a little tricky for those unfortunate to get seats in the back, but few complained. The tree was magnificent to look at all year long, and much more interesting than Amory starring in *The Man Who Came to Dinner.*

For music I'd booked the Sno-Tones, an elf vocal quartet accompanied by a jazz trio. As I walked in, they were in the middle of a peppy version of "Let It Snow," which of course was accompanied by an echo of people humming and singing along. Santalanders can't resist joining in on a snappy tune.

Midge greeted me at the door. It was impressive that she was stage-managing the bazaar, given that the big fireworks show was taking place at her home that evening.

"Don't you have your hands full getting the lodge ready for the fireworks show tonight?" I asked.

"Are you kidding? Tonight is Amory and Butterbean's show, right down to the refreshments." Her tone conveyed that she was not entirely happy with that arrangement.

"That's good, isn't it?" I asked.

Her mouth turned down. "I don't know. It's weird to be sidelined. Ever since Amory fell under Butterbean's spell, he's been like a teenager. It's the world's biggest bromance since Bert met Ernie."

I laughed. "Well, everyone's looking forward to the fireworks, and if it's less work for you, so much the better."

She glanced down at her clipboard. "Let me see . . . where did I put you?"

"Nowhere," I said. "I dropped out."

"Nooo . . ." She studied her chart and then tapped her pencil on a spot she'd found. "No, you're at booth B-2, right next to Louella's Pine Cone Creations."

"Jingles said he would explain everything to you," I said.

She smiled tightly. "Generally we don't encourage outsourcing our volunteer booths, but in your case we're making an exception. We understand that you've been busy, and we appreciate your going out of your way to meet your tea cozy obligation."

I made myself smile even as confusion roiled inside me. How could Jingles have put up a booth when there were no tea cozies to sell? "Of course." I swallowed. "B-2, you said?"

She pointed me in the right direction. My stomach churned

uneasily as I passed booths of handmade candles and soaps, ornaments, and other arts and crafts. The aisles were thick with
shoppers wandering from booth to booth. The Sno-Tones
were singing "Rockin' Around the Christmas Tree" as I approached my booth. Jingles was standing behind a table with a
sign taped to the front made out of butcher paper and lettered
with magic markers: *Mrs. Claus's Tea Cozy Corner*. In front of
it Jingleini was set up, decorated in a wig and frilly red-and-
green apron. He held a tea tray, although the little tea pot was
covered with something that looked an awful lot like . . .

I sucked in a breath. Were those Sherry's hats?

Elspeth Claus stood feet away from me, clad in a candy
cane sweater with red leggings. Her fists were planted on her
hips, and from the way her chest was rising and falling, she
looked close to hyperventilating. "What. Is This?"

My face reddened. "Um . . ."

"Tea cozies," Jingles announced proudly.

"Jingles," I said, "can we talk for a moment?"

Unfortunately, we didn't have a moment. "Those things
don't look like tea cozies to me," Elspeth said. "This is outrageous! How could Midge have let this happen? I put in my
application for a booth *months* ago. I told them it would be
called *Elspeth's Tea Treasures*: tea towels, trivets, cozies, and
spoon rests. I worked on my booth for months, only to be
stuck next to the washroom while your vomity pile of wool
and felt gets a better spot."

Jingles's jaw dropped, and he darted out from behind the
booth. *"Vomity pile?"* he sputtered in indignation, even though
he had made a similar comparison earlier this morning.

At that moment, Jingleini blurted out, "Would you care
for some tea?"

Elspeth glared at the robot, then turned to me and poked
a long-nailed finger into my chest. "And you're not even

manning your own booth—you've got some elf and a robot doing everything for you!"

Jingles lifted his chin. Technically, he was an elfman, so being dismissed as "some elf" rankled. "April isn't just some rank-and-file Claus nobody. She's Mrs. Claus—she *delegates*."

"Um, Jingles . . ." That was *not* helping.

Elspeth poked me in the chest again. "Just because you're with the hoity-toity castle Clauses, you're always getting special treatment."

"Elspeth, it's just a booth."

"Just a—" She was speechless with indignation. "I'm going to speak to Midge about this." She snatched a hat—I mean a cozy—off my booth, turned on her heel, and stormed off.

"Hey!" I called after her. "You can't just take that."

She waved the hat-cozy at me in defiance and sped away.

"Would you care for some tea?" Jingleini repeated.

I glared at the Selfy and pulled Jingles aside. "Have you taken leave of your senses?" I pointed to the pile of Sherry's hats. "Those aren't tea cozies, they're hats."

"So?" he asked. "What are tea cozies if not hats for teapots? I cut little slits in them to accommodate the spouts and handles." He demonstrated with his hand, so that his thumb poked out of one end as the spout. "Ingenious, wasn't it?"

To be honest, it *did* look better as a tea cozy than a hat. "There's only one problem," I said. "I didn't make these."

He gaped at me. "What?"

"I *bought* them, Jingles."

He looked down, aghast—not at what he'd done, but at my bad taste. "*Why?* Why would you have done that? They looked so awful, I just assumed you must have made them yourself."

"Thank you."

"You know what I mean."

Unfortunately, I did. I was so not crafty. "These are counterfeit cozies. I'm in so much trouble."

Jingles drummed his fingers worriedly. "Perhaps after Elspeth calms down, the whole thing will blow over."

At that moment, Elspeth was steaming back our way with Midge, Mildred, and Pamela in tow. And if that wasn't bad enough, Sherry herself trailed after them. I cringed. In a few moments, I would be exposed to the world as a tea cozy fraud. I felt the sudden urge to swipe all the hats off the tabletop and run for the exit.

"What are you doing with my hats?" Sherry demanded.

"Sherry, there's been a terrible mistake," I said.

"Mistake?" She turned to the others. "She bought up my entire stock just the other day. She didn't tell me *why*."

I tried to say something, but my mouth felt bone dry. *Because I felt sorry for you and wanted you out of the way* probably wouldn't go down well as an excuse.

"Hats!" Elspeth said, her outrage amped up another notch.

"Would you care for some tea?" Jingleini burped out.

Poor Sherry gaped at the robot. "Really? As if being displaced by a Selfy at work wasn't bad enough—you bring one here to mock me?"

Elspeth would not let her own grievance be upstaged. "You plotted to upstage my Tea Treasures booth, and you didn't even have the decency to make genuine tea cozies?"

"I didn't plot anything," I said. "This is all just a big mistake."

"April, how do you mistakenly put together a fraudulent tea cozy booth?" Midge asked, lips pursed in disapproval.

"Jingles and I got our wires crossed."

Jingles was already dismantling the booth—preparing to flee.

Sherry looked wounded. "I told you they were hats. Why

would you do this? I even signed up for a booth here at the bazaar. Are you trying to make me a laughingstock?"

Before I could speak, Pamela chimed in, "What happened to the adorable tree pattern I helped you learn to knit? With the jingle bells and the stars?"

There was nothing to do but confess. I apologized profusely to everyone and promised to make amends in any way they could think of, which didn't seem to unruffle many feathers. The fact that no one had yet bought one of "my" hat-cozies was no consolation to Sherry.

"They haven't bought any at my booth, either," she said.

"Well, at least she's already a regular at the Depression Center," I said to Mildred as I watched Sherry walk away despondently.

Mildred frowned at me. "What are you talking about? Sherry sells hats outside the center, but she's never come in for help."

Outside. I laughed. Apparently I'd bought a whole bag of pity hats for no real reason.

Midge and Mildred exchanged looks and then Midge took my arm. "Come on, April. Let Jingles take down your booth. I'm repurposing *you* to the cleanup crew."

While I was performing my janitorial penance, Claire wandered in, carrying a bag from the candy cane popcorn concession.

I smiled. "Where did you run off to?"

"The Gingerbread House."

The Gingerbread House was a small inn near Peppermint Pond that Jake stayed at whenever he was in Christmastown. "You were there all this time?"

She swallowed a piece of the popcorn. "Golly doodle, this stuff is good." Her eyes widened in amazement at the words that had issued from her lips. "I'm beginning to sound like an elf." She tilted her head. "Check my ears?"

"They're still not pointy. But they do seem red."

"It's cold out there. I've had to do the walk of shame a few times in my life, but never in a place where I needed snowshoes instead of stilettos."

I knew she wasn't being literal, but I couldn't help glancing down at her feet, clad in the fleece-lined ankle booties she'd bought specifically for this trip. She wasn't in the clothes she'd worn to the ballet, so she'd obviously swung by the castle at some point. "How did you know how to get here?"

She laughed. "How do you think? Jake drove me."

"Jake's here?" I looked around.

She shook her head. "No, he dropped me off and then went to find Quince and Pocket."

I squinted at her. "What are they up to?"

"Quince and Pocket were out Snomaneuvering this morning, and they said they ran into some elf from the Farthest Frozen Reaches—a wild elf, Jake said. Whatever that means."

"Elves are a little different across the border."

"Well, this elf—Shaggy, I think his name was?—said he'd been working for the Brightlows, along with some other wild elves."

"Here in Christmastown?"

She nodded. "That's what I wondered. I talked with all the elves at the Brightlow Christmas party and danced with half of them, and I think I would have remembered a wild elf."

Interesting. "Bet you didn't dance with a Selfy, either."

"What are you talking about?"

"Sherry the hatmaker said she'd been replaced by a Selfy at Brightlow Enterprises. But I didn't see any Selfies being used there, did you?"

Her eyes narrowed in thought. "No . . ."

"So where are the wild elves and the Selfies doing their work?"

"I think that's what Jake's trying to find out."

As I wrung out my mop, wondering about this, Claire flopped down on a bench that had been carved out of a tree trunk. She stretched her legs, crossing them at the ankles, and let out a long, contented sigh. "Is it always this heavenly here?"

At the moment I was feeling far from heavenly, but I didn't want to harsh her mellow.

"You're so lucky," she said.

Uh-huh. Obviously, our heads were in different spaces, but it didn't take a mind reader to understand why she was seeing Santaland through candy cane–tinted glasses.

Which, I had to admit, was how I'd wanted her to view my adopted home when she came for this visit. Now, though, the dreaminess in her eyes gave me pause.

"You know, Jake isn't really from Santaland. He lives in—"

"The Farthest Frozen Reaches." She growled in frustration as if I'd brought her thumping back down to unwelcome reality with one sentence. "I *know*."

"It's sort of inhospitable there."

In lieu of replying, she gobbled down a handful of popcorn, munching it fiercely. I'd hesitated to try it myself, but done right it's a magical blend of mint, sweetness, and salt. I was also discovering that it was a lot of trouble to sweep up. The kernels stuck to my broom.

"Jake keeps reminding me about his home," Claire said. "He says I wouldn't like it there."

So they'd already discussed the possibility of her visiting him? I mean, he'd arrived only two days ago.

My surprise must have shown. She swallowed another bit of popcorn. "Don't worry. Jake is just as convinced as you are that he and I are just a holiday fling."

At least one of them was keeping a cool head. Naturally, that would be Jake.

"When I suggested his coming to Oregon with me, you know what he said?"

"You asked him to Cloudberry Bay?"

"Why not? You yourself said the Farthest Frozen Reaches isn't a place for me."

"I know, but—" Curiosity stopped me. "What did he say?"

"He said he'd melt down there." Her eyes narrowed in thought. "Do you think he was speaking literally?"

"I'm not sure."

"I mean, it's not like the Oregon Coast is Florida."

"But what would he do in Cloudberry Bay? Would he be able to apply for a detective's license?"

She crossed her arms. "I just mentioned a visit, not loading up a U-Haul." A smile played at her lips. "Although I think he'd be a natural in the ice cream business, don't you? I could teach him the trade. Mr. Frost's Ice Cream. How does that sound?"

I hesitated to say what I was thinking, but my filter has always been unreliable. "Maybe Jake's just trying to avoid getting deeper into a relationship that he knows won't work out."

"That's what I told him—that he's a coward." She wadded up her paper bag. "A big, good-looking, sexy coward."

"Sometimes you have to be realistic, though."

She shot me a withering look. "Right. I'm sure you were just being practical when you married Santa Claus."

Touché.

She scrunched down on the bench. "Of course, Jake doesn't have a castle. Or any family that he's mentioned to me yet. Maybe he *did* hatch from an iceberg."

Now that she'd mentioned the relationship between Nick

and me, I thought back to our courtship, when he'd been a guest at my inn in Cloudberry Bay. Before I knew who he was, we'd had a whirlwind romance, too. Then, when I finally learned his true identity, I'd been skeptical that a relationship between us would work out. It hadn't taken me long to realize I didn't want to live without him, though.

How did I know Claire and Jake wouldn't reach the same conclusion?

"Well, you've got a couple of days to figure things out," I said.

"A couple of days." Tears sprang to her eyes. "What are a few measly days? And then I'll have to go back to Cloudberry Bay. Which is a nice place, of course, but it's not the same there now, April. I mean, you're not there anymore. I miss you. Most of the time I'm busy with the shop and involved in goings-on around town, but I can't lie. Sometimes I feel so lonely, going to live in an ice house with wild elves, polar bears, and snow monsters all around doesn't sound so bad."

A lump formed in my throat. I dropped my mop and plopped down next to her. "I miss you, too. That's why I wanted you to come up this Christmas."

"And look what happened. Doomed love."

I thought about Jingles's story of Snowbell and Blurf. Surely there was some way Jake and Claire could avoid crashing through the ice.

My commiserating seemed to have a calming effect on her. She crushed the bag in her hands some more, eyed a nearby trash can, and made a perfect three-point shot. "Don't look so woebegone," she told me. "You and Jake are probably right. It's just a holiday fling. I've survived them before, right?"

I nodded, then pushed off the bench to resume mop-up duty.

She laughed. "Here, Cinderella. Let me help. The sooner we can get out of here, the more time we can spend getting ready for this evening."

I tried to remain sanguine as we cleaned up glitter, pine needles, and eggnog sploops. Claire had survived holiday heartaches before.

What neither of us knew was that we would both be fighting for survival in more than the metaphorical sense before the night was out.

Chapter 20

Kringle Lodge was just a couple of miles from Castle Kringle, but the trip along the winding road up Sugarplum Mountain could take a while, depending on the weather conditions. This evening was clear, but I wanted to get to the lodge in time to talk to Amory before the festivities began. I left my sleigh in Nick's capable hands, so he could drive the rest of the castle contingent up to the lodge while I hitched an early ride with Claire and Jake.

"As soon as I get to the lodge, I'm going to corner Amory and ask him what kind of financial shenanigans he's been up to concerning Brightlow Enterprises," I said from my usual position in the back of the snowmobile.

"I thought you were playing in the band," Claire said.

My stomach flipped. With all that had been going on, the performance of the *1812 Overture* kept slipping to the back of my mind. "I'm counting on Butterbean's fireworks to drown out my percussion performance." I scooted forward. "The thing is, I can maybe see Amory crashing a drone-deer. I can't see him as a murderer, though."

"You know him better than I do," Jake said.

"Did you run across any more wild elves today?" I asked Jake.

He shook his head. "Not so far. I told Quince and Pocket to keep an eye out and follow them if they see any."

"Have you ever heard of a place called Snowbell Pond?"

He nodded. "It's close to the border of the Farthest Frozen Reaches."

"I'm wondering if the Brightlows have somewhere out there."

Claire swiveled to look at me. "Why would the Brightlows want to build an alternate site somewhere so inconvenient?"

"To take advantage of wild elf labor?" I leaned forward further, draping myself over the back of their bench seat like a kid from road trips in the old days before car seats. "Juniper mentioned that Blinky brought her some dried buttercups that grow out that way."

Claire gasped. "He brought them to her that night for her chowder. But she said they were too bitter."

Jake looked at her, impressed. "Good clue memory."

She beamed as if he'd just dubbed her Nora to his Nick.

The timberline of the Christmas Tree Forest—the trees that wound across Santaland like an evergreen garland—ended just before we reached Kringle Lodge. The lodge boasted only one tree, its Christmas tree, which stood like a sentinel a hundred yards away from the lodge itself.

I don't know why, but the sudden absence of trees along the patch made the world seem twenty degrees colder. I'd dressed in double layers of wool, and my coat, gloves, and accessories were all down- or fleece-lined, but I still shivered.

Maybe that shiver was a premonition.

The traffic grew thicker as we approached the lodge. Every motorized conveyance available had been mustered to haul people and elves up the mountain for this big event. One sleigh passed us driven by Luther Partridge, the concert band conductor. He was hauling our music stands and boxes of percussion equipment in back and the sousaphone in the passenger seat.

The sprawling old wood-and-stone lodge came into view, its glowing lights radiating warmth. Jake drove around to the parking area in the back of the lodge. Then we walked back around to the front, where people and elves were starting to gather. A deep covered porch stretched all across the front of the lodge house, with lights winding around the railings, windows, and doors. It would afford comfortable viewing of the fireworks, and to accommodate the concert band, Amory had erected a tent in the front yard, complete with portable heaters.

"Greetings, Mrs. Claus!" Butterbean hopped in front of me, looking unusually dapper in a crimson-and-white outfit fashioned to look like a tuxedo up top. His pants only went to his knees, showing off festive green-and-white stockings. His elf booties had been polished until they resembled patent leather, and the toes were elaborately curled.

"So glad you could make it," Butterbean said. "I need to speak to you about the cues."

I frowned. "Cues?"

"The fireworks cues. I spoke to Luther, the band leader, briefly. We decided the fireworks will begin on your cymbal crash."

While Butterbean was speaking, I was looking over his head to see if Amory was out front. I didn't spot him. He must be inside. I could hear the Wonderland Winds doing a rendition of "It's Beginning to Look a Lot Like Christmas," and it was a challenge not to sway along to it. I noticed Claire had slipped away with Jake to go dancing.

"He was looking for you, actually," Butterbean said.

"Amory?"

Butterbean looked confused. "No—Luther. He said you would need to set up the percussion."

Right. But first I wanted to find Amory. I asked Butterbean if he knew where he was.

"Probably inside, listening to the wonderful music. There's a buffet in there, too," he informed me.

"Are you going in?" I asked him. He looked like an elf who'd appreciate a buffet.

"I'm too keyed up. This fireworks show, it's just the beginning."

I'd already started to walk away, but his words brought me up short. "What did you say?"

He bobbed excitedly. "It's just the beginning—Butterbean Pyrotechnics. It's always been my dream to be a full-time creator."

I stared at him, forgetting for a moment what I was supposed to be doing. Blank confusion must have shown on my face, because Butterbean prompted, "You said you were looking for Amory?"

Right. I gave myself a mental shake and hurried my steps toward the lodge house. It was blessedly warm inside. The grand fireplace of the massive main room held a roaring fire, and lodge elves threaded through the crowd holding trays loaded with mugs of hot beverages. People and elf couples were dancing to "I Saw Mommy Kissing Santa Claus." I was trying to see if Claire and Jake were dancing when, out of the corner of my eye, I spied Amory retreating into his study.

I hurried over, cracked the door open, and peered inside. Amory was unlocking a cabinet. I frowned. What was he up to?

As soon as he pulled the cabinet's door open, I stepped into the room. "What are you doing?"

He whirled, eyes wide. Then he pulled out a bottle of

amber liquid. "Whiskey—Toasty Elf, 1932." He held the bottle out for me to inspect the label. "Care to join me? I've been saving it to celebrate."

I couldn't decide what exactly made this a red-letter evening. "What are we drinking to?"

"To success—and my finally becoming a standout Claus." He twisted the top open from the bottle, then reverently poured two glasses as if it were liquid gold. "You have no idea what it's like to be in my position. Never going to don the red suit, never the star of the show."

Understanding dawned. "Tonight's your night." The way Christmas night belonged to Santa Claus. The difference was, Nick didn't seek out the limelight or want to bask in adoration. "Shouldn't you be sharing this moment with Butterbean?" I asked when he handed over a glass.

He chuckled. "Butterbean's too jittery tonight to stand still. Besides, all he cares about are the fireworks, while I . . ."

Amory had already scored a coup by having so many people trek up the mountain to his party. It was the biggest social event of this Christmas season, and Amory was acting as if he were Cinderella, the prince, and the fairy godmother all rolled into one.

We clinked glasses. "To the best fireworks display Santaland's ever seen," he said, and tossed back his whiskey in one gulp.

I took a sip. Usually when drinking spirits I brace myself for the kick, but this liquid was so smooth it barely delivered a gentle nudge. The rich flavor warmed me all the way down. Amory was already pouring himself another, and I was contemplating it myself. I wasn't sure if I should risk it. Cymbals required a clear head.

So did investigating.

"What was your relationship to Virgil?" I asked.

Amory pulled his gaze from the amber liquid in his glass. "That elf who got himself killed?"

"That elf who worked at Brightlow Enterprises, the company you invested a lot of money in."

If he was surprised at my knowing his business, he didn't show it. "And lost a lot of money in," he pointed out.

"Were you angry about that?" I asked.

"I suppose I was. I—" His mouth snapped closed, then he backtracked and asked, "You don't believe *I* killed that elf, do you?"

"Why did you invest in Brightlow Enterprises?"

"Why does anyone ever invest in anything? I imagined making a bundle. I met Dabbs when we were on the Christmas Tree Forest Conservation Commission together, and he convinced me that his company was about to come up with something huge. And when I heard about the drone-deer, it sounded like something that would be useful, especially up here at the lodge. Make it easier to get messages down the mountain, that sort of thing."

I nodded.

"I bought one of the first drone-deer to come out of their factory," he continued. "On its maiden voyage, it nose-dived into a tree. After that I realized Dabbs had sold me a bill of goods. I told him he'd never get another penny from me."

"That sounds reasonable."

"And you sound disappointed." He sniffed. "Are you so desperate to find an alternate suspect for this murder your friend's accused of that you're willing to pin it on your own family? I know we're only related by marriage, but I thought we were friends." He shook his head.

"I just want to know the truth," I said, and added, "and to free Juniper. She didn't do it."

"I should be tending to my guests," he said, putting his bottle away. I'd ruined his moment of quiet celebration. "The ones who *aren't* accusing me of elficide."

He walked out, and after downing the last of my drink, I followed.

The main hall at the lodge was stuffed with revelers now. I squeezed my way through, greeting everyone I knew— which *was* practically everyone. That realization warmed me almost as much as Amory's whiskey had. When I first moved here a year and a half ago, I hadn't imagined that I would ever feel at home in Santaland. Tonight I felt like I belonged.

I looked over at the dance floor and saw Jake and Claire swaying slowly to "Have Yourself a Merry Little Christmas." In contrast to the crowd around them, both had contemplative expressions. What was going through their minds?

I felt a tug on my arm. It was Nick. "Shall we dance?" he asked.

The crowd parted for him to lead me out on the floor. That was one advantage of being with the guy in the red velvet suit. This was probably the closest I'd ever come to being the belle of a ball—a thought that made me smile as he took me into his arms.

"Something wrong?" he asked.

I looked up into his eyes, loving him for being so in tune with me that he could sense when my inner workings were out of whack. "This song is always so sad—I always hear Judy Garland's voice in my head. And then I was looking at Jake and Claire, and feeling sad for them because they're from two different worlds. Love doesn't always work out. We're lucky."

"Yes," he said, pulling me just a touch closer. "I've told myself that every morning I've woken up with you beside me."

His words nearly caused me to dissolve into a puddle, but I looked over and saw Pamela eyeing us from the sidelines.

A Mrs. Claus doesn't burst into tears at a party, she would have told me.

And I couldn't forget that Nick had his own issues he was working through. He might be putting on a jolly show tonight, but I could swear there were more lines around his eyes than there had been this morning.

"Is the reindeer situation still unresolved?"

"Let's just say it's good that we have an alternate plan."

"Butterbean's surplus helicopter?"

He sighed. "Don't mention it to anyone. I'm still hoping we won't have to use it." He lowered his voice. "It's parked in an old sleigh shed outside Christmastown."

I really hoped the reindeer came to their senses before tomorrow night.

The music ended, and while we all clapped appreciatively for the Wonderland Winds, I glanced someone unexpected through the large windows of the lodge.

Holly Silverpick.

What was *she* doing here?

I told Nick, "I need to go out and help get the band ready."

He nodded. "Yes, the fireworks will probably be starting soon."

I slipped away, waving at Claire and Jake, who hadn't broken apart from their slow dance even when the music stopped. Now the band was playing "I'll Be Home for Christmas," and they were locked in the same slow sway.

On the porch, I nearly ploughed into Butterbean. He hopped out of my way. "Nearly time!" he shouted, practically levitating with excitement. "What a night!"

"Have you seen Holly Silverpick?" I asked him.

"I'm so stoked!"

"Never mind." I spotted Holly out on the snow-covered

lawn, heading toward the bandstand. Did she have some plan to sabotage the concert?

I sped toward her. "I need to talk to you."

She rolled her eyes. "No, you need to talk to Luther. He's been asking about you for fifteen minutes. The concert's about to start and you left Bobbin to put out all your percussion."

What? Bobbin was a piccolo player, and he didn't have a key to the percussion instrument box. "How did he manage without the percussion box key?"

"Luckily, I had my doohickey with me," she said.

"What doohickey?"

She dug into her parka pocket and pulled out what looked like a Swiss army knife, although it had the Brightlow Enterprises logo on it. "Dabbs created it last year and Brightlow gave it to all the employees as a favor at our Christmas party. He was so proud—he acted as if he'd created a cure for cancer instead of, you know, something that had already existed for a hundred years."

I opened it and looked at the various files, corkscrews, and even two sizes of skeleton keys. So Holly Silverpick had the capability to pick locks. That freaked me out a little more.

"Why are you here?" I asked.

She blinked. "I'm playing baritone."

"You're in the symphony, not the concert band."

She responded with the patience of a kindergarten teacher talking to a toddler, "Yes, but Luther asked me to sit in because you're short on low brass."

"Oh."

Not here to sabotage us, then. Still, how was I not supposed to be suspicious when she lied all the time?

"You really need to find another Suspect Number One," she said, laughing. "I'm not the elf you're looking for."

I opened my mouth to apologize, but one second I was looking at Holly, the next Luther had stepped between us, his face twisted with impatience. "Where have you been?" he said. "You need to check your setup—Bobbin put everything in place. He's going to double on bass drum tonight. You can handle everything else, right?"

"Right," I said, with a lot more certainty than I felt. I hurried over to the tent area.

Bobbin, a toothpick of an elf—he was as skinny as his chosen instrument—had the furry-tipped bass drum mallet in a two-handed grasp, like he was Babe Ruth at home plate. To be fair, the mallet looked gigantic in his tiny hands. "Is this right?" he asked, his voice almost a squeak.

"You could probably manage it one-handed."

Doubtfully, he unclasped his left hand and gave the bass drum a cautious tap. The sound made him jump back. "That's loud!"

"You get used to it."

Guests were migrating from the lodge hall to the porch in anticipation of the show, and Amory was already walking out to make his speech. I headed over to where my percussion was set up: snare, triangle, timpani, bells, cymbals—everything where it was supposed to be. I had no idea how I would manage all this, even with Bobbin handling the bass drum. *Pick your battles,* I thought, frantically scanning the music that had been placed on the stand.

Luckily, Amory was long-winded. He thanked everyone for coming, singled out special guests, gave an account of how the fireworks spectacular had come about, and—of course—finally delivered a heartfelt tribute to the brains and imagination behind the event: Butterbean.

Butterbean hopped on a chair and waved to the crowd. "So excited!" he said, so wound up at this point that he was unable to do more than incoherently belch enthusiasm.

And then the concert began.

When anyone thinks of the *1812 Overture*, they probably just remember the last several minutes of bombast, which, on top of being played at national celebrations, has been used to sell everything from puffed rice to submarine sandwiches. But before the wow finish there are ten minutes of quieter music, some fiddly bits, and some flirting references to *La Marseillaise*. Then, after a few foreshadowings of the rousing finale, *pow*. I kept up as best I could, doing a martial rat-a-tat on the snare, switching to the triangle, running over to the bells as the music started to swell.

All the while, though, my mind felt strangely disconnected from the music. As I tapped the triangle, I sifted through the clues that were still standing out in my mind like jigsaw pieces that wouldn't slot into place. The broken glass at Virgil's. The lone book he'd been reading. The piece of a letter from Blinky. The clattering of footsteps heard by Juniper's landlord. Wild elves. And the warning that had seemed to set off this series of unfortunate events: *This is only the beginning!!!*

Butterbean had said the same thing. Could *Butterbean* be a killer?

That didn't make sense at all.

Finally, though, it came time to get ready for the big cymbal crashes at the end.

I took up my cymbals and looked out over the audience. Nick was easy to spot on the porch, as was Pamela, with Christopher standing between her and Tiffany. Missing Claire, I frowned until I spotted her and Jack strolling off from the lodge, obviously hoping to view the fireworks away from the crowd.

The band—which sounded pretty good, if I do say so myself—was winding up for the big thunderous moment when the fireworks would begin. I held my cymbals, my eye on

Luther, waiting for my cue, which would also be Butterbean's cue to start the fireworks show.

When Luther's hands gestured my way, I braced myself and crashed the cymbals. That crash was probably the last thing many of the people and elves would hear for a while.

The fireworks were supposed to last five minutes. Instead, a thick column of light streaked into the sky, followed by a brief delay, and then a fireball that hung overhead like a supernova for the briefest of moments before a thundering crack accompanied it. It felt like an Armageddon-worthy bomb exploding.

The surprised cries coming out of people's mouths were swallowed by that deafening clap of sound, and then a percussive blast unlike anything I'd ever felt. The tent pole nearest me collapsed. I dropped my cymbals and dove out of the way of falling canvas, landing on the snowy ground. I sat, dazed and disbelieving, twitching my head to see if I could rattle my ears back to working order. All around, band members had either hit the ground or were likewise scrambling to get out from under the half-collapsed tent. A glance at the audience on the porch showed a similar traumatic reaction. People and elves were either on the porch, or flat against the porch railings and walls, clinging to one another in shock.

After the crash, everything seemed eerily silent except for the ringing in my ears. I'm still not quite sure how much time elapsed that the group stood in shock at what had just happened. It might have been minutes, or just seconds. All I know is that I heard and felt nothing until the ground beneath my feet rumbled. Good heavens, did Butterbean's fireworks foul-up cause an earthquake?

Instinctively, I sought out Nick in the crowd and found him just as his gaze zeroed in on me lying in the snow. He said something to Pamela, who was clinging to a porch rail, and then he ran toward me. I wanted to call out that I was fine, but before I could, a movement caught my eye. Standing next to me, Bobbin thrust his bass drum stick in the direction of the rise toward Sugarplum Mountain's summit. A huge swath of snow had dislodged and was now tumbling in a deadly fury down the mountain, picking up speed and churning up snow as it headed directly toward the lodge. Toward us.

My eardrums were still in shock from an entire fireworks display going off in one *kerpow*, but I had no trouble reading Bobbin's lips, or seeing the terror in his eyes as he yelled, "Avalanche!"

Chapter 21

What followed the realization that disaster was rushing toward us like a thick white river of snow was pure mayhem. The avalanche billowed powdery snow as it raced down—a cloud that looked like it would devour everything in sight. Elves in the band fled the tent, running with saxophones, trumpets, and even a tuba. Sheet music floated in the air, caps flew off heads. Elves were sprinting, sliding, and tumbling toward the lodge. The crowd bottlenecked at the entrance as people frantically tried to reach some shelter from the icy deluge headed our way.

I was still pushing up from the ground when Nick's hand clamped around my arm. He pulled me up and in the next second we were running around to the lodge's closest side entrance, beckoning a swath of the stragglers at the back to follow us. Once I was almost to the door, Nick stopped and directed more people to follow. I hurried inside, looking around for Claire.

Then I remembered seeing Claire outside as the concert began, strolling away from the lodge with Jake. I turned back around but now there was a stream of elves and people swarming in all the doors. I needed to go outside and find

Claire. I headed in the other direction, thinking I could make it out of a back door. I dashed down a hall and was just reaching a door when Lucia appeared, tugging Quasar in behind her as a furious white cloud of snow and ice rushed toward them.

Lucia slammed the door shut and barred it. The three of us were huddled in the hallway when the avalanche hit the lodge. The building trembled, and glass could be heard shattering. At least my hearing was back.

"Weeping walruses!" Lucia exclaimed. "Was Amory trying to kill us all with that fireworks bomb?"

"It was Butterbean." Almost burning a château down wasn't enough for him, evidently. He was going to take an entire mountain out this time. "He's a menace. Before the concert he was all puffed up and telling me that this was just the beginning of his career of pyrotechnical design."

"He's definitely better at selling himself than the follow-through," Lucia said.

No kidding. I was *not* letting Nick ride in a helicopter with that elf.

My brain froze. *Selling himself.*

At the same time, I saw that banner in my mind's eye, red letters against white: *THIS IS JUST THE BEGINNING!!!*

Understanding hit me with the force of—well, an avalanche. How had I missed it? That drone-deer banner hadn't been a warning at all. It was advertising. Advertising for a product that went wrong—just like Butterbean's fireworks venture. And knowing that, I was pretty sure I understood everything. Or almost everything. Only now I couldn't do anything about it. I was stuck at the summit of a mountain. And my best friend was out in the snow. I had to find Claire.

"I've got to go outside." Before Lucia could stop me, I scooted around Quasar, unlatched the door, and yanked it open. And faced a solid rectangle of snow with the imprint of the door on it.

"Whoa," Lucia said from behind me. "Is the lodge buried?"

It couldn't be. "Claire's out there. I saw her and Jake walking toward the Christmas tree just before . . ." My throat closed.

Lucia didn't say anything, but she didn't have to. Her thoughts were plain on her face. She thought Jake and Claire were goners. Of course she did. Any reasonable person who'd seen that churning mass of snow barreling down the mountain at us would think that.

Despair welled inside me. I'd convinced my friend to come up for a holly-jolly vacation in idyllic Christmastown, only to have her follow me around while I investigated an elf murder. And then I introduced her to a guy she would have a doomed holiday affair with. And then maybe die with.

Quasar walked to the door and gestured down with his muzzle. "L-look."

Near the floor, the curled toes of a pair of sharp black elf booties were sticking through the packed snow and ice.

With a gasp, Lucia and I started clawing at the snow. Something burgundy peeked through. Lucia finally was able to get a handhold on the frozen elf's ankles. "Grab hold of my shoulders and help me tug," she commanded.

Quasar and I both leapt to help, grabbing her to create more pulling power. She blew her breath out and in, like an Olympian preparing for a gold medal luge run. "Ready?" she asked. "Pull!"

The three of us yanked with all our might, but the victim must not have been packed in as tightly as we'd feared. He popped right out of the snow door like a champagne cork, sending Lucia, me, and Quasar stumbling backward. I landed on my butt against Quasar, and Lucia fell on top of me.

The elf we'd rescued, Butterbean, landed on top of Lucia, but he sprang back to his feet immediately, sucking in a deep breath. "Thank you!" He shook snow off his good suit like a dog, and came out looking, infuriatingly, less disheveled than the rest of us.

As soon as I could untangle myself from the pile, I was on my feet. Rage flared in me. "You crazy elf, what have you done?"

Eyes bugging, he shook his head. "A mistake was made somewhere."

"Yes—by *you*."

He drummed his fingers together anxiously. "I must not have set the sequence properly."

I was ready to strangle him, but Lucia's hand on my shoulder stopped me—as did another thought. "Did you let anyone else near your equipment today?"

His head shook vehemently. "No—no one but myself and Amory had access to it. I'm sure of that." He drew up to his full height. "I'm very careful!"

"Right. Except when it comes to blowing the tops off mountains." I thought about Claire, who was probably still out there, maybe even more deeply buried in snow than Butterbean had been. How was I ever going to find her? And how much time had I already wasted saving Butterbean?

My frantic feelings must have shown on my face. Lucia grabbed both of my shoulders. "April, let's go find your friend." We all turned to go, even Butterbean, but Lucia rounded on him. "You might want to lie low for a bit," she said. "You're not the most popular elf on this mountain right now."

"It was just a mistake," he said in a forlorn voice.

Lucia, Quasar, and I backtracked through the corridor to the main hall.

It was darker in the room than it had been earlier. The power lines were obviously down, and the windows allowed no moonlight in. Like the back door, they were covered solidly in snow. The top of one had broken, sending a snowbank spilling into the lodge. The high arched doors at the front of the building had not been closed when the avalanche hit, so a wave of snow had also poured in there, and with it a jumble of elves who'd been on the porch. A crew including Christopher, Luther, and others were tugging elves out of the snow, while others were scooping snow into pails and hurrying it away. Where they were disposing of it, I didn't know. Was there any egress that wasn't a wall of snow now?

Luckily, the large hearth fire was still roaring. Elves and people milled around seeking out friends, some weeping with relief to have found one another. Witnessing one of those reunions, I felt my chest constrict with a mixture of longing and uncertainty. Mayor Firlog had set himself up as traffic director and information center. He stood on a chair, calling for calm and announcing that there was a triage room for anyone who needed help. Lodge elves circulated, providing hot beverages to the shell-shocked assembly.

Lucia examined the scene and shook her head. "We're not getting out this way. Come on."

She headed toward the stairs. On the way, I spotted Amory standing by himself, his face ashen.

"You haven't seen Claire, have you?" I asked him. I wasn't expecting a positive response, but he didn't respond at all. There was something zombielike in his blank expression. "Amory?"

Lucia put a hand on her cousin's shoulder. "It'll be okay, Amory."

What was she talking about? It wasn't okay—Claire was missing. Then I remembered that Amory's parents had died in an avalanche. No telling what memories were rattling around in his head.

He looked up. "Butterbean swore it was safe."

"It probably would have been, if Butterbean hadn't set off an entire display of fireworks in one explosion," I said.

Pamela and Midge were standing by the buffet, which was still laden with food as it had been before the explosion. Midge was marking off elves and people against her guest list. But I imagine there were probably a lot of people at the top of the mountain who weren't on the official guest list.

"Go talk to Midge, Amory," Lucia said, giving him a nudge in that direction. "Get something to eat."

At the staircase, we ran into Nick, his brow furrowed. "We got everyone in, I think." He nodded toward the door. "Except the elves still being pulled out of the porch pileup."

"What about Claire and Jake?"

His expression drooped. "Claire and Jake?"

My hopes plummeted with a *thunk*. He'd forgotten about them—and probably no one else here had thought to look for them, either.

"I'm going to find her," I said.

"I'll go with you."

We all hurried upstairs—I couldn't understand why until Lucia opened the door to the second-floor deck that was built over the ground-floor porch. There was just a foot of snow up here. We tromped out onto the snow to investigate what seemed like a world that looked as foreign as the lunar surface. The Northern lights cast a bright, multicolored gleam on the brilliant snow, making it seem brighter out here than it had been in the lodge's hall.

The lodge seemed to have served as a bit of a break for some of the snow's slide, but snow now covered what had been the lawn—the tent was wiped out completely, which gave me a shudder. The back of the lodge had also been buried—the roof of a small outbuilding was all that peeked up through the powder. No evidence anymore of all the motor-ized sleighs and snowmobiles that had got us up here.

From the highest point I could find, I pivoted, peering out as far as I could. And then, finally, I spotted something in the distance—a flash of peacock blue. "That's her!"

It was a strange thing for us all to go trooping off the sec-ond-story roof as if we were on terra firma, but the snow was pretty densely packed. It was going to take Amory forever to get the lodge de-iced.

I practically fell the whole way down the incline of snow and slogged and stumbled toward Claire. She was only about a hundred yards away, but running through that snow was like moving through icy quicksand. Every footfall landed me in snow up to my knees. I needed snowshoes, I thought in frus-tration. And why wasn't Claire heading back to the lodge? I could see her moving, and yelled out for her.

Lucia let out an oath, and a moment later she was lifting me by my armpits onto Quasar's back. He had sunk into the snow, too, so she didn't have to lift too far. "Go," she di-rected. "We'll catch up with you."

I'd never ridden a reindeer bareback. I hadn't even ridden a horse bareback since camp when I was ten. I looped my arms around Quasar's neck. "Okay," I told him.

Never the strongest or more graceful of reindeer, Quasar nevertheless pushed and leapt his way up out of the snow. In a jolting lurch, we were airborne, his nose flashing red as we sailed over the snow. We were only off the ground a few mo-ments, though, before we came crashing down again. I fell off immediately and went rolling off into the snow.

"Thank goodness!" Claire said.

Or maybe I said that as I fell into her arms. We clasped each other. "I was so afraid," I said. And then I saw that Claire was still afraid. Her eyes were wild with panic.

"Help me, April. Jake's under here somewhere."

I looked at the snow and noticed the little piles everywhere from where she'd dug with her gloved hands.

"When the avalanche came, we knew we'd never make it back to the lodge in time," she said. "He told me to take cover in the Christmas tree. He practically tossed me up into it. But that's the last thing I remember. He must have been swept away, and . . ." She choked. ". . . buried."

Lucia and Nick, who were both in thick boots, finally arrived.

"We'll find him, Claire," Nick promised.

"Yes, but—"

I could tell what Claire was thinking as she looked across all that snow. How soon could we find him? And how could he possibly still be alive?

Foolishly, I kept thinking of Jingles telling me about Snowbell and Blurf. Doomed love.

She swallowed. "He saved me, but risked his own life. And I was the one who wanted to walk out to the Christmas tree so we could be alone. So stupid!"

Lucia had broken off a branch from the tree and stripped it down to one long, sharp stick. "Stop yakking at April and start poking this into the snow to see if you can find him." She thrust her stick at Claire.

There was nothing like being bullied by Lucia to knock you back to your senses. Claire took the stick numbly and did as directed. The rest of us started working on making our own sticks, while Quasar pawed the ground.

"I-I think I smell something," he said.

We all gathered around him, poking frantically into the ground.

"I see a black outline here," Lucia said.

We all dropped to our hands and knees and started digging. Soon, we could make out Jake's form.

"We need an ambulance," Claire said, her voice edged with hysteria.

The rest of us exchanged grim looks. There would be no ambulance coming up this mountain any time soon. All the vehicles were buried, and the road was blocked by a bank of snow.

"There are some injured elves and people inside," Nick said. "Midge and I designated a room to triage the people who need help."

A triage room was well and good, but I didn't remember seeing Doc Honeytree among the guests tonight. Someone would need to get him up here.

Of course, this was assuming that Jake was still alive.

As soon as we'd dug enough around Jake to get hold of his arms, Nick reached down and began to tug him out of the trench we'd created around him. It isn't easy to dislodge someone from snow, especially when they're as stiff and lifeless as Jake was.

Claire wept silently as she helped Nick extract him. The detective was frozen as solid as a log. His face had turned an alarming shade of blue, and his limbs were as stiff as icicles.

"Jake, you can't die," Claire cried.

Lucia stood, whacking her palms against her jacket to knock off the excess snow. "He'll be fine."

"*Fine?*" Claire rounded on her. "Look at him. He's a block of ice—a man cube."

Nick lowered his ear to Jake's chest. "Heart's still beating."

"It would take more than a few minutes in the snow to kill Jake Frost," Lucia said. "He's from the Farthest Frozen Reaches. Plus, he's . . . well, whatever he is."

Claire leaned down where Nick had lain Jake out on the

ground. "Jake," she said, her mittens touching his blue face. Nick took off the large red parka he'd been wearing and laid it over Jake. She tucked it around him.

"Even if he is a Frost," Lucia said, "he'll probably thaw out faster back at the lodge."

With an invaluable assist from Quasar, we carried Jake back to the lodge. With its bottom floor buried in snow, Amory's house now resembled a ranch house with an especially large roof. We retraced our tracks up to the second-story porch. The triage room was also on the second floor, and we took him there and set him by the fire to defrost. Claire stayed by his side.

Outside the room, Nick and Lucia conferred on what to do next. "Someone needs to get the doctor, and bring more help to get all these people back down the mountain. We don't know how long it will take to dig vehicles out."

"Or if they'll work once we do," Lucia agreed.

"I could ski down," he said.

She shook her head. "You've got to stay here, Nick. I know this is Amory's house, but he's still shell-shocked from the explosion and the avalanche. People are looking to you to direct them and keep them calm. Besides, even if we can find our way clear to the road down Sugarplum Mountain, we don't know what shape it's going to be in. There might have been additional slides farther down."

"What we need is a summoning horn," Nick said.

Summoning horns were used in emergencies to call the reindeer herds to Santa's aid. On Christmas Eve the horn was blown ceremonially before the chosen nine reindeer were hitched to the sleigh. But, even if the horn was sounded, would the reindeer be inclined to answer the summons? Given how things stood with the strike, that was a big question mark.

"Does Amory have a horn here?" I asked.

"He should," Lucia said, "although I doubt he's ever used it."

Nick's expression grew more troubled. "Amory's not in a good state to think about things like that right now."

"I know where it is," said a voice behind us.

It was Butterbean. He was no longer buzzing with excitement, although he did seem eager to help. Maybe he wanted to redeem himself. In my book, that would require more than locating a trumpet.

"I saw it in the attic studio Amory set up for me," he said. "I can take you there, Santa."

"Thank you, Butterbean," he said.

"While you're summoning the reindeer with the horn," Lucia said, "I'll go down to Christmastown to see if I can rustle up more help, and maybe some supplies."

"How will you go down the mountain?" Nick asked.

She turned to Quasar, who was standing in the hallway next to me. "Quasar can make it down, can't you?"

The question tapped his Rudolph instinct. He lifted his head, his nose fizzling red with eagerness. "Y-you bet."

There really wasn't much choice. Quasar was the only reindeer on the mountain at the moment.

Nick reluctantly agreed to the plan, and Lucia and Quasar wasted no time heading out. Nick hugged me. "I was so worried about you. You must have been freezing out there."

For once, I hadn't even noticed the cold. And I knew that I'd probably be colder before this night was over. I wrapped my arms around him, feeling awful for what I was about to do. In our short marriage, I'd never lied to Nick. I wasn't lying now, exactly, but I wasn't telling him what I had in my mind. As Lucia said, Nick had a role to perform. Usually my place was beside him, but right now I had a more pressing concern than performing Mrs. Claus duties. I had an injustice to right.

"I just remembered something I need to tell Lucia," I said, giving his lips a quick kiss. He needed to get going, too. "I'll be back."

Nick returned the pressure, his dark eyes twinkling at me before I broke off and hurried back out the second-floor balcony to find Lucia.

Chapter 22

I followed the reindeer tracks, catching up with them as Lucia was about to hoist herself onto Quasar's back. "Wait!"

She turned to me. "Something wrong?"

"I have a favor to ask." I heaved in a breath, winded from running through thigh-high snow. "Let me go in your place."

She let out a husky laugh. "No. Not happening."

"Please? I have to talk to Crinkles," I said. "It's important. I think I know who killed Virgil."

"Who?"

I'd gotten in trouble before by blurting out my suspicions too precipitously. "I need to tell Crinkles before I broadcast it," I said. "I'm going to go through proper channels."

Lucia's brow furrowed. "You've never ridden a reindeer."

"I just did tonight."

"Right, and you fell off as soon as he touched ground."

That was unfortunately true, and I'd probably have the bruises tomorrow to remember that fall by. "The important thing is to get help, not how clean my landing is."

"I-I can try to be more careful," Quasar said.

His implicit agreement to the plan had more influence on Lucia than my arguments. She wavered. "If you break your neck, Nick wouldn't like that."

"Neither would I," I assured her.

She bit her lip. "You didn't tell Nick about this, did you?"

"You were right—he needs to tend to all the people stranded up here. He can't be worried about me."

That answer seemed to sway her a little more. But not quite enough. I decided to sweeten the pot. "I'll owe you one, Lucia. Anything you need me to do . . ."

She crossed her arms. "I need help refereeing reindeer games."

Oh, God. Really? I couldn't imagine dragging myself out of bed at dawn to stand in a snow-covered field with a stopwatch. But if it would get me down to Christmastown tonight . . .

"Okay," I said.

Lucia eyed me to see how serious I was. Apparently the dread in my face convinced her. "Let me give you a leg up."

As she helped me onto Quasar's back, she rattled off a list of instructions—when to lean forward, when to lean back, how to squeeze my knees to try to stay in place, how I should keep my head down except for the moments when I needed to straighten or even lean back . . .

I nodded through this litany, absorbing about ten percent of it. I had been all action minutes before, but now that I was on Quasar's slightly sway back, and remembering anew the momentary heart-in-mouth feeling I'd experienced just an hour earlier on the short hop to reach Claire, action gave way to panic.

"He'll need to stay above the treetops," Lucia was saying, "so if you're afraid of heights, don't look down."

I wondered if I could just close my eyes all the way down the mountain, but I didn't ask her that.

"And Nick will be blowing the summoning horn soon, so don't let that throw you, Quasar. You *don't* want to answer the summons."

Quasar lowered his head in acknowledgment. Lucia turned back to me and explained, "That horn is a rallying cry for reindeer. Quasar will probably have a hard time resisting it—you might need to urge him on."

"Okay."

"Ready?" she asked.

"I guess so."

"Take-offs can be rough. It might take Quasar a few bounds to get going."

"I-I'll do my best, April," Quasar promised.

"Don't worry about me," I said.

With that, Lucia gave him an affectionate pat. "On, Quasar!" she called.

The words were like a pistol at a racetrack starting gate. The "few bounds" Lucia had warned me about turned out to be bone-jarring lurches that threatened to unseat me before we'd traveled ten feet. What had Lucia said? *Squeeze the knees.* I squeezed, but I belatedly wished I'd asked her to lash me to Quasar's back with a rope or something. Quasar let out a frustrated snuffle. For a moment I worried we would simply not make it off the ground, but just as soon as that fear crossed my mind, the bucking stopped, and with a sickening plummet in my stomach, we were airborne. Reflexively, I let out a whoop and leaned forward. I wished he had a mane to hold onto. I had to make do with trying to brace my hands on his neck.

As Quasar gained height, a fanfare sounded behind me, as if from a hunting horn. I turned to see Nick atop Kringle Lodge's roof, holding the curved brass horn toward the moon. Could he see me? He must be able to. But of course he just assumed I was Lucia.

Beneath me, Quasar shifted, almost as if he were throwing on the brakes. His withers twitched and he snorted peevishly. I could see why. The horn resonated right through me, I could just imagine what it did to a reindeer.

Our altitude started to dip, and I remembered Lucia's instruction to keep Quasar going forward. "On, Quasar!" I shouted, and to my shock, he stopped mashing on the brakes—or whatever reindeer had. Soon we were soaring above the trees, and all thought of closing my eyes left me.

I always thought the view from the old keep's tower at Castle Kringle afforded the best views in Santaland, but that was nothing compared to the view from Quasar's back. I could see so much—the lights of Castle Kringle directly below us, and then beyond that, the lights of Christmastown, and farther east, Tinkertown. After we passed over the castle, most of the mountain below us was dark, except for the decorated Christmas trees standing before the various châteaus of Kringle Heights. Forgetting Lucia's admonishments not to look down, I tried to pick out the individual houses. Decorations made it easy to spot various homes, especially Mildred's place with the inflatables Olive had secured to the roof.

Soon after we crossed over Mildred's, Quasar called back to me. "Reindeer ahead!"

I looked up. Sure enough, a reindeer was headed straight at us. I guessed there was no air traffic control for reindeer.

"You there!" the approaching reindeer shouted at Quasar. "Where was the explosion?"

"By the lodge," I answered. "There was an avalanche."

As he passed, the reindeer—the same Comet who'd spoken at the all-herd meeting a few nights ago—shook his collar and shouted, "LODGE!"

It was then I noticed that he was followed by a whole battalion of reindeer flying in formation up the mountain—they were answering the summons! My throat constricted. Not out of fear, but because I finally understood. It wasn't just Quasar who had that heroic spirit. The reindeer were setting their grievances aside to help out.

Quasar veered down to give them plenty of room. "L-look," he called back to me.

Below us, a ribbon of lights showed a trail of sleighs and sleds drawn by reindeer starting up the mountain. Sitting shotgun on one of them was old Doc Honeytree, his medical bag in his lap. At the back of the procession, snowmen on those terrible Snomaneuvers pulled wagons of what looked like supplies from Christmastown Hardware. Quasar and I had been sent down to get help, but all of Santaland was already pulling together to rescue the elves and people at the top of the mountain.

This was *not* a good time to have tears in my eyes. At this altitude, temperature, and speed, having one's eyelashes freeze together was a real possibility. And Quasar and I were fast approaching Christmastown.

"Where to?" he called up to me.

We didn't need to find Doc Honeytree, at least. "The constabulary," I said.

As we closed in on our destination, I went clammy with fear. We were going too fast—didn't Quasar realize that? It almost felt like we were dive-bombing the constabulary.

I braced myself, but I wasn't sure how well that would work. Just when I thought Quasar was going to face-plant us into the street, he pulled up again, and then rose a little, slowing our speed as he then banked in a circle. He dropped a little lower, and when his hooves finally achieved touchdown, we actually made an okay landing. That is, my fall off his back was no more traumatic this time than it had been earlier by the lodge's Christmas tree. The snow wasn't as thick here, though, so I hit harder ground and felt the crunch in my bones to prove it. Gingerly I stood up, hoping nothing had broken. I took a few experimental but successful steps.

The constabulary door was yanked open before I reached it. Juniper gaped at me. "What the bejeebers is going on?"

"The fireworks all exploded at once."

"We saw it," Smudge said. "We wanted to see Butter-bean's fireworks, so the constable and Ollie let us up on the roof," Smudge said. "But then we saw a light flash and heard a thunderclap."

Juniper nodded. "And the summoning horn!"

"Crinkles and Ollie are on their way up the mountain to see what went wrong."

I must have missed them. Shoot. Now I couldn't tell Crinkles what I'd pieced together about the drone-deer crash, and my theory about who exactly had killed Virgil.

"I'm sorry you came all this way for nothing," Juniper said.

"Not for nothing. I wanted to see Dabbs Brightlow anyway."

She frowned. "Dabbs? Why?"

"Because I think he was responsible for the drone-deer crash . . . and maybe more."

Her eyes went wide. "Virgil's murder? Dabbs had an alibi."

Yes, he did. But with only Velvet Sprucebud and Cookie, the Brightlow Enterprises security guard, to back him up, how reliable was that alibi? "Another elf said she was there that night, too, but she didn't mention seeing him. I'm not sure I can prove he murdered Virgil, but I can at least get him to fess up to crashing the drone-deer so that it's not muddying the murder investigation."

"You're going to go out there tonight?" she asked, alarmed.

"I could see Brightlow's lights on when Quasar and I were flying in. I'm betting there's someone there."

"We'd better go with you," Smudge said.

"No, you'd better not. I don't want to be accused of springing prisoners when the constable's back was turned. But I'll text you when I get there and when I leave."

"You'll be careful, won't you?" Juniper asked.

"Of course."

"A–and I'll be with her," Quasar added.

We left Juniper and Smudge rattling around the constabulary, unguarded prisoners on their own, and headed over to Brightlow. I could tell Quasar was tiring, and he was probably hungry. We covered the distance to the Brightlow building in several bounds instead of one sustained flight. I managed to hold on until the final landing, and this time I looped my arms around Quasar's neck so that I rotated off his back more than simply falling.

I texted Juniper that I'd arrived. Then I turned to Quasar. "Wait out here," I told him, probably unnecessarily. It wasn't as if Cookie the guard was going to let a reindeer wander through Brightlow Enterprises at night. For that matter, I wasn't sure *I* was going to be allowed in. Quasar immediately wandered off toward nearby trees, pawing the snow to see if there was food underneath.

The strange thing was that when I opened the door to the building, no one was on duty. The lights were on, but no one appeared to be working. Surely there would be one or two industrious elves toiling away on last-minute drone-deer orders before Christmas? I decided to check the executive offices. Only after I'd shut the elevator door and it began its ascent did I question the wisdom of what I was doing. *Maybe I should leave and come back with Crinkles.*

I'd just about decided to turn back when the elevator stopped. On the other side of the cage door stood Velvet, looking as tense as I felt. Recognizing me, she let out a deep breath. "So it *is* you."

"You were expecting me?"

"I saw you on the security camera."

"The guard wasn't at his post downstairs," I said. "Where is everybody?"

"Cookie wanted to know what all the ruckus was up on the mountain. He left to find out."

"I could have saved him a trip," I said. "I just came from Kringle Lodge. There was an avalanche."

Her lips twisted. "I bet you could use a drink, then," she said, opening the cage door. "I know *I* could use one. And some company, too. Being in this old place by myself was starting to give me the willies."

I could see how it would. At night, the place was eerily silent, and had an echo. She turned and tapped down the hallway in her high-heeled booties, just assuming I would follow her.

Which I did, of course. I scooted to catch up with her. I was relieved that Dabbs wasn't here, honestly. I might be able to get more information out of Velvet.

She ushered me into the office I'd visited before, Dabbs's office, and went straight to a cabinet containing bottles and glasses.

"I came here to talk to Dabbs."

"He's out at the moment." She opened the cabinet door and brought out a fat bottle of brandy, holding it up happily for my inspection. "Fortunately, his liquor cabinet isn't kept locked."

"It wouldn't matter if it was, would it?" I asked.

She blinked at me, and then her eyes narrowed. "Excuse me?"

"You all have those little Swiss army things that were given out as party favors last year. Dabbs's big contribution to the company."

Her jaw set as she poured two snifters a quarter full. "I think you have the wrong impression. Dabbs is *very* important to this company. He is the future of Brightlow Enterprises."

I'd never met anyone with such a tendency to launch into

PR-speak. She must have been born for this job. I looked around the room. "Is Dabbs at your other work site?"

Her eyes narrowed. "Pardon?"

She turned her back to me and busied herself putting the bottle away, but she wasn't fooling me. "There's another Brightlow Enterprises work site, isn't there? You had to know it would be discovered eventually."

"Oh, you mean our research-and-development lab." She crossed toward me with my glass. "We've kept it under wraps so far. This place is rather old, you know. Outdated. Between you and me, we're thinking of transitioning it to being our retail-only site."

Interesting. Maybe that alternate site was where all the workers were tonight. "Is that where Blinky has been hiding out, the alternate site?"

She handed me my snifter and raised hers. "Cheers."

Avoiding the question.

I doubted the brandy would be as good as the whiskey Amory had offered me. Still, I knocked it back gratefully enough, letting the fire of it thaw my frozen bones.

Velvet leaned back against the desk. "What did you want to talk to Dabbs about?"

"I know that Brightlow Enterprises was responsible for the drone-deer crash at the ice sculpture contest."

Her lips turned up in an indulgent smile. "And how do you know that?"

I told her my theory about the banner. "You were advertising something." That would have been her department, after all. "But your PR attempt went haywire that morning— as you should have expected it to. The drone-deer crash was pretty on-brand for drone-deer, from what I've heard."

"That's not true. It's an excellent product. Or *was*, I should say. Your husband came here to talk to us, and now we're going to have to rebrand the drone-deer. It's so unfair. The reindeer in this country have gone nuts. Why we should give in to their blackmail and whining is beyond me."

"Nice try to pivot the conversation from your faulty product. Amory Claus described his drone-deer failing just like the one that hit the Blitzen statue."

"You can't believe what *he* says. Amory's just disgruntled."

"Sounds like he had reason to be. He lost a lot of money investing in your company."

"He wouldn't have lost anything if he'd just stuck it out for a few more months. He's been very short-sighted."

"You were selling a faulty product, and sometime in the past weeks you started hemorrhaging employees. Did you think word of that wouldn't get out?"

"But that's the whole point of—" Her mouth snapped closed.

"The whole point of what?" I asked.

She shook her head. "Never mind." She held up the bottle. "Have another?"

I held up my hand, palm out. "I'd better not." I worried about getting back up that mountain again. It was hard enough staying on a reindeer's back when I was sober, and this brandy was strong. Very strong. I already felt a little fuzzy.

I was glad to see Velvet pour herself another one. Drink loosened the tongue, and, absent Dabbs, I was hoping she could tell me some of what I was hoping to learn about what had been going on around here. She crossed back to the desk and leaned against it again. I had a feeling she didn't want to sit down because she enjoyed being in a position to look down at me. I was okay with that, too, as long as I got the information I wanted.

"Is the alternate site where you've had the elves from the Farthest Frozen Reaches working?"

Her eyes widened. "Who told you *that*?"

"It's true, isn't it?"

She shrugged. "We've let most of them go. We decided it might be best to find some outsiders to do the construction work on the project. You know how Christmastown elves are."

"How?"

Her lips turned down. "Gossipy." Her brow raised. "Just like the people in Kringle Heights. You've evidently been picking up on all sorts of worthless tittle-tattle."

"I'm not sure how worthless it is, given that it all seems to be accurate."

She sniffed derisively. "You have no idea what's going on, Mrs. Claus. You really don't. Brightlow Enterprises is on the cutting edge of Arctic innovation. We're going to bring—"

"—Santaland into the twenty-first century," I finished for her. She was like a sloganeering windup doll. My tongue felt heavy. I needed to get out of there, but my limbs were leaden. "Was that the reason this company wouldn't simply fess up to having their advertising drone-deer crash?" I asked. Talking was easier than moving. "You were afraid the crash would ruin your reputation as being cutting-edge inventors. You were willing to let Santalanders remain in conflict, thinking one of them had arranged the crash to send a message, because you were too cowardly to admit that it was just a mistake of your own faulty drone."

Her eyes flashed. "The company never lied."

"You never told the truth, either. Just like you never told the truth about where Blinky was. Why couldn't you simply say he was at the research-and-development site?"

"You don't understand."

"No, and I don't understand why you set up my friend for Virgil's murder, either."

Velvet put her glass down. "That's ridiculous. We never did any such thing. How could we?"

She was used to using the royal "we" when talking about

Brightlow Enterprises, but this time I could tell she was simply referring to herself and Dabbs. And I assumed that was appropriate, because the two of them were in this together up to their elf ears. "Dabbs killed Virgil—I don't know why," I said. "But I'm assuming it was he who called Juniper at the library, breathless. Maybe all the messages Juniper and I were leaving for Virgil that day drew his attention to her. But that evening after Virgil went home, Dabbs followed him home and when Virgil let him in and even prepared an eggnog for his unexpected company, Dabbs bludgeoned him."

She crossed her arms. "You're not making any sense. The murder weapon was Juniper's."

"Juniper's landlord said he heard footsteps clattering on the stairs that night." I looked down at her high heels. "Probably like the sounds your heels would make."

Her lips twisted. "Plenty of elves wear high heels—Juniper might have been wearing them."

"Not that night. I saw her footprints in the snow by Virgil's house. I didn't know at first whether they belonged to a male or a female elf. *You* stole that fireplace poker from Juniper. She'd been a thorn in your side for a few days with her questions about Blinky, and when Dabbs saw that Juniper and Blinky had some kind of history, the two of you decided you could get her out of the way by implicating her in your crime. So you stole her poker, and for good measure you planted a scrap of a note from Blinky—written to Dabbs, probably—that, in the context of being discovered in Juniper's apartment, made her sound like an unhinged stalker."

"Now how would I have known to steal a fireplace poker from a librarian's apartment?"

I frowned. I didn't know. My brain felt like a wet sponge.

She shook her head almost pityingly, and picked up the Christmastown Chamber of Commerce Good Citizenship award—the Golden Icicle. "Do you know what this is?"

I blinked, straining to focus. "Yes . . ."

"Do you think they give this out to murderers?"

Really? She was going to use that stupid award as evidence that she and Dabbs couldn't have done what I'd just accused them of?

Evidently so, because she hugged it, and then took a few steps toward the bookcase behind me, as if to protect it from my unappreciative gaze. Or maybe she was getting it out of the way in advance of Dabbs's return, so they could have another desktop tryst. If I had my druthers, the next time they met face-to-face they would be behind bars. The challenge now was figuring out how to summon Constable Crinkles. The problem was, my brain felt so sluggish. *The brandy.* It was either very strong or very spiked with something.

As things turned out, I didn't need to worry about summoning Crinkles. And I was completely wrong about Velvet's intentions regarding the award. With ninja-like agility, she pivoted and bashed the Golden Icicle Award against the back of my skull. The blow knocked me out of my chair, and turned the world around me to black.

Chapter 23

"Mrs. Claus?"

At the sound of my name, I geared up to squint one eye open defensively, fearing a piercing light that might make matters worse in that painful land beneath my skull, yet needing to know where I was. Cold penetrated down to my marrow, and I seemed to be lying on a carpeted floor.

When I looked up, would Velvet be swinging that award at me again to finish me off? A tiny corner of my brain wondered if I *had* been finished off and would open my eyes to the great hereafter—though I sincerely hoped the afterlife didn't involve splitting headaches.

What I wasn't prepared for was having a completely new face peering down at me. The elf looming over me had thick black hair cut short on the sides, large ears, and wore round wire-framed glasses that magnified his already big brown eyes. In his white lab coat he looked like a cross between Beaker the Muppet and Barton Fink.

Even as my brain clawed back to consciousness, the elf's face recalled a recent cover of *Santaland Today* magazine. "Blinky Brightlow, I presume?"

He looked surprised and a little relieved. "Juniper told me you were a friend of hers," he said.

Juniper. I tried to sit up, wondering how long I'd been out. Evidently long enough for the long-lost Blinky to finally make a reappearance in Christmastown.

Or had he? As I took in my surroundings, the first thing I noticed was that I was *not* in Dabbs's office. In fact, I wondered if I was at Brightlow Enterprises at all. This place didn't seem like the old Christmastown pottery building. The walls were sheetrock, not brick and plaster, and painted flat white. One wall was papered with black-and-white pictures that had been printed up on paper and pinned to it. The industrial-grade carpet still emitted a chemical smell reminiscent of new tires. The room around me was bare, like an office that hadn't been moved into. Two plastic chairs provided the only furnishing. Blinky perched on the edge of one.

I shut my eyes to give them a rest, and to see if it would help me process what on earth could be going on. Nope—didn't help. I struggled to sit up, trying to ignore the chorus line of elf cloggers stomping and jangling in my head. I focused on Blinky. "Do you have any idea how worried about you Juniper's been?"

He pushed his glasses up the bridge of his beaky nose. "I texted her."

"I saw that text." I shook my head. "You could have elaborated just a little bit. Explained where you were, for instance."

He blinked at me in confusion. "I was here. As you know, we're not supposed to talk about this place."

I swiveled to see where "this place" was, but there were no windows to clue me in. The sparseness of the decor gave no hints of whether we were in Christmastown, or Tinkertown, or an office park in the suburbs of any North American city. All the same, I could make an educated guess.

"Is this near Snowbell Pond?"

He drew back. "Dabbs said we weren't supposed to tell."

"I pieced a few things together on my own. You gave Juniper those buttercups, remember?"

"You guessed from that?"

"That and a few other things," I said distractedly. Now that I was able to focus, I could see that Juniper was in some of the pictures on that wall. Blinky must have taken them at her apartment. There were repetitive shots of her doing mundane things—feeding Dave, sweeping, dusting her mantel . . . They were lined up according to activity, as if Blinky were documenting the process of how her body moved doing specific actions, like those nineteenth-century Eadweard Muybridge photographs documenting a horse's movement as it galloped.

Why had Velvet brought me here if it was supposed to be a secret? That question was something I needed to reckon with. Right now, though, I was still curious about what Blinky had been up to. "Were you really just going to dump Juniper?" I asked, angry for my friend, who'd been so worried about him. "During Christmas week?"

"I didn't dump her." Red blotched his cheeks. "It hasn't been a good time for pursuing a relationship. I've been very busy."

"So busy that you were going to let her rot in jail?"

"*Jail?*" Behind the glasses, his eyes bulged. "Is Juniper in jail?"

I remembered Holly telling me that Blinky lived in his own world. Dabbs apparently hadn't let much outside information penetrate that world. "She was taken there on suspicion of murdering Virgil. She was set up."

Blinky bit his lip. He looked like he was trying to piece a few things together himself, and not having much luck. "I heard about Virgil, but Dabbs never told me Juniper had been arrested."

"So you've been in contact with Dabbs?"

His mouth opened in surprise at the question. "Of course.

He's always checking in. I've been working very hard, you understand. Even when I met up with Juniper at the library that first evening, I was supposed to be working. But one thing led to another, and—"

"Working at what?" I asked.

"Motion studies of household tasks. I'm a bachelor, so it was good to be able to observe someone in her home. Juniper displays admirable economy of movement."

I wondered for a moment if he was pulling my leg. But no, he was serious, and he had the photos to prove it. "And this admiration for her economy of movement led to a one-night stand."

He frowned. "Is that what Juniper called it?"

"No, that's just what anyone would assume after you cut out on her after she made you snailfish chowder, then stood her up for your next date, and then didn't even show up to the ice sculpture contest after mentioning you would."

He pushed his glasses up his nose. "I told you—I've been busy."

"Please, it's Christmas week! All of Santaland is busy. You can't start a relationship and then just flit off to—" What *was* this place?

His face tensed. "I've really messed things up, haven't I? I just assumed—and still hope—that we'll have more time after the project is launched." He cleared his throat. "Of course, if she's in jail for Virgil's murder . . ."

"She didn't murder Virgil."

He sat up straighter and nodded. "She doesn't strike me as the murdering type."

I was wondering how good he was at recognizing that type—or how good any of us were. "Where is your brother?"

"He went off to talk to Velvet after they brought you in, injured. They said they found you passed out in Christmastown. Lucky for you."

I rubbed my head, unable to agree. I feared this was going to prove to be the unluckiest day of my life. And Dabbs and Velvet had brought me. Had Dabbs been in Christmastown— or even in the Brightlow Enterprises building? I shouldn't have trusted Velvet.

"When did I arrive?"

His face scrunched in thought. "About an hour ago? They hauled you up here and told me to keep an eye on you. Then they went off to talk." His thin lips turned up in a half smile. "Those two steal off to 'talk' a lot."

"In this instance, they're probably really talking. Feverishly."

So after she clunked me on the head, Velvet had seen fit to find Dabbs and drag me out here. Why? I was afraid of the answer. I knew too much, and I'd been all alone when I spouted off my theory about Virgil's death to Velvet. Meanwhile, half of Christmastown was trapped at the top of Sugarplum Mountain. My whereabouts weren't of paramount importance to anyone at the moment. Except . . .

I patted my pockets. Darn. My phone was gone. There was no way I could text Juniper or anyone else.

"Is something wrong?" Blinky asked.

I almost laughed. For a genius, he was slow on the uptake. "The reason I passed out was that my skull had a close encounter with the Golden Icicle award Velvet was holding in her hand." I pulled the knit cap off my head.

He almost jumped back. That must have been some wound. "Are you saying that Velvet hit you? Why would she do such a thing?"

"Because I guessed who killed Virgil."

He frowned. "You think *Velvet* killed Virgil?"

"It wasn't her alone," I said. "She and Dabbs did it."

He shook his head, remembering something. "This is just what they were warning me about. Dabbs and Velvet said you might start talking off your head. You've probably got a concussion."

"It's not the concussion talking. Virgil was killed—but not by Juniper. Someone wanted to set her up for the murder, and it has to be someone connected with Brightlow Enterprises. Work was Virgil's life." I narrowed my eyes. "I even wondered once if you were the culprit."

He gaped at me. "Why would you think that?"

"You disappeared."

"I've been right here," he argued.

"Right. Hidden away at a secret site, forbidden by your brother to tell anyone where you were or what you were up to."

"I just wanted to improve the Selfies," he said.

"The robots?"

He nodded excitedly. "So you *do* know what we're doing here."

"We've got a Selfy at the castle. It's even less impressive than the drone-deer."

"You've got a prototype," he explained. "I told Velvet it still had some bugs, but she thought having one in the castle would be good PR."

"It might have, if it had been more reliable than a Ford Pinto."

He shook his head. "We've made all sorts of improvements since the first crude models came out. The new Selfy is cleverer, more dexterous, and altogether more capable. Soon, they will do away with the need for all labor except what's required to program them." A fire lit in his eyes. "It will change life for everyone."

He sounded like something out of Virgil's sci-fi book, which had been all about robots taking over the world, and it didn't work out too well. It couldn't have been a coincidence that Virgil, anxious about Brightlow's pet project, had picked that title to read.

Blinky hopped to his feet. "Let me show you."

He took my hand and helped me up, which was only marginally less painful than I expected it to be. My head throbbed, but at least I didn't feel dizzy. He scurried to the door, opened it, and waved impatiently for me to follow. "You have to see this. You'll be amazed."

I traipsed after him. In the corridor, I discovered that we were high up. The building had been designed on the model of the Brightlow building in the old pottery: the second-floor offices overlooked a large work floor. Except this floor, unlike the one in Christmastown, was far from under populated. There were dozens of Selfies below, all of which resembled Jingleini in shape but lacked his distinctive features. Their white plastic bodies had *BE* stamped on their middles and their only facial features were black circles for eyes and mouths.

Though physically identical, they were performing specific tasks at workstations that had been constructed for them on various platforms. Their robotic arms moved in even, efficient motions. Several were constructing various toys on an assembly line. One side of the floor was devoted to sewing. Another crew formed a gift-wrapping station. Other Selfies pushed supply carts. Two were on a hydraulic lift, cleaning the plate glass we were looking through. On the other side of the building was a test kitchen, where Selfies were busy cooking and baking. When a flour spill occurred, a Selfy drove an industrial vacuum over to pick up the mess. The machine was an enormous suction tube attached to a large electric cart. The Selfy driver seemed able to manipulate the nozzle from behind.

There was so much going on at once, I had a hard time focusing on it all—Selfies working at desks, Selfies driving around the floor in a sort of modified golf cart, a Selfy working at a cash register, ringing up non-existent purchases. The robots all navigated the test lab in the same slow, dazed way, as if Velvet had slipped something into *their* brandy.

My attention was drawn to another section of the warehouse floor, where a small assembly line of Selfies was creating more Selfies, perpetuating the mechanical species. It was all like a nightmarish, North Pole version of the movie *Metropolis*. An assembly line of thoughtless beings making treats, making toys, wrapping presents . . .

"Anything an elf can do," I murmured.

Blinky nodded excitedly. "Isn't it fantastic?"

Fantastic? I looked down at those automatons and could only see a soulless futuristic hellscape of toys cobbled together without artistry, of mass-produced baked goods, and a million headaches when any of them started to malfunction. Jingleini might be an early model, but he hadn't been able to perform even basic tasks successfully. Sure enough, while I was watching, a Selfy toppled off a ramp and lay on the floor like a beetle on its back.

I had a feeling Virgil had visited this site, and had seen what I was seeing: a nightmare. No wonder Brightlow Enterprises had started letting employees go—they were preparing for a future of no workers at all. And they had hired elves like Shaggy from the Farthest Frozen Reaches to construct this site, because they knew if word got out about what was going on here, the elves would be up in arms.

I thought of the cobblers who created fantastic booties for Walnut, and the wonderful elves who whizzed around Sparkletoe's Mercantile helping customers. Most of all, I thought about the lovingly made creations at Puffy's All-Day Donuts and Merry Muffins, and the warm camaraderie at the We Three Beans coffeehouse. What would it be like to go into those places and find Selfies instead of my friends?

"You can't do this," I said.

Frustration crossed his face. "You don't understand. This is the future. And it's here."

"Exactly. It's here, hidden, because *no one* wants this. Maybe you, Dabbs, and Velvet thought you could simply implement a robot coup d'état, but it won't work. The elves of Santaland won't stand for it. This place has already resulted in Virgil's death. Isn't that enough?"

His gaze narrowed. "What do the Selfies have to do with Virgil's murder?"

"He must have seen this place. He looked frantic the two times I saw him before he died. He was reading dystopian books about robots, and was very nervous when Juniper and I went to Brightlow Enterprises to enquire about your whereabouts. He was acting jumpy, and Juniper and I probably didn't help matters by peppering him with messages we left at his office. We thought he could tell us where *you* were, but Dabbs and Velvet must have worried that Virgil was considering telling us about this place. They killed him before he could spill the beans, and they set Juniper up for their crime."

"That's preposterous," Blinky said. "Dabbs wouldn't do that. He couldn't—he didn't even know her."

"He met her after you disappeared. And all he had to do was visit here once to see those pictures of her on your wall. He would even have been able to notice her very unique set of fireplace utensils—just the thing to set her up for a murder."

His jaw worked. "Others might have seen her apartment."

I sighed. "Did you ever send Juniper a letter telling her to leave you alone?"

"No."

"A scrap of paper allegedly in your handwriting saying something to that effect was planted in her apartment. The deputy found it."

He frowned. "Dabbs is always pressing me to hurry. I wrote him a letter once asking him to leave me in peace."

"That was the one," I said.

"But . . ." His voice trailed off. "I don't understand."

"Dabbs killed Virgil because he was going to tell people about this place before Dabbs and Velvet were ready. They had just had one PR nightmare when the drone-deer crashed, and they were watching how modernization was upsetting Santalanders. They wanted to make sure that this rollout took place on their terms. Virgil sounding the alarm would have thrown a monkey wrench into their master plan."

He shook his head. "What master plan?"

I gestured around the showroom. "They're going to replace elves, and put Santa's Workshops out of business. Your mother came close to announcing that the Brightlows intended to wrest control of Santaland from the Clauses."

"A total takeover of Santaland? That's preposterous."

"Then why operate in complete secrecy? Why hire elves from the Farthest Frozen Reaches to construct the building?"

"Selfies are labor-saving devices. We're supposed to be making elves' lives easier. Murder? No one ever said anything about that to me."

"Of course not. You're immersed in the la-la land of your inventions. You don't even seem to care that your erstwhile girlfriend was set up for murder."

"Of course I care."

"Then *do* something about it."

"But . . ." He rubbed his hands across his face, flummoxed. "Well, it's simple enough to test your far-fetched accusation. We'll just go downstairs and talk to Dabbs."

"Oh sure. Dabbs will be certain to fess up to everything I've said."

But Blinky was already marching down the corridor, lab coat flapping. I tripped after him, my gaze scanning our surroundings for anything that I might use for self-defense. I didn't want to face Velvet unarmed again. There weren't any weapon-like objects in view, except those plastic chairs. I imagined myself facing off with Velvet like a lion tamer approaching a large, feral feline.

When we reached a steel door marked *Stairway*, he put his hand on the knob to turn it. But the door didn't open. He rattled the knob. "It's locked."

Fear gnawed at me. "Is there another door?"

He nodded and charged off down the adjacent corridor. Along the way to the next corner, we passed the pair of window-washing Selfies on a platform wielding sponges and squeegees to clean the viewing glass between us and the warehouse floor. I didn't give them good odds of not falling off that platform, but I supposed that was the appeal of a Selfy. One could fall and another would replace him.

At the next exit, Blinky again looked shocked as he rattled another immoveable doorknob.

"Do you have a key?" I asked.

He shook his head. "These doors have never been locked before."

"Do the windows open?"

He laughed. "You can't be serious. We aren't going to have to climb out of a window. Besides, there are no upstairs windows."

Of course not. This was an industrial building, meant to be secret. "Do you have a phone?"

He brightened. "Of course, it's"—he deflated—"downstairs on a worktable. I was so surprised when they brought you in, I didn't think to pick it up."

This was not good news.

"Blinky, we need to find a way out. Now."

He shook his head. "Dabbs will be back up soon."

"Don't you understand? Velvet drugged me, clunked me on the head, and then she and Dabbs dragged me out here in the middle of nowhere. They kidnapped Mrs. Claus, and now

I've seen their secret plans for wresting control of Santaland from the Claus family and replacing all the elves with robots. They're not going to let me out of here."

"You mean they would"—his Adam's apple bobbed over his collar as he swallowed—"kill you?"

"And you, too."

That really shocked him. He might be good at getting robots to duplicate the movements of elves, but he couldn't guess his brother's next moves at all. "Why?"

"Because you have a conscience," I said. "Would you let him get away with hurting me?"

"Of course not." He frowned. "Oh."

"Also, Dabbs still sees himself as the unappreciated Brightlow genius. He was humble bragging over a jar opener. With you out of the way, he'll be able to take credit for this entire plan."

"But I invented the Selfies, and perfected them."

"And now that they're perfected, you won't be needed anymore."

"But . . ." He shook his head. "You can't honestly think he'd want to *kill* me."

"Blinky, I have a lump on my head the size of a bowling ball. I saw Virgil after he'd been bludgeoned. I know you're family, but given that those two have killed before and now have locked us up in a secluded site no one knows about, I'm just going to assume that what they have planned for us isn't good."

He stood frozen, finally letting it soak in.

"We need to find a way out of here," I said. "Now."

We examined the doors, which were constructed of steel and dead-bolted. Trying to bash our way through one was definitely not going to work. Remembering lost hours of my youth spent watching *Mission: Impossible* television reruns, I looked up to see if there was some duct work we could crawl through. But the ceiling was all exposed pipes and fixtures, and far too high to reach. That just left one option.

"We need something heavy enough to break glass."

He looked over at the glass-squeegying Selfies and understood immediately. "I have an old wooden chair."

The office chair in his little office couldn't have looked more out of place. It reminded me of the one behind the reception desk at the Coast Inn—an antique, made of solid oak with leather on the backrest and the seat, and rusty casters. I glanced at him in surprise.

He sent me a what-can-I-say shrug. "I like old things, too. It's my lucky chair."

It was lucky for us that it was there, that was certain.

We rolled the chair out into the hallway, where the Selfies were now busy cleaning another section of plate glass. Those robots might look super creepy, but I had to admit they were doing a good job making that glass shine. I almost regretted having to ruin all their hard work. Moving in perfect tandem, Blinky and I hoisted the chair up between us. I was taller than he was, but he was surprisingly strong. Which was fortunate, because that chair of his weighed a ton.

"Count of three?" I asked.

He glanced at the Selfies across the glass, their eyes and mouths dark Os almost of surprise. I read Blinky's hesitation to hurt his own creations and gave him a shake with the chair. "Life or death," I reminded him.

He nodded. "One . . ." We started swinging the chair. "Two . . ." We hauled back, and on when we said, "Three," both of us heaved the chair at the glass with all our might.

The wall of glass shattered, and the chair sent both Selfies flying backward like bowling pins. With my boots, I ninja-kicked some of the remaining shards of glass out of our path so we could climb out onto the window-washing platform. It was shakier than I expected, with no rail, and for a moment

Blinky and I grabbed each other and stared down at the floor twenty feet below. Like ants seeing a bread crumb fall, several cleaner Selfies swarmed below to sweep up the broken glass and the bits of one Selfy that had broken apart on impact.

Despite my dizziness from looking down from our precarious perch, I was impressed. "That's amazing."

The Selfy with the giant vacuum drove over and sucked up glass through its tube mouth like a giant caterpillar. Unfortunately, it also hoovered up all of the Selfy.

Blinky frowned. "Oh dear."

"We don't have time to worry about Selfycide," I admonished him. "How do we get off of this platform?"

"I wasn't talking about the Selfies." He directed my gaze to where Dabbs and Velvet stood glaring up at us. My heart stopped. Dabbs was holding a rifle.

"You can jump down, or we can help you," Dabbs called out to us.

I felt sick. I should have known that the noise from the broken glass wouldn't leave us much time. "Shoot us, you mean?" I think I preferred to take my chances jumping. But then I looked at the maw of the industrial vacuum. If Blinky and I fell to the ground, would the Selfies see us as just another mess to clean up?

Velvet smiled tightly as the predicament played across my face.

When Blinky spoke, his voice cracked. "Dabbs, you're my brother."

Dabbs snorted. "Right. Brother to the *genius*. Everyone always assumes that you're the brain, and I'm just a bean counter. I'll show them!"

"You'll never get away with this!" Blinky called out.

"With what? An unfortunate industrial accident?"

"Killing Mrs. Claus will be bad PR for the launch of your Selfy Workshop," I pointed out.

Dabbs laughed. "It would be if they ever found you. Snowbell Pond is nearby. You might join Snowbell and her family at the bottom, below the ice."

As he said the words, I imagined myself added to the pile of bones in that icy deep. Frozen. Maybe being snarfed up by an industrial Selfy vacuum wouldn't be so bad after all. Or, if we didn't break our bones when we fell to the floor, we just might be able to outrun the machine before it sucked us to our doom.

Not that I held any illusions that Dabbs wouldn't shoot us anyway. If dropping me into Snowbell Pond was his plan for me, it wouldn't matter if I was riddled with bullet holes.

"Made your choice yet?" Dabbs called up to us.

I glanced at Blinky and could see in his eyes that he agreed with me. It was jump or nothing. "Count of three?" he asked.

I turned. Took a breath. "One."

"Two," he said, barely audible.

When I opened my mouth to say "Three," an entirely different voice echoed around the warehouse.

"Dabbs Brightlow!" an amplified voice shouted. "This is Constable Crinkles! This warehouse is surrounded!"

Dabbs and Velvet stiffened in panic, while my knees went noodle-limp in relief. Rescue! If I got out of this alive, I would never criticize Constable Crinkles again.

Except . . .

"Release your prisoners!" the voice called through the megaphone. "Put down—Ouch!"

I frowned. That voice, though familiar to me, did not belong to Constable Crinkles. In fact, he'd sounded like . . . Smudge.

A moment later, Smudge and Juniper frog-marched in, dressed in the constable's and deputy's uniforms. They were poked into the warehouse at harpoon point by a burly, disreputable-looking elf with stringy hair and an eye patch. The constable's megaphone dangled from one hand.

"I found these two outside."

Dabbs laughed. "Nice going, Shaggy. Keep your eye on them."

Juniper and Smudge were gawping at the gleaming white-and-stainless-steel Selfy factory they found themselves in.

"Golly doodle!" Juniper exclaimed. Then she caught sight of Blinky and me. "Blinky!"

Blinky managed a halfhearted hand wave.

"I *told* you Blinky was in danger," Juniper said to Smudge.

Blinky shook his head. "You shouldn't have come here, Juniper."

"I had to find April." She sent an apologetic look up at me. "I'm sorry, April. I panicked when we didn't get another text from you. But we didn't think we'd actually need weapons."

How had she found me? No one else knew about this place.

"It doesn't matter," Smudge said with admirable bravado. "In a few minutes, the building *will* be surrounded."

Velvet, positioned safely behind Dabbs and his gun, laughed. "Yes, that's what you were telling us a few moments ago." She looked at Shaggy. "Did you see anyone else?"

The wild elf shook his head.

How had they gotten here? Only one possibility occurred to me: Quasar. He must have seen Velvet taking me out of Brightlow Enterprises and followed her.

"I guess we'll have four of you to dispose of now," Dabbs said. "Luckily there's plenty of room at the bottom of Snowbell Pond."

Juniper gasped. "You'll never get away with that. And even if you do, how will you live with yourself?"

"Very comfortably," Dabbs explained, "once Dabbs's Santa-land Workshop is fully functional and has put those old Claus factories in Tinkertown out of business. I'm offering a way for elves to be free of being busy all the time. Soon, elves will live like Clauses, and I will be known as the elf who liberated them."

Smudge shook his head. "Hard for me to get excited about that if I'm not alive to see it."

Dabbs had wound himself up into an almost messianic fervor. "Once my Selfy factories are up and running, generations of elves will thank me—Dabbs Brightlow. *I'll* be living in a castle."

"Why wouldn't they thank Blinky?" Juniper said. "He's the one who's done the work, I'll bet."

Does she want to get us all killed immediately? If there was one thing that set Dabbs off, it was comparing him unfavorably with his brother.

He cocked his rifle. "Blinky is a mechanic. A tinkerer. It was *my* vision that came up with all this."

I looked sideways at Blinky. His jaw was tight. "We never meant the Selfies to take over Santaland, Dabbs."

His brother's eyes flashed. "*You* never meant them to—because for all your so-called genius, you lack imagination. You're a putterer. Who's been the visionary of this company? Me. That's what Mom's never understood. *She'd* probably like to give you all the credit, too."

His voice had tightened, and his agitation would have been frightening even if he hadn't been armed.

Velvet shifted her feet. "Can we get this over with? This has been an exhausting day."

Panic gripped me. Were they really going to kill us all? Shaggy nudged Juniper and then Smudge with his harpoon until they were standing underneath us. "Lower the platform," Dabbs commanded Velvet.

She about-faced and crossed to a control panel on a nearby wall. The platform beneath Blinky and me dropped, and soon we were with Juniper and Smudge at floor level, surrounded by Selfies on an assembly line making plush toys. Fearful though I was, I couldn't help noticing that Selfy craftsmanship was even less impressive up close than it had seemed when viewed from above. The eyes on the stuffed bears were crossed, and I doubted that seamwork would have passed muster with my late grandmother, who'd been a home ec teacher.

"You have a long way to go before you'll be able to replace real elves with these sham ones," I said. "Those teddy bears are not Santaland quality."

Dabbs scowled and stepped over to check one out. "What's wrong with it?"

"It's cross-eyed, and its nose is way off center."

He frowned.

"I bet the candy canes don't taste like real peppermint, either," Smudge taunted.

Dabbs glared at Blinky. "I put you in charge of quality control!"

"I told you we were still working out a few problems . . ."

Dabbs stamped a bootied foot and threw the bear at his brother. "You're always undermining me!"

Velvet put a hand on his arm. "It's okay, Dabbsy. We can fix it. The bones are all here."

"*No!*" Dabbs vibrated with anger. "Not if we can't even make cockadoodie teddy bears!"

Shaggy speared the bear with the tip of his harpoon and inspected it. "I like," he growled.

"See?" Velvet said soothingly to Dabbs.

"Of course *he* likes them," he said. "He's a barbarian. I will not go down in Santaland history as a maker of mutant teddy bears!"

"Shh!" Juniper lifted a hand, interrupting his tantrum. Her head was cocked. "Hear that? I told you help was coming!"

Everyone stopped and mimicked her tilted head stance. All I heard was factory noise, but elf ears are more sensitive. Could they detect Quasar flying around overhead?

Velvet smirked. "Nice try."

"I really do hear something." Juniper turned to Smudge. "Don't you?"

While everyone's attention was diverted, Blinky sprang into action. In a flash of white, he rushed forward in an attempt to tackle Dabbs, but he failed to wrestle his brother to the ground. The two elves were locked in a struggle over Dabbs's rifle.

Smudge, not to be outdone, whirled and grabbed Shaggy's spear, which still had a teddy bear impaled on its tip. Juniper joined the struggle, which soon resembled a tug-of-war, with a spear taking the place of a rope. I was watching two separate struggles, and not sure which one to join in—or how to join in, either.

In the fight over the spear, it was two against one, but Shaggy was a strong elf and might have held out a long time. But when the rifle fired behind him, he yipped in terror and released his grip, sending Juniper and Smudge sprawling backward. They collided with Blinky and Dabbs, and all four landed in a heap.

I looked around. Shaggy had fled. The rifle had fallen on the floor, and I lunged for it. Holding it in my left hand, I set about untangling elves from the pile with my free hand. I pulled Smudge off first, then Juniper. At the bottom of the pile, Dabbs had been thrown backward onto the floor and appeared to be unconscious. But on top of him lay Blinky—with a red stain spreading across his white lab coat.

Juniper looked down in horror and fell back on Blinky

again, this time to pull him off his brother. We turned him around and discovered that he'd been shot during the altercation. He appeared to have lost a lot of blood.

"*No!*" Juniper cried. "Blinky—please say something."

His mouth worked for a few moments, and Juniper bent down, her ear close to his lips. She frowned.

"What did he say?" Smudge asked.

Bewildered, she said, " 'Velvet.' "

I looked up. *Where* is *Velvet?* Turning in a half circle, I saw a terrifying sight: the proboscis of the giant vacuum bearing down on us—Velvet had taken the wheel from the Selfy sitting next to her. I could feel the suction power from twenty feet away, and she was gaining ground quickly. From the mad look in her eye, she was headed right for Juniper, Smudge, and me.

"Run!" I yelled.

It didn't take Juniper and Smudge long to figure out where my panic was coming from. Smudge grabbed Juniper's arm and pulled her up, and then we all scrambled for the exit against the drag of Velvet's hellish suction machine chasing us.

We hit the doors running, but they were automatic and stayed open after we ran through them, allowing Velvet to come right after us. Being chased by a giant vacuum was disorienting enough, but when we hit the cold air, it was being stirred up like a whirlwind by a giant helicopter landing just in front of the building. My jaw dropped, although I shrugged my scarf against my face. The way the helicopter churned up air and snow reminded me of the avalanche bearing down on Kringle Lodge—except this was noisy. The *whomp, whomp, whomp* of the rotor blades stopped all of us in our tracks—even Velvet.

"Holy moly!" Juniper yelled. "What's that?"

"Butterbean's helicopter."

The door opened and out spilled Nick, Crinkles, and Butterbean. The cavalry had come to our rescue. I whooped with delight. But then I saw Velvet go tearing off in the vacuum machine. Did she actually think she could get away?

I sprinted after her, unable to keep up, but then the machine bogged down in the icy snow. Panicked, Velvet jumped off the machine and legged it. She might have had a chance at escape, but she ran into something she wasn't expecting coming from the opposite direction: a diminutive snowman on a Sno-maneuver. They collided, and both Quince and I tackled her.

I sat on Velvet while Quince saw to Pocket, who had broken apart a bit during the collision.

"How did you get here?" I asked Quince.

"Jake told me to follow the first wild elf I saw. We saw Shaggy and followed him to this place. But when I texted Jake, he didn't answer back."

I told him about the avalanche.

Back in the workshop, we found materials to tie up Velvet and Dabbs for their trip to the constabulary. Crinkles was taking them out to await the snowmobile that Ollie was supposed to be driving in from Christmastown. Quince also remained outside, patching up the damage Pocket sustained in bringing down Velvet.

Smudge put his arm around Juniper as they stood over Blinky's lifeless body. There would be no patching up Santaland's most famous inventor.

Juniper sniffled. "He died saving us."

Someday, I would have to tell her that she'd been right all along about Blinky, but at the moment I ceded the comforting duties to Smudge. For once, he seemed not to be messing things up.

Nick put his arms around me. "You gave me a scare."

"Those two ghouls gave me a scare," I said, nodding to

the doors Crinkles had just escorted his prisoners through. "How did you get here in time?"

"Quasar saw Velvet and Dabbs drive off with you from Brightlow Enterprises in Christmastown. He didn't realize at first what was happening, but decided to follow. When he saw them come out and carry you into this place, he flew back to Christmastown to the constabulary. Juniper and Smudge tried to contact me, but the cell and phone service is out at the top of the mountain. So Quasar flew up and delivered the message in person. Comet took us to the old sleigh shed where the helicopter was."

"I'll never complain about Butterbean's boneyard helicopter again."

He laughed. "Well, you don't have to worry about tomorrow night. The reindeer are back onboard."

Butterbean bounded over to us. "But I'll still be on standby, just in case."

Even after his colossal foul-up earlier, I was ready to forgive him. I wasn't sure Amory ever would—but Amory hadn't almost been sucked up by an industrial vacuum.

"Is Jake okay?" I asked Nick.

He nodded. "Mostly thawed now. He wanted to come, but Claire put her foot down. The road down Sugarplum Mountain is cleared, so they should be back at the castle tonight when we get home."

Home. That sounded so good. I sighed, looking around at the dystopian Selfy work floor around us. Most of the Selfies seemed to be running out of juice—as if they were all at the end of their charges. Their slow-motion movements made them seem mournful. Maybe they sensed their days were numbered. At least, they would be if I had any say in the matter.

"What do you intend to do with this place?" I asked Nick.

He shook his head. "I'm not sure."

"I think we should blow it all up," I said. "For everyone's peace of mind."

Hearing opportunity knock, Butterbean hopped to attention. "I can help with that!"

Of course. After blowing up the top of a mountain, demolishing a Selfy warehouse would be a piece of cake.

Nick and I exchanged looks, then laughed. It was such a relief to smile. It felt good to be alive, and to know that all the people I loved most were safe.

Chapter 24

The summoning horn—the original, ornamental one—sounded again the following evening, but this time its purpose was purely ceremonial. Santa's great carved sleigh, polished so that it glistened, stood loaded and ready. Helper elves clambered over the attached wagons, taking their places. In front, in shining harness, stood nine reindeer impatient to be underway.

All around Christmastown City Hall a crowd teemed, spilling through the streets and all around the park surrounding Peppermint Pond. The symphony played "Sleigh Ride" from the band shell, and the entire crowd seemed to be hopping, humming, and singing along with it. On the sleigh, Nick and Christopher stood and tossed candy to the excited elf children below. Christopher wouldn't be accompanying Nick this night, but in nine years, this job would be his and he was already enjoying some public duties.

I stood on the steps of City Hall and looked over the crowd, flanked by Pamela on one side and Claire on the other. Next to my friend stood a thoroughly thawed Jake Frost. Juniper and Smudge were in the crowd just below, dancing with the rest of the throng.

Christopher hopped off the sleigh, and the next time Nick

blew the curved brass horn, the crowd parted to give the sleigh room for takeoff. I watched with my heart in my throat as he called out the names of all the reindeer herds represented by the animals pulling the sleigh. A cheer went up at each name, from Comet to Rudolph. And with a ceremonial crack of the whip, Nick mushed the team forward.

It always seemed impossible to me that such a load could lift off the earth, but within seconds the sleigh was airborne, and the crowd surged after it, cheering and whooping as the few helper elves from Tinkertown waved back from their precarious perches.

Just as he was clearing the rooftops, Nick turned and blew me a kiss. I blew one back.

"Holy Moses, you were right." Claire turned to me, eyes shining with excitement. "The whole Santa–Christmas Eve bit is real."

"I told you so."

"Is it always like this—amazing?"

"Always," Pamela and I responded in unison, and then laughed. Seeing my husband take off on a round-the-world voyage would never not make me nervous, but it was hard not to be joyful this evening. All of Santaland was united and jubilant.

"Tonight's a festival for the whole country," I said. "And tomorrow we rest."

I would rest once Nick got back.

Claire sucked in a deep breath, as though the euphoria in the air intoxicated her. "And the day after tomorrow, I get to take a walk on the *really* wild side."

I looked over at Jake, who was shaking his head but smiling. After seeing him frozen, Claire wasn't inclined to let him go—and he was warming up to the possibility that something might work out for them. She was extending her vacation and had talked him into taking her to the Farthest Frozen Reaches. Not my idea of a vacation—but Claire had always been more adventurous than me.

"Let's all go to We Three Beans for an eggnog latte," she suggested.

Now I knew Santaland had her in its clutches. I laughed. "No thanks—but don't let me stop you."

She didn't. She took Jake's hand, and they threaded through the crowd.

I sighed happily, watching for a moment as Lucia and Quasar swayed in time to "Jingle Bell Rock." I took a step down to join them, but was stopped when Jingles slipped in front of me.

He rubbed his gloved hands together. "I just wanted to let you know that I've solved our help problem."

"I don't want to see another Selfy for as long as I live," I warned him.

His eyes widened. "Oh no. I've decommissioned Jingleini for good. I'd like to hire someone better."

"Who?"

Like a magician pulling a rabbit out of a hat, Jingles snapped his gloved fingers and Butterbean hopped in front of me.

I drew back. *Maybe I should take back what I said about the Selfies.* I might have forgiven Butterbean for the avalanche enough to let him demolish the Selfy warehouse, but I didn't want him demolishing Castle Kringle. "I'm not sure this is a good idea."

"Amory let him go," Jingles said. "So Butterbean's free to seek other employment. And he has some ingenious ideas about improving life in the castle."

Butterbean bobbed on his heels. "Lots of ideas! I'm excited for the opportunity!"

Jingles leaned forward with a gleam in his eye I recognized from talking to Amory a few days ago. "Butterbean was telling me about a system for bringing up your bedroom ceiling lights in the morning by putting them on a timer that would mimic dawn light in the time zone you were used to."

Hm.

"We could even have the slow increase in soft light be accompanied by light morning birdsong," Butterbean said, his hands mimicking birds gently twittering.

It *was* a soothing idea.

"What did you call it?" Jingles asked him.

"A twinkle timer," Butterbean said. "We could even rig up the hearth to self-start at a designated hour."

"Twinkle timer," I repeated, burrowing deeper into my coat. *Birdsong. Gentle light. Warmth.* I envisioned myself waking up as if I were a nymph in a warm forest glade. "You've got yourself a new assistant, Jingles."

Butterbean all but somersaulted in happiness. "Merry Christmas, Mrs. Claus! You won't regret it."

Right. What could possibly go wrong?

"Merry Christmas," I returned, and skipped down the steps to join the dancing.

Visit us online at
KensingtonBooks.com
to read more from your favorite authors,
see books by series, view reading
group guides, and more!

Visit us online for sneak peeks, exclusive
giveaways, special discounts, author content,
and engaging discussions with your fellow readers.

Betweenthechapters.net

Sign up for our newsletters and be the first
to get exciting news and announcements about
your favorite authors!
Kensingtonbooks.com/newsletter